COMMON GROUND

Also by Andrew Cowan

Pig

ANDREW COWAN

COMMON GROUND

Harcourt Brace & Company

New York   San Diego   London

Requests for permission to make copies
of any part of the work should be mailed to:
Permissions Department, Harcourt Brace & Company,
6277 Sea Harbor Drive, Orlando, Florida 32887-6777.

Library of Congress Cataloging-in-Publication Data
Cowan, Andrew.
Common ground/Andrew Cowan.
p. cm.
ISBN 0-15-100265-7
I. Title.
[PR6053.0942C66   1997]
823'.914—dc21   97-11307

Printed in the United States of America
First U.S. edition
A B C D E

For Lynne and Rose

Author's note: I have a Mum and Dad, and a brother.
They do not appear in this novel either.

ACKNOWLEDGMENTS

I am grateful to the Scottish Arts Council for the award of a bursary whilst writing this novel, to the K. Blundell Trust for the award of a grant, and to Jennifer Kavanagh for making everything possible.

Doug's journey in this book was made by Alastair Whitson and Joanna Leevers, and Doug's words began as Alastair's. Ged Lawson provided the woods, Tony Drane found the beetle, but nothing would have been written without the love and support of Lynne Bryan, who read every line twice, and changed them, twice.

COMMON GROUND

SEPTEMBER

THE WINDOW shook in its frame and then the rain came. Ashley wrapped himself in a blanket and stood closer to the heater. He faced into the street. On the opposite kerb a red car had been abandoned beneath a shedding sycamore. With each damp gust of wind a shower of leaves fell to the bonnet and roof and stuck as if glued. The car was new, a model advertised everywhere on roadside hoardings, in bus shelters and train stations. It was designed for the city. The windscreen lay like a sheet of crazed ice across the front seats. The rear tyres were flat and the bodywork was dented. As he looked down, two girls paused on their way to the top of the street and pilfered what little remained to be taken – a cassette tape and window wipe, a bottle of oil from the boot. Twenty yards up the road they dropped all three in the gutter.

He turned to Jay and said, 'I'll bet you fifty quid you're not.'

'You don't have fifty quid, Ashley,' she replied, and raised one knee to the height of her shoulder. She was sitting on the edge of their bed, carefully shearing her toenails with a pair of dressmaking scissors.

'I have employment,' he reminded her. 'I work.'

'Okay,' she shrugged, and for a moment she faced him. 'But I'm serious this time.'

Her gaze was direct, defenceless, and he felt a lift of excitement, almost elation. He sensed it was £50 lost, but would not admit it, feared his disappointment if she was mistaken. 'You're pregnant every other month,' he told her. 'You feel sick and you're pregnant, you forget your dates and you're pregnant, your period starts and you say you've miscarried. You owe me hundreds already.'

She didn't respond. The gas heater hissed softly in the silence between them, outside the rain eased and came stronger. He turned back to the window and watched a small boy straining to remove a wing-mirror from its bracket. 'So how do you know?' he asked finally.

'I keep crying,' she said.

'You do that anyway, Jay.'

'I feel nauseous,' she added. 'And miserable.' She dropped the scissors to the floor and heaped herself beneath the bedclothes. 'Constantly nauseous,' she said. 'And really fucking miserable.'

The mirror came free with an audible snap, like a branch breaking, and the boy looked up to their window. He was eight or nine years old. As he climbed on to the car's bumper he steadied himself with a hand on the bonnet and leaned forwards, suddenly hurled the mirror at the shattered windscreen. He ducked, but the net of glass absorbed the impact with barely a sound and the missile rolled under the dashboard. With another glance up to Ashley the boy rocked himself on the bumper and dropped backwards.

Ashley crouched for Jay's scissors and then lay on the bed at her side. It was a Saturday afternoon. From the house next door there came the furious whining of grand prix engines, a commentator yelling above them. It sounded like an argument. He slipped a finger and thumb through the loops of the scissors and snipped at the air. 'Where'd you get these things?' he asked. 'They're lethal.'

'A box,' she mumbled, and flapped an arm in vague indication. Ashley nodded, but didn't look round. There were boxes and bin-bags in every room of their house, and in several other homes too, in squats and caravans, friends' attics and cupboards. Jay's belongings were casually accumulated, sometimes casually abandoned, but he couldn't persuade her to sort through them, discard what she'd outgrown or might never use. She was resistant to persuasion. Slowly he brought the point of the scissors towards his forehead, felt a tingle of anticipation in the bridge of his nose. Yawning, he said, 'Suppose you are pregnant, Jay. Will you keep it?'

She sighed. It became a groan and she turned around, took the scissors away from him. 'Maybe,' she said. 'I won't know till I know.'

'But you are going to a doctor?'

She gave a nod.

'I'd like you to keep it,' he said.

'I know,' she murmured, and tucked the scissors under her pillow. She considered him closely, deliberating, half-frowning, then lowered her head to his shoulder. 'I know you do, Ashley,' she said.

He cradled her awkwardly against him. Her hair was dark and as fine as a child's; it curled in wisps where she'd been lying. He blew on it. Outside the leaves scuffled in the breeze. She shifted to make herself comfortable, and he said, 'I don't suppose I can tell Douglas?' but she didn't reply. He turned his face to the sky, the blanket of cloud over the roofs of the flats opposite. Jay's breathing became even and slow. He heard the car's horn sounding, a long blare and then silence.

The light of its indicators shimmered in the rain on the window.

Do you realize, Dug, the Met Office has 100 categories of British weather condition and not one of them is 'sunshine'? If you wanted to imply sun you'd have to say, '00 – Cloud development not observed.' Did you realize that? Here in our minor metropolis today we've had another 59, or 'drizzle and rain, moderate or heavy', whilst the previous fortnight has been an even more miserable 65, 'rain, not freezing, continuous, heavy', so I doubt I'll be implying sun again this year, nor my own personal favourite, which is 06, 'widespread dust in suspension in the air, not raised by wind at the time of observation', which is the weather of new-town heatwaves, as you'll remember. Or maybe not. Can you remember it? Doesn't it make you even a little homesick?

As you haven't yet written, I don't suppose it does, and I don't suppose you're too interested in our weather either but you can rest assured I'll be keeping you posted on all matters meteorological whilst you're away, like it or not, because I've now got access to the Met. Office computer through my BBC micro at work – screens and screens of fascinating statistics – and it's important, I think, that you remain informed and in touch with all that really matters to us.

In which vein, here also is a tree – or at least a paper representation of such – a birthday present from Jay. She adopted it in your name for a fiver (concessions £2). In fact, she herself printed this and 2,000 other certificates on her baby Gestetner at work – such is her commitment to the cause – and still had to pay a fiver. I hope you are properly grateful, because from now on, no matter where you may roam in the world, a part of this island will always be yours. Or sort of – the adoption, ahem, 'does not confer legal ownership', it merely creates 'a personal and familial link with a threatened tree'. I have formed a personal and familial link with two threatened trees (although I've yet to make their actual acquaintance), as has Jay, as have – apparently – 'over three hundred and sixty other protesters' – ie 361. The official Public Inquiry into our bypass is now under way incidentally, and bone-crushingly tedious it is too. It seems the Objectors won't get their chance to be objectionable until the Government's spokesfolks' batteries run out, which could take weeks, if not months.

In the meantime, we hope you'll be able to find a decent cake-and-beer shop on the road from Katmandu to Jodhpur. I did think of sending a proper card with a picture of a racing car but Jay didn't think you'd have packed a mantelpiece to put it on. We have a mantelpiece now (I screwed it into the wall myself, and drilled the holes for the screws before that, and bashed out the mock-effect real-brick fire-surround before that), on which there sits a toast rack in the form of five little piggies standing in a line, just the job for storing and displaying picture postcards from around the globe. Currently empty.

The mantelpiece was the first of my home improvements not to have gone wrong at any stage and you must remind me to describe in greater detail how it was done the next time, if ever, you visit. In the meantime, the kitchen is like a builder's yard, it'll be another year at least before the decorating is over, and the fabric of the building is crumbling all around us – out the back there are cracks wide enough to swallow a man, or woman, or both at once. Providing that neither is pregnant, of course.

There are cracks everywhere. Our house is deeply fissured. The widest are the ones beneath my slippers because the boards are all tongue and no groove, or all groove and no tongue, especially in the bedroom, where there used to be a perfectly adequate orange-swirl carpet, which Jay insisted we dump outside with all the other junk and raw sewage. So now we're about to paint the boards, and even as I type Jay is stuffing the gaps with events from around the globe. She sat up here all last night tearing a month of Sunday papers to shreds and stirring the shreds into goo, and now she is stuffing the goo into the timber. And really I ought to be helping her, maybe come back to you tomorrow, by which time you should've climbed another mountain, forded another stream . . .

Or 'trekked', I should say – there's an article in today's travel pages about 'trekking', in which it's claimed that 'the countryside of Nepal looks like the Scottish countryside, cubed' (not including the hanky-hatted English holidaymakers, I suppose), and which also says this: 'A generation ago, it was to the Himalayan passes of Nepal and the dope-filled bars of Freak Street that earnest young Westerners went to discover themselves. Mostly they were destined for failure, finding not wisdom but strange new styles of dress and fellow travellers from Sydney to visit in the following year . . .' So, I trust you shan't become all bearded and baubled or develop an Australian accent, and I hope you shan't have the misfortune to discover yourself. I can't think of any surer way to spoil a nice view than a sudden flash of self-knowledge. But enough . . .

In the morning they were woken by the hissing of a punctured tyre, although for several seconds they could not locate the sound. It might have been the radio downstairs, caught between stations and raised to full volume; or the television unplugged from its aerial. Fleetingly Ashley imagined intruders. 'Where's those scissors?' he whispered, and grabbed for his jeans as he stood, already aware he was mistaken. The noise was everywhere, filling the house like daylight. He stopped beside the heater and listened for gas.

'It's coming from the street,' Jay told him, and swung her feet to the floor. She moved swiftly to the landing, shielding her mouth with her fingers. The hissing subsided as she hurriedly descended the stairs.

Ashley drew back the curtains. Outside the sun shone low across the chimneys and lamp-posts, dividing the street into strips of amber and shade. A young boy with spectacles was crouching beside the flattened front tyre of the car, a skateboard upended beside him. There was a shard of glass in his hand. Behind the steering wheel an older boy was trying to pull the dashboard casing apart. The rubber seal from the doorway lay in a coil beneath the rear bumper. The windscreen now sat on the roof, buckled as if it had been jumped on. It made a shape like a pair of veined wings. Ashley gathered his clothes and went down to the kitchen.

'Did you throw up?' he asked, and Jay puffed out her cheeks as she nodded. She sat watching the kettle, shivering in a nightshirt and cardigan. A step-ladder straddled the table beside her and there were tins of gloss and emulsion beneath it, paint-spattered sheets on the floor. The ceiling was half white and half beige. Ashley stood by her side and massaged her shoulder but she shrugged him away.

'The milk's gone off,' she told him.

'I'll get a newspaper,' he said.

The morning was heavy and warm. A slow breeze carried the stench of the sewage works from the west, where the city became warehouses and factories, a long industrial plain by the river. As he closed the front door an old man touched his arm and said, 'They tell us that's a healthy smell, son!' He coughed thickly, a roll-up pinched between his forefinger and thumb. There was a dog-chain dangling from his jacket pocket. Ashley smiled, and offered his hand to the dog as he passed it.

On this side of the street there were no trees. The pavement was narrow and the flagstones were broken, in many places missing or subsiding, tilting at angles. The houses formed a yellow-brick terrace, the last in a half-mile parade of similar rows which began where the nearest park ended. At the backs there were stone yards, small gardens, an alley the width of an ash cart. And on the opposite side of the road, behind a curtain of sycamores, there stood a long, continuous block of four-storey flats which had been built in the Sixties, in the year that Ashley was born. The street was called Telegraph Lane.

A bread van pulled in from the junction and stopped at the shops on the corner. The road was wide and dipped steeply into the kerbs, the surface no longer continuous but patched and relaid, repeatedly excavated and mended. There were potholes of rubble, and ruptures caused by the roots of the trees. In places the asphalt appeared to be flaking like the bark on the trunks. Ashley stepped over a runnel of water and crossed to the other side, walked in the shadows of the trees and parked cars. The flats resembled the comprehensive school where he taught, the same grid of windows and coloured partitions, concrete struts at regular intervals. As he approached the newsagent's he surveyed the windows along the first landing until he found an old woman gazing out. She was dressed for church in black and starched white, her grey hair like a hat of fake fur. When he lifted his hand she raised hers in return, but her expression was fixed, vacantly staring. She was always there, and always waved.

The delivery man obstructed the entrance to the shop, a tray of rolls on his shoulder. He wore a white hat and white coat, and he spoke at a shout. 'We always wanted our boy to do something ordinary,' he was saying, 'so we'd know where he was at. But he works for British Airways, and he's obsessed. He's a nutcase. He knows the timetable by heart, cover to cover. Keeps sending us brochures with the flights all marked in red pen. But we don't want them. Why would we want to go anywhere?' A quieter voice replied from inside, and the man answered, 'But we're not abroad kind of people. No offence, but we're not interested in abroad.'

Ashley stared at the display in the window. There was a box marked *Hey Girl Fun Range Neon Fashion Purses,* and another of *Squirt King Glitter-Glo Water Pistols.* A few pegboard shelves supported a collection of toys in cellophane wrappings, a group of china ornaments. Beneath them stood a random arrangement of aerosols and toiletries, and a notice taped to a ten-pack of nappies:

OWING TO PRESENT CIRCUMSTANCES
ALL £20–£10–£5 NOTES
WILL BE CHECKED
Ajaz

Ashley went inside, ducking beneath the bread tray as the delivery man departed. The interior was narrow and dark. Sacks of potatoes and onions were slumped against the magazine racks; the counter was flanked by tall cabinets. From a transistor radio at the back of the shop there came a distant murmur of Indian voices, a conversation conducted through static and the local interference of taxis. A small, tubby woman watched Ashley closely through a pair of thick spectacles, her husband seated mildly beside her. She laid Ashley's newspaper on the counter before he could ask for it, and said, 'Anything else? Milk? Rolls?' Then the man rose to ring open the till.

Jay was standing on their doorstep when he returned, her bicycle propped against a lamp-post. 'What's happening?' he called, and she looked at him glumly. Her anorak was ripped at the sleeve and there was a crust of mud on her boots. She strapped a helmet under her chin, and he said, 'Where are you going?'

'Alison's. There's a meeting.' On the other side of the road a small girl with red hair smashed the car's brake lights with a stone

'That's not till this afternoon,' said Ashley.

Jay shrugged. There was an outline of kohl to her eyes. It was the only make-up she wore, and the effect was unsettling: enticing when she was happy, but distancing now. It emphasized her pallor, suggested the peep-holes of a mask. As she stepped across to her bike she avoided having to touch him.

Ashley said, 'Shouldn't we be having a talk or something?'

Jay mounted the bicycle and glanced over her shoulder, as

if about to pull out, then sat very still. She took a long breath, concentrated her gaze on the road. When she spoke her voice was almost a murmur. 'I'm going to keep it, Ashley,' she told him. 'You needn't worry about that, but it's scary for me, you know. I haven't done this before, and I need some time on my own. I need to think through how I work in the world.'

A police patrol van eased into their street and cruised to a halt as it approached the wrecked car. The small girl hid her hands in her pockets and stepped back to the pavement. There was a crackle of radio. Moments later the van sped away. Ashley said, 'Well, thanks for discussing it anyway, Jay,' but she didn't reply. They watched a leaf skittering over the road. He rummaged in his carrier bag. 'I've bought you a present,' he said. 'It's supposed to cheer you up.' Beneath the bread and milk and newspapers there was a plastic purse and a water pistol. He presented them both on one hand. 'Choose,' he said.

Jay lifted the pistol from his palm and slipped it into her pocket. 'Thanks,' she said.

He waited. 'So what shall I do with the purse?'

'Start saving?' she suggested, and pushed off from the kerb, wobbling a little as she cranked through her gears. 'You owe me fifty quid,' she shouted.

Ashley watched until she had turned from their street, then he called to the girl with red hair and pitched the purse towards her.

OCTOBER

O *F COURSE, what I didn't mention last time were my
sperms. An astonishing thing about sperms: in the average
ejaculation there are 400 million of them, half the population of
India in every four millilitres of seminal fluid, twenty times the
population of Nepal in a blob on a teaspoon. In Jay's ovaries
meanwhile there resides a mere half-million egglets, less than the
population of this city, and only 325, the population of this terrace, ever actually come out, ever. But one did come out quite
recently, just about the time your plane took off, and so did a few
hundred million of my sperms, and thus as you descended the
steep valley walls into the bowl of Katmandu, there swam my
sperms for Jay's womb; as you touched down on the runway, so
my sperms sped along Jay's cervical canal; as you queued in
reception for your entry stamp and banknotes, there wriggled my
sperms on the brink of Jay's ovum; as you wilted from heat and
fatigue, so did my sperms in their hundreds of thousands; as you
staggered into sunshine and the tumult of taxi drivers, there went
my solitary surviving sperm through Jay's outer membrane and*

the jostle of her fatty yolk droplets; as you haggled a price, so my
nucleus paired up with hers; and finally, as you spluttered towards
your hotel, there floated our twinned cells to find a bed in the
lining of her uterus. So now you're up a mountainside and we're
up the duff.
  No joke. We shall be three in the spring!

The classroom wall was blistering. It had begun the previous term with a single patch of flaking paint behind the
aquarium, but had festered and spread through the long
summer break, corroding in layers to the concrete. A flossy
mould had also appeared, cotton-wool white with blue and
green flecks, like the fungus which grew from his fish. Recently the janitor had wedged a bucket between the fish tank
and the computer trolley to catch a leak from the ceiling.
In places the plaster above them had started to collapse,
exposing the damp lath beneath. It was dripping rainwater
now – Ashley was watching it – but it was impossible to hear
in the hubbub.

The children were measuring distances on maps, the
lengths of rivers and coastlines, roads and railways. Many
were standing. They were using sheets of scrap paper, marking from one kink in a line to the next, rotating their sheets on
the points of their pencils, realigning, marking, and pivoting
again. It was a physical activity and some were rotating themselves round their desks. Others had abandoned their maps
for tussles and arguments, or simply to sit, looking out at the
rain and the road. Ashley ignored them. They were first-years
and naturally noisy, easily distracted.

Yawning, he reached for the document on the edge of his
desk and drew it towards him. It had been there for weeks,
since the start of the term, and it was called *A Charter for
Quality.* There were thirty-two pages in a sleeve of blue-
tinted plastic. Ashley unclipped the spine and tugged out the
paper, then dropped the sleeve in his rucksack to take home.

He squared the pages before him. A few minutes later he started to read.

A mystique often surrounds the concept of 'quality', it said. These are some of the definitions we may use. 1. We do not possess quality; we only practise it; 2. Quality is conformity to specification; 3. the continual effort to improve; 4. what the client says it is; 5. everyone's responsibility. Educationists sometimes object to the concept of 'conformity to specification' as being too mechanistic and production-orientated. Other words can be used but the principle of 'doing what we set out to do' is inescapable for any organization, whether producing consumer goods or a more intangible service such as education.

Frowning, Ashley tried to read the paragraph again, then skimmed to the foot of the page. He scanned the remaining headings and subheadings and leaned forwards, crossed his legs and folded his arms. After a moment he laid his head on the text. He closed his eyes. The print smelled of Jay, the sharpness of the ink she used in her work. It was the smell of the certificates and campaign leaflets that lay piled in their living room; the smell she brought home on her hands, in her clothing and hair. It reminded him too of sitting for tests, huddling at his desk in the hush of a classroom, a sheet enclosed in the curve of his arm. At school he had been what his parents expected of him, well behaved, unnoticed. He never volunteered an answer in class and was rarely chosen to run errands. His reports produced good grades but few comments. There were similar children in every group he taught now, versions of his younger self – diligent, shy, and steadily progressing. He fought hard with himself not to dislike them.

When the bell rang for lunch a chair fell over and several maps slid to the floor. In the clamour for the door a girl screamed and then laughed; others shouted. Ashley raised his head and saw a group of boys pressing another to the wall. The victim was holding a satchel high to his throat, his hair fanned against the poster behind him. Ashley sighed. He bent for his rucksack and searched out his sandwiches, heard the poster tear from its tacks, the boy's assailants spilling into the corridor. Only two girls remained in the classroom. They were called Stacey and Clare and they weren't much taller standing than Ashley was seated. The cuffs of their blazers obscured their hands, their socks were bunched above shiny workboots. 'Nice sleep, sir?' asked Clare, and briefly narrowed her eyes. She was pale and dimpled, her friend much thinner, brown-skinned and freckled. They came to the side of his desk.

'Don't call me sir,' said Ashley.

The girls inched closer together and squared their shoulders. They had a question but hadn't decided who should ask it. As he waited, Ashley saw the day-cleaner standing in the doorway behind them. She held up a cigarette and indicated the girls with a glance. Ashley nodded and the cleaner closed the door behind her, crossed wearily to a desk at the rear of the classroom, striking a match as she went. She opened a window and sat down, unbent her back as she inhaled. Clare watched her, and said in a rush, 'You see your fish, Mr Brook? We were wondering, can we be the monitors? You needn't give us badges or anything.'

'Do they need monitoring?'

'They're pregnant,' said Stacey.

'The guppies are going to have babies, Mr B.'

'How do you know?' he asked, and took a hasty bite from his sandwich. He felt himself reddening and got to his feet. 'Show me,' he mumbled.

The cleaner tapped her ash in an inkwell and looked out of the window. Her name was Janet and she spent her days touring the corridors with a bin-bag, picking up wrappers and cans, or pushing a brush, a damp mop, sometimes an industrial vacuum cleaner. She was short and stocky and always faced the ground as she worked, seldom smiled or spoke. As the girls explained about guppies, she waved a hand at her smoke and quietly shivered. She didn't look away from the rain. 'You see how fat they are, Mr B.?' whispered Stacey. 'And the big dot on their bellies? That's the eyes of all the little fish inside them. They don't lay eggs, it's all live births.'

'Really?' said Ashley. He lifted a map from the floor, folded it fatly against its creases, then retrieved another.

Clare told him, 'Her dad's got a whole room full of tanks, Mr B. Right up to the ceiling. She knows all about it. Look,' she insisted, and he put down the map, dragged a chair to the tank.

A murky film of algae darkened the glass and for a moment it was hard to see what she was pointing to. Then in the dimmest corner of the tank, where the pump emitted a constant fountain of bubbles, he noticed a group of five or six grey females, heavy-jawed and motionless, unexpectedly bulbous. The much smaller males occupied the widest stretch of clear water in the centre of the tank, their bright lacy tails fluttering behind them. Other varieties dashed and glided amongst them. Stacey said, 'They're all up there because your filter needs cleaning. There isn't enough oxygen in the tank. That's why the males are all panting, see? They're gasping for air.'

Ashley nodded, and stared into the water. He had inherited the tank when he had first arrived at the school, eighteen months previously. Then it had held only crisp packets, some gravel and rocks. A yellowing pot-plant had sat in the dust on the lid. There was an air-pump and thermostat in the drawer of his desk. It was spring and his first teaching post, and in the following weeks he had brought dozens more plants from home, lining them up on the window ledge and book cabinets, underneath the aquarium. He had not grown them himself – Jay had taken the cuttings, and supplied him with soil, plastic saucers and pots – and he was surprised when they thrived. Each morning he travelled with a pot on his knee, and each evening his bus stopped outside a shop in the city called *Aqua Interiors*. One stifling hot day in May he had crossed four lanes of stalled traffic to go inside. In the cool submarine quiet of humming motors and bubbles the only illumination had come from the surrounding tanks and the spotlamp over the till. Twenty minutes later he had left with a lump of bogwood and a collection of water-filled bags which the fishkeeper had called his basic starter community.

'So what about my neons?' he asked Stacey.

Only two had survived of the original eight, a fluorescent shoal of darting reds and blues. One by one he had found them dead on the surface at feeding time, half-eaten, their colours dulled in the air, a flossy mould on their bellies. Stacey leaned a little closer and curled her lip in disgust. 'Don't know,' she said. Then, 'Check this, Clare, it's gruesome.'

Ashley rose to gather the remaining maps and atlases. The girls followed him back to his desk. 'So can we be your monitors, Mr B.?' asked Clare. 'We'll change the filter for you, if you change the water.'

'And we'll bring a breeding trap for the guppies.'

'Come again?'

'For the babies,' said Stacey. 'If you put the pregnant ones in the trap, then the babies can swim to the bottom when they're born, so the mums can't eat them.'

'Might be for the best if they did,' sighed Ashley. 'Are you sure you want to bring any more creatures into the world, girls? It's a big responsibility, you know.' He rolled the *Charter for Quality* into a cylinder and attempted to twist it, as if wringing a cloth. 'It's a lot of hard work and heartache,' he told them. 'They get diseases and die. They dirty their water and drink it. They chew each other's tails off. All kinds of disgusting things.' He rocked back in his chair, tapped his knee with the charter. The girls watched him steadily. He said. 'Change the filter, you say?' And Stacey nodded. He looked at the tank, the layer of sediment on the gravel, the tidemark on the glass where the water level had fallen. 'Okay,' he conceded, and tossed the cylinder to his bin. He opened his drawer and gave them each an enamelled badge marked *Monitor*. He had several. 'Fine. Babies it is.'

'Brilliant!' cried Clare. She yanked her friend by the sleeve and immediately backed away to the door. 'You won't regret it, Mr B. Guaranteed.'

Ashley listened as their footsteps receded in the corridor. A drop of water fell from the ceiling. In the silence that followed he heard the tearing sound of wet tyres on tarmac, a rumble of heavy lorries, kids shouting. He picked up his sandwich, saw Janet grinding the last of her cigarette into the inkwell. She forced the window to close and carried the well to his litter bin, tapped it against the metal rim and cleaned inside with a dampened finger. 'More mouths to feed, Ashley,' she said grimly, her voice hoarse and smelling of smoke. He thought then she was about to smile, but she returned the well to its desk and walked to the door without meeting his eye. 'Congratulations,' she said.

How about that? It's an actual fact and I owe Jay fifty squids. And what's even more weird and wondrous, she has already begun thinking way off in the long term, up to one year ahead at a time, giving unfeasibly serious consideration to the tax and benefit and maternity side of things, the type of birth and midwifery available, the potential costs, human and fiscal. And she's attended her first antenatal clinics at the health centre round the corner where she was awarded an official Certificate of Pregnancy and given a pat on the head for being such a 'good girly' because it seems as soon as a woman is about to become a mother she gets treated like a child herself, they want to take all her decisions for her, they forget her name, and they seem to assume that I shall want nothing whatsoever to do with it – I've not been invited to a single consultation, presumably because all they talk about is breasts and female body functions, to which I'd be only too happy to lend an ear, or two, given the merest encouragement. So instead I've made a casual assessment of the Camcorder range in town, a must for all modern fathers-to-be, and found myself transfixed by the babyfood shelves in the supermarket. I almost bought some cotton buds last night, because I feel it's my duty to play a part, however small that part may be.

Many men don't, you know.

However, when Jay isn't being so rational and sensible and quite unlike herself, she does still cry for no apparent reason – once every couple of days she has a sudden mood change and gives forth a flood of tears – it comes on like a Met. Office 99, the air cools, gets darker, and whoosh! crash! run for cover! 'Thunderstorm, heavy, with hail at time of observation'. Then all is rosy again. She also burps and farts a lot and has round-the-clock nausea, for which eating appears to be the only cure, but otherwise she is blooming, not to say burgeoning. The 'expected date of confinement', since you ask, is April 24th, before which, at eighteen weeks, there'll be spina bifida tests and a chance to listen to 'baby's breathing' which is 'always exciting'. And as for names, since you'll want to know this too – if it's a girl, she will be called Milly or Maggie or Madge, and if it's a boy, Thing.

I expect you're highly excited and not a little apprehensive, as indeed are we, as is perfectly natural and normal. It's in all the manuals. Not that this applies to Jay's mother – Daffy Daphne, aka 'Dee' – who remains unnaturally, abnormally cool and moon-like about everything. She is somewhere in lunar orbit, of course, but this is where she habitually resides. 'That's really nice,' she intoned on the earth-to-satellite link-up last week, not in the least apprehensive or excited. 'Yeah. That's really good, Jay. Really nice.' A flute (honest) and some miniature ethnic headgear arrived in the post soon after.

And our mother, Douglas, what did she say?

'Congratulations' perhaps?

Or, 'Oh, what wonderful news'?

Or even, 'Oh, what a worry'?

In fact she said, 'Damn. I've forgotten what I was going to say now, I'll call you back next week.'

End of conversation, she hung up.

She has since phoned several times, if only to ask what she should be feeling, though never in so many words – she tells me what a miserable bastard ('so and-so') Dad is, what a waste and a mess you've made of your life, what a trial and a burden her own life has been – all the usual stuff. And then somehow or other she works her way round to mentioning Jay and the baby without ever actually saying what's on her mind. There are things she just can't confide to British Telecom, no matter how quickly she speaks, and so she's written me a letter instead – in which she says all the usual stuff, what a waste and a mess you've made of your life, what a trial and a burden her life has been, what a miserable so-and-so ('bastard') Dad is. But also this:

'Don't please think I'm not pleased about baby, etc. I am pleased but somehow just can't seem to get all enthusiastic like others. It's just me. I've never been that way about babies, not even you two, but it's not that I'm not pleased, etc. I suppose I'm just not an enthusiastic kind of person but I will be thinking of you often and keeping fingers crossed in case of bad news or bad fortune . . . ' (etc.)

What you can't see is her handwriting, which looks as though scrawled on her knee on a bus through the Himalayas during major tectonic realignments – her hands were not merely trembling, Douglas, but <u>quaking</u>.

Dad was also so moved by the news he actually picked up the telephone. Were you aware he could do this? <u>And</u> *press the correct numbers?* <u>And</u> *speak into the right end? She must've been out of the room at the time – there's no way she'd willingly forfeit her right of interruption. Not that he had much to say. 'Are you getting hitched now or later?' was the gist of it. I told him neither.*

So he said, 'Are you just being unconventional for the sake of it?'

And, 'Have you thought about surnames?'

And, 'What about Jay, doesn't she want to get married?'

Which was quite an eruption of conversation from Pa Brook, wouldn't you say? He's convinced the only reason we're not yet man and wife is because I am totally lacking in moral fibre and don't have the common manful decency to make an honest woman of her. So I said, 'Shall we get married, Jay?' and suddenly she came over all nauseous, not to say thunderous.

Incidentally, Mum's two pages of squiggle arrived in the exact same post as your picture postcard of Mt Nilgiri – it was the Saturday morning before last and the weather was up there in the sixties again (rain, continuous, heavy) and so we switched on the smelly gas heater, made two mugs of tea, and snuggled up with our magnifying glass to read it. We held off from looking at the front of the card until the very last moment, at which point I expleted something obscene and Jay choked on her Earl Grey – she may even have belched, or farted, or wept buckets, or even all three – but on reflection we decided that the view must be a figment of your fevered (bearded, baubled, bobble-hatted) imagination, no where on earth looks like that. The next time you write you may dispense with the photo altogether and concentrate on keeping your wordage up. You may also address me as O Great Spermy One. In the meantime I hope all continues to go well out there, no mishaps or lurgies or life-threatening landslides. I leave you fraught with anxiety. This is only the second time I have ever written to a poste restante, ever. I guess it's an adventure for us both, huh?

NOVEMBER

*O*N AN IMPULSE, the next postcard said, *I checked my high-tech digital watch for the time back home and it was quarter past nine on a Monday morning! That really whacked me up. By the way, how is the job?*

Outside the rain fell in vertical drifts; the traffic drove with dimmed headlights. Ashley gazed across the staff carpark to the slope of green behind the science block, where a solitary cherry tree grew from a mat of fallen leaves, its branches glistening wet, almost purple. Three girls in football kit were sharing a cigarette in the shelter of a fire exit. Beyond them were railings, a zebra crossing, and then a long hill of large houses, some shielded by screens of tall conifers, many visible through a lattice of birch trees and poplars. The houses were spaced widely and the roads between them bordered with hedges, lit by ornamented lamp-posts. It was a private estate. On the far side of the rise there was a ribbon of farmland and, within half a mile, the edge of Hogslea Common.

Although inside the school's catchment area, very few children from these homes were on the school roll. Most came from the newer estates which converged from the south and the west – the first a warren of prefabricated blocks and concrete enclosures, overseen by a field of high-rise towers; the other a tidy expanse of semis with gardens, formerly Council and now mostly mortgaged. Ashley could rarely tell which of his pupils came from which area, though he knew that one of his sixth-formers – a tall, pallid boy called Euan Eliott – lived in the nearest of the tower blocks and claimed to see the canopy of the Hogslea woods from his bedroom, the city centre from his kitchen.

It was Euan who came last to the classroom this morning. Self-conscious but unapologetic, he lifted a chair from the desk by the door and carried it down to the fish tank. He sat facing the glass and tugged a packet of crisps from his pocket. 'You're not with us then, Euan?' said Ashley, but the boy made no reply. Careful not to remove his eyes from the fish, he slumped lower in the chair and stretched out his legs, propped his feet on the computer stand. 'Well, enjoy your breakfast,' Ashley said.

The other pupils resumed their conversations. The group was entrusted to Ashley for this one period each week, his head of department being occupied elsewhere. There were four boys and three girls, already five fewer than at the start of term. When the first two girls arrived promptly on the bell they sat always in the seats furthest away from him. Quiet and unobtrusive, they often passed him in corridors without acknowledgement; he frequently muddled their names in his lessons. The other girl was called Christobel Mimms and placed herself immediately before him, close enough for her sighs and yawns to be audible, for her attention to unsettle him. A few rows behind her sat a blazered prefect called Kashif, whilst the remaining two boys, both overweight and untidy, occupied a desk each in the middle of the room.

When the footballers outside had finished their cigarette, Ashley pencilled some marks on his register and stood at his blackboard. He rubbed his eyes with his fists. 'Right,' he yawned, 'what are we doing?' The girls at the back removed the caps from their pens, flipped opened their notepads. The other faces glared neutrally in his direction. He nodded, and made a channelling gesture with his hands. 'Well, maybe we could start by pushing some of these desks together. I don't like you scattered all over the room like this.' But there was no response. Christobel fingered the leaves of the pot-plant beside her. 'Fine. As you were then,' he said.

It was important to keep moving, however slightly, and so he rocked sideways and back as he spoke, made short, tentative steps in one direction, half-strides in the other. 'I'd like to do the impact of tourism,' he told them, and pushed his hands in his pockets. 'But this is no longer on the syllabus, which is a shame because I was going to let you read my brother's postcards. However, Mrs Gumley has suggested we do models of urban structure instead, which *is* on the syllabus, and so that's what we'll do. But please don't hesitate to yawn if you find it all rather boring.'

He craned forwards to examine his toecaps, listening expectantly, but there was silence.

'Urban zone models,' he said briskly. 'These are attempts to represent the structure of cities in the form of diagrams, the earliest of which was devised by an American called Burgess in the 1920s and was based on Chicago. You could say it resembles a target – like so.' He drew five concentric rings on the blackboard. 'A series of circles, more or less, with the central business district, or CBD, here at the bull's-eye. This is surrounded by the twilight zone – or transitional area – where you find light industry edging out slum housing and where you also get your highest concentration of recent immigrants and other disadvantaged groups because the rents here are cheaper and because there's loads of manual employment right on the doorstep. Or at least in theory, but write that down anyway.'

He was speaking too loudly, he knew, and far too quickly, but volume and speed disguised the tremor in his voice, the breathlessness with which his sentences ended. He felt the damp beneath his arms; dimly registered the widening stain on the ceiling over his fish tank. With the exception of Euan his class was busily writing, heads bowed, and when the first of these looked up he continued more slowly.

'Around the twilight zone there's an area of low-class housing. Which is where the slum-dwellers aspire to move to. The houses aren't so old, and the rents – or mortgages – tend to be dearer. This is pretty much where I live. And if you like, you can pattern this circle with dots, like so, to represent all the dogshit on the pavements.' He tapped rapidly at his diagram with the tip of his chalk, heard whispering behind him, the name of the park nearest his home. 'This is surrounded by middle-class housing – otherwise known as the medium-class residential zone. Very few dots. And finally the posh folk, like the ones on the hill over there, which is an area of high-class residential housing. No dots.' He watched as Euan crumbled some crisps into the fish tank and quietly lowered the lid.

'So,' he exhaled. 'Anyone see any problems with this model? Kashif? You girls at the back?' His throat was dry, a scratchiness that would worsen over the course of the day and with which he now woke most mornings. He strolled down an aisle, saw a copy of his diagram on each pad, hastily written annotations, a few doodles. No one faced him except Euan, and quietly he said, 'I wouldn't sit so close to the fish – you might get splashed.'

'Ha ha,' replied Euan.

'I'm serious.' Ashley pointed to the ceiling but Euan leaned forwards, examined a shoal of silver fry with exaggerated interest. The plaster overhead was fleshy with moisture, raised in a weal and weeping where it was cracked. A droplet of water fell to the janitor's bucket.

Ashley switched on the lights. He saw his classroom double into its reflection, three rows of white globes appear against the thickening sky. His plants acquired shadows, seemed momentarily to swell. A flurry of rain hit the window. 'Well,' he continued, 'one obvious problem is that Burgess assumes a perfectly flat area. There are no rivers or hills – no morphological features whatsoever – that might have an influence on settlement. And you will notice, if you bother to look, that he doesn't allow for the influence of roads or transport systems either. In other words, it's all too neat and simple. Isn't it?'

There was silence. Ashley met each gaze in turn but found no response until Christobel, who smiled sympathetically. 'All right,' he said, turning back to the board. 'After Burgess there came another American – called Hoyt – who developed a more complex model, based on sectors. So our target now begins to resemble a simplified dartboard, with rings and wedges, and bits knocked out, like this.' He sketched some radials over his circles, rubbed away a few lines with his thumb. 'Which makes for a prettier design, I think, but why an improvement? Anyone care to chance an opinion?'

His students fixed their eyes on the board. Some propped their chins on cupped hands, all frowned in contemplation, but no one stirred to answer. 'A demonstration of independent thought, anyone?' he asked. In another room a teacher was shouting. There was laughter, chairs scraping the floor. He swallowed and said, 'Euan? How about you? Any observations?'

'Your fish are pregnant again,' Euan told him.

'I know,' Ashley sighed. 'The fun never stops.'

Arms folded, he leant against the rim of his desk and considered the city on his blackboard. He wondered whether to continue. The drips from the ceiling were falling in rapid succession, becoming a trickle, and he recalled a detail from his brother's first letter, a wood-heated shower in a lodge in the Himalayas, a river in full spate below. The letter had arrived on a Saturday. The same morning a flat-bed lorry had rattled to a stop beneath their bedroom window, a small beetle-like caravan in tow. Jay's half-sister Hazel had jumped from the cab and hammered on their front door. She wasn't expected, and when the lorry eventually departed she installed herself in their living room, the caravan unhitched at their kerb. She told Jay she wanted to help out with the road campaign, she wanted to speak at the Inquiry. She read Doug's letter, and told Ashley that Nepal was being overrun by trekkers. She said every wood-heated shower required the felling of three trees, and that the country would be deforested by the turn of the century. She was angry because he hadn't known this. *You're a teacher!* she'd told him. *You ought to know that!* She was not yet fifteen, younger than any of his sixth-formers.

Christobel raised an arm, one finger extended. She jigged her head until he saw her.

'Chrissie?'

'Can we yawn now?'

'Yes, of course. Please do.' Ashley located a sheet of squared paper behind him, his notes for the lesson. 'But there's loads more of this stuff to get through. We're supposed to discuss prevailing winds and the rise in car ownership. There's Ullman and Harris, and a man called Mann. All vital for your personal development.' One of the girls at the back was packing her bag, slowly and carefully, as if not to be noticed. 'But if you like,' he said, 'we could easily skip it.' He pulled open his drawer, slipped his lesson plan under some folders. An apple rolled forwards. He began to eat this as he wiped down his board. He drew another wide circle. 'This is my own personal model,' he said. 'Devised in my own personal head.'

'Do we have to copy it?' a voice asked.

Ashley divided his circle into twelve numbered segments, spoke over his shoulder. 'You don't *have* to copy anything, Kashif. But we've got to fill the time somehow. And this,' indicating his diagram, 'is a clock face. With my house just about here, south of the river at nine o'clock, inside Burgess's third ring. Whilst you lot live up here at about eleven o'clock, north of the river, in the fourth ring. And the famous Hogslea Common sits at three minutes to midnight – like so.'

He continued through a mouthful of apple, chalking over the imprint of his previous drawings. 'The Common makes a sort of down-turned wedge shape, with the fat end outside the clockface, like this. Now imagine what's going to happen when the new road is built. It begins at about seven o'clock down here, then comes up over the river, around the circumference, way past midnight, and shoots off towards that map on the wall. Suddenly a new ring of development happens – what used to be urban fringe becomes part of the city, what used to be countryside becomes urban fringe. You get superstores, factories, new houses, and these attract more stores and factories and houses. The life is sucked out of the city, and the Common is severed in two.'

As he chewed he attacked the board with his chalk, shading and deleting, layering detail on detail, until his diagram resembled a densely worked scribble, an infant's vigorous drawing. 'The thin pointy end of the Common,' he concluded, 'finds itself surrounded by concrete and cars and quickly chokes to death. Whilst the fat end is now half the wood it was – though not half as important – and before very long this is also swallowed up by the city, or at least overrun by picnickers and birds'-nesters and people dumping their old fridges. In theory anyway.' He turned to the class and stretched out his arms, aimed the apple core at his bin. 'Any comments?' he asked, smiling.

Euan was facing him now, and said, 'Why do you bother doing this job, Mr Brook? Seriously. What is the point?'

Your letter from the mountains arrived safely, Dug, and gave cause for much gleeful whistling and yodelling, but your handwriting is decipherable only when recognizably English. Where you are at any one time is rather a mystery, I can't make head nor tail of the place names. Which is a pity, as we'd like to follow your progress on our inflatable globe. One very curious thing about your being so far away – and I think about this a lot – is that really you're no further away than you ever were, or at least no less accessible than you ever were. We could no more have popped down to your place in London of a Sunday lunchtime than we can now hop on the next bus to Rajasthan. But because you are always on the move, on the other side of the world, somewhere or other, and not of a fixed address in a place which I'd recognize, we think about you more often, and wonder about you more often, which means in effect you are with us more than you ever were, not taken for granted, not neatly marked on our mental map of the universe, which means that your absence is felt more, which means you are missed more. Thus by going so far away you have come closer to home, in a manner of speaking. And what's really amazing is that I think these thoughts without the aid of a Himalayan peak to sit on. I would certainly like to sit on a Himalayan peak, however – 'they were cold, white, beyond life, and wiped you clean'. Give me some of that!

Hazel wore a grey pinafore which might have been a school dress. Her hair formed a ridge of green along the top of her head, like a hedge between two fields of stubble. It was shaved at the sides and dyed corn-yellow. As she spoke she stared into the fire and spread some tobacco along a channel of paper. 'The last site was shite,' she told him. 'It was in a valley by a road – this dual carriageway – and it was like non-stop lorries and cars, twenty-four-hour traffic, with all these stupid *knobwits* leaning out and yelling at us, like *we* were the ones fucking up *their* atmosphere. They killed my dog too. She was only four months old.'

Ashley steadied himself at the top of his step-ladder. He loaded his brush and glanced down.

'I saw it happen,' she said. 'I was trying to get her back, but she just went smack into this car. He stopped, the guy actually stopped and got out. But all he did was check his bumper – I was screaming at him, but he just shook his head and drove off, like he didn't even *see* me.' She rolled the paper, tucked and smoothed it into a cigarette, ran her tongue along the gum.

'We buried her on the hill. We climbed up in the afternoon and it was really beautiful, fields and woods and the sun shining, a few rabbits – sheep. Great place to be a dog. We dug a hole and covered her with leaves, these big autumn leaves – they were really lovely. But that was it, time to go. There was only six of us left and it was *awful*, fucking awful. But it's the same wherever you go now, you end up stranded in some shitty lay-by or you get evicted. Seventeen times I've been evicted this year.'

Ashley shook his head, and Jay said, 'Ours could be number eighteen, Hazel.' She was sitting high in a rocking-chair by the fireplace, her knees wide apart and touching the armrests. A book lay open in the hammock formed by her skirt.

Hazel said, 'I'll just smoke this, Jay, and that's the last, I promise.' She held the roll-up near her mouth, lit it when Jay looked away. 'I could've gone to Wales,' she said. 'I still might, but last winter was so *grim*. You'd get these amazing frosty mornings, Ash – they were really magical, really, really beautiful – but then it snowed for ages and everything just froze – I had a bottle of vodka and even *that* froze. Eggs, toothpaste – and when you went to the shit-pit you'd have to dig two feet of snow just to find the ground, then *that* was frozen as well. Nightmare.'

Ashley smoothed his brush along the ceiling coving. A tape was playing softly below and he hummed to himself.

'But I can't handle cities either,' she sighed. 'It's like, fucking hell, man, what's happening. There's so many people, so many attitudes – it's a buzz, for a while I really like it, but then it gets so *manic*, you end up completely stressed out. I need that feeling of being in touch with what the weather's doing, knowing you can just look up and the sky's all around you. In the city everyone has their own little piece of sky. They have their own little piece of ground, and their own little headspace. They don't know what's *real*. Everything's so *easy*. They've got too much time on their hands and they end up going crazy. It's like when Mum decided we were going to be normal and she got us into this Council estate. Everyone was totally paranoid, no one spoke to anyone. You'd wander round at nights and all you'd see in the windows were colour tellies. It was like this huge mental asylum where everyone's either totally wired or watching the box – electric valium.'

Ashley descended, repositioned his step-ladder and re-mounted.

'There was a school there as well and that was the worst-ever. The teachers never showed you any respect – they all expected it, but they never showed it, they just wanted obedience. That's all they taught you, how to be normal and nice. It's mind control, so the kids all hate anyone different. Everyone in a school has to be the same, they're like sausages coming out of a machine. There was one in Wales last year, that was good, they let me hang out in the art class, but most of these places, everyone's the same, it's really strange. They all want to be *like* everyone else, but they all want to be *better* than everyone else. They're competing to see who can be the most *ordinary*.'

Ashley sighed but said nothing, squinted into his paint-work. A cobweb was smeared in the gloss. His neck and arm ached. The tape had ended.

I think I've done the Met. Office a disservice, Douglas. For 'weather codes' I should've said 'precipitation codes' because there's a separate list for wind, called the Beaufort Scale, as every schoolchild knows. I taught this to my third-years last week when we were experiencing a highly poetic Force 5, which is to say 'Strong breeze: large branches in motion; whistling heard in tele-graph wires; umbrellas used with difficulty'. Jay is generally a Force 0 these days, or 'Calm: smoke rises vertically', but does occasionally get up to a Force 3 — 'Moderate breeze: raises dust and loose paper; small branches removed'. She still precipitates, of course, or, rather, precipitates copiously in short bursts, but mostly she sits contentedly sewing jumpsuits.

Her belly is quite rounded already, which I approve of, but she also talks to it, which I'm not so sure about, and drums on it, which I definitely don't like, it makes me squeamish, I'm sure she'll do the infant some serious inner-ear damage. Always assum-ing it has an inner ear. It does have an outer ear — we've seen it, because last month we went to the maternity hospital over the river for an ultrasound scan. The infant has a very big head, a pounding heart, and at least one fully functioning limb, with five perfect fingers. Probably also a thumb. It was then exactly thirteen weeks and six days old. The estimate is calculated from its length in millimetres and is, apparently, entirely accurate, which means we were also able to calculate the exact hour of conception — July 20th, a Saturday, no doubt between the hours of ten and eleven am, leaving me just enough time to fetch the paper and cook up two bacon rolls before the ITV Chart Show, such was the nature of our Saturdays in those hazy, carefree times. Consulting my diary, in which I compile fully comprehensive lists of all I must do for each day of my life, I was able to discover that I spent the rest of that day arranging our finances into box files, finishing the ironing, stripping the bedroom wallpaper, and — significantly! — traipsing round a garden centre helping Jay choose seeds for her window boxes. I expect I also had a lie-down to replenish my sperms, it's not every day a guy conceives a baby. Especially not the day before his gal's period, which, miraculously, was when it happened, at least according to Jay's diary, which is less than fully comprehensive, or reliable. So how about that?

After the scan Jay went to be examined by her consultant and was told her pregnancy is 'unremarkable in every way', which I thought was some bloody cheek, but apparently means all is going swimmingly. The expected time of arrival is now the third week in April, and we are currently at week eighteen. According to the manuals this ought to be our Honeymoon Period when Jay has never felt so wholesome and wonderful and never wanted so much sex but in fact she feels little different from the Sicking-up Period, except that she doesn't sick-up. At nights she now sleeps with a pillow to support the bulge, but doesn't sleep very well. She can't seem to work out what to do with her arms, she grunts and sighs, turns one way then the next, and usually wakes all out of sorts – eg this morning when she actually swore at our unborn child. After breakfast, however, she was improvising an Egyptian love dance in the kitchen with Hazel, the sort-of-sister, our latest unpaying guest, who is – on the Beaufort Scale of things – a definite Force 6, which is to say, 'Whole trees in motion, inconvenience felt when walking'. Inconvenience felt, full stop. She is a very inconvenient person.

Apparently, since she arrived I've spent an embarrassing amount of time scurrying up and down ladders, paintbrush in hand, so at least she's spurred me to some serious nest-building. Also apparently, since Jay and I began sharing our bed with the pillow, I've stopped wriggling in the night and now keep pretty much to my own side of the mattress. Evidently my sleeping self thinks the pillow's a baby, which just goes to show how little I know. In fact, the first night Jay brought the pillow to bed I had my first dream about baby. I dreamt Jay fished under the sheets and pulled out a pudgy girl-child swaddled in white. I was furious. 'Why didn't you tell me you'd put her down there? I could've rolled over and squashed her!' So I went to set up my ladder in the living room, but left the door open so I could watch *the baby crawling around in the hallway. Suddenly she got off her knees and ran full-tilt at the door. 'Jay! Jay! She can run!' I yelled. But then she ran straight into the door and fell over backwards, unhurt, like a wind-up toy. 'But she doesn't know how to stop yet!' I shouted.*

You will notice that she is a she – a Milly, a Maggie, a Madge – and that Hazel's camp-bed does not occupy our living-room floor when I'm dreaming.

DECEMBER

THE INQUIRY featured often in the regional paper and TV news, and sometimes in the national media, but the building that housed it was not a prominent one. Set between spreading horse-chestnuts, the hall had once been a chapel, a Council depot, and recently a community centre. On a signboard under the eaves a thin wash of paint concealed the words *Bathesba Gospel Church*. Notices for a summer playscheme were posted in the grilles on the windows.

When the Inquiry had opened in late August the chestnuts had formed a solid mass of green against a clear sky, but now the bare branches merged with rain-laden clouds, a vaporous grey blur above the roof tiles. As he approached the hall from the bus stop Ashley trod through a mulch of dead leaves. A thin yellow light came from the hall entrance and he noticed a woman giving an interview, a reporter mechanically nodding. On the forecourt two men were loading metal cases into the back of an estate car. A presenter from the evening news was standing with them, hugging herself in an overcoat. Ashley edged past them and down a narrow passageway to the rear of the building, where Hazel's cream-and-green caravan was stationed as a base for the bypass objectors. It was decorated with cellophane-wrapped posters and route maps. A sign on the door said *Information Point*, and Ashley entered without knocking.

Inside, a large kettle steamed gently on a two-ringed cooker; a gas heater burned in one corner. The surfaces were wood-veneer and moist with condensation, pinned with documents and notices. Jay sat alone on a bench by a window and widened her eyes to acknowledge him. She was tugging the sides of her mouth, stretching the soft flesh of her lips to reveal her gums. It was painful 'and she closed her eyes, but continued to pull, breathing slowly as her lips lost shape and colour, became outlines, until finally she gasped and let go. Ashley unzipped his coat.

'What are you doing?'

She pressed her lips to a pout and gingerly touched them. A dog-eared book lay open beside her. 'It's like having your fanny stretched apart,' she said. 'I was practising.'

'Here?'

'No one's looking.'

Ashley moved the book to one side and sat with her. She hooked a leg over his and reached an arm round his shoulders, tried to draw him closer.

'How was school?' she asked.

'No one turned up,' he said. It was the last day of term, five days before Christmas. 'I bunked off.' He wiped a sleeve through the damp on a window and peered out at the hall, the grubbily rendered rear wall. Finally he asked, 'How was your media event?'

'Okay.' She smiled. For the previous three months Jay had been working in a neighbourhood centre near the route of the new road. She went several days each week and provided lessons in screen-printing and stitching, organized a project to make wall-hangings. The themes were road building and lost habitats, and that afternoon her group had unfurled their banners to the Inquiry. It was their official submission against the road scheme. The Inspector was scheduled to close proceedings the next day. 'We're going to be on the telly,' she said.

'Nice.'

'The papers and radio came too. Then Hazel started shouting her mouth off, so that sealed it – plenty of pictures.'

Ashley nodded. He fastened his coat, slipped Jay's book into his pocket. 'Are you coming in with me?'

'I'm on duty,' she said, and pointed to a rota. 'But you go – you might catch the beetle man. He's very sweet. He's found a rare species that only lives in the oak trees. It's very, *very* rare. You should go and support him – most of the rest have gone home now.'

'Hazel too?'

'She's still there,' said Jay, then hurriedly added, 'but so are the banners. You could just look at the banners, forget the beetles.' Ashley began to stand, and she said, 'Only, can I have my book back, please?'

'If you keep your fingers out of your mouth.' Her lips were unnaturally red. As he bent to kiss her she pulled the book from his pocket.

'My fingers, my mouth,' she said.

In the dim-lit lobby of the building there was a smell of floor mops and detergents, a clutter of old furniture and sports gear. A second set of double doors opened into the hall. Ashley raised a hand to push through but found himself guided inside by a suited official, the door closing softly behind him. The man's open palm indicated a receptionist, who rotated a register to face him, laid a biro beside it. An electric fan-heater hummed at her feet. Jay's banners were propped in procession along one of the walls.

As the woman copied Ashley's name on to a sticker the official folded his arms and sat on the edge of her desk. He bowed his head and studied Ashley's entry in the register. Like the receptionist, he was quietly, expensively dressed and seemed far superior to the task he was performing. Ashley nodded at the banners and said, 'Can I look at these?'

'You may,' said the woman, and proffered the sticker on the end of one finger.

The proceedings took place inside an enclosure of display stands that occupied most of the hall. Along the entire outer length of the screens there was an exhibition of photographs and diagrams, statistics and captions. The lights overhead descended on thin, rigid stalks, the clouded bulbs further darkened with dust. Additional lamps had been clamped to the uprights of the boards, angled to illuminate the exhibition. The wall-hangings faced the screens across a distance of four or five yards.

Ashley's shoes squeaked on the linoleum-tiled floor. He paced slowly past the banners, then retreated to view the four as a group. At the far end of the hall a door opened and closed and he heard the muffled sweep of a photocopier. From within the enclosure there came a shuffling, contemplative silence not broken until the copier had ended its cycle. At last the door reopened and a voice hesitantly resumed, 'I think this should make things clearer . . .'

The name of Jay's organization, *Northside Community Arts*, was embroidered into the first of the banners, and a treescape appeared in the upper panel of each, changing colour and density to signify the seasons. The four lower panels ran together as a single scene composed of appliquéd vehicles and buildings, people and wildlife. Many of the figures and objects were crudely outlined and stitched, whilst a few were expertly padded and sewn. Combinations of transparent material had been layered to represent clouds and sunshine, the reflections in water. Other details were drawn in felt-tip. As he listened to the voice of the naturalist, Ashley realized he was staring at a large quilted beetle, the vivid green of its wings shot with blue and gold thread, red beads for its eyes and cords of silk for its legs.

'There's a range of species in the area,' the man was saying, 'mostly fairly common, and I've provided a list of these. They're bound to exist in similar communities elsewhere, but this particular beetle is extremely rare. There's some literature in Europe, but it hasn't been seen here since before 1830. It's an outstanding find. I've photocopied the relevant page from *Stephens* . . .'

Ashley turned to the official display. He stood before a blaze of red, yellow and green, a swathe of young trees in autumn. The photograph was familiar. Beneath it a caption read, *Since 1963 the Department has planted a total of 30 million trees in England and Wales, a vital contribution in the effort to replenish the nation's stock of trees in the aftermath of Dutch elm disease.* Other images depicted motorways as they swept through open countryside; ribbons of grey winding through valleys of conifers; cars and campers parked in summer glades. *Trees enhance the visual appeal of roads for the motorist,* he read, and remembered lingering at this point on his first visit to the Inquiry, arrested by the compositions and bright colours, the smooth, clean arcs of the roads. On the adjoining screen there was a selection of computer elevations and cross-sections, projections of the road as it would bank and cut through the contours of the land. Each graphic was decorated with tree symbols of differing sizes and shapes: triangular, circular and elliptical; short, medium and tall. A box of text began, *Trees reduce noise disturbance and conceal traffic and prominent structures . . .*

At the entrance to the enclosure there was an aerial view of the city, and he wondered momentarily how he might acquire one for his classroom. Its sprawling boundaries bore little resemblance to the model he had drawn on his blackboard; the woodland was revealed as tiny in relation to the whole, its outline far from geometrical. The new road, a thick cord of red, arched around the western suburbs and through the Common before veering northwards. There it joined the motorway which also served Ashley's home town of Ravensby, ninety miles further on. He searched for his and Jay's house. Where his parents had previously faced an arduous drive into the congested heart of the city, the new route would carry them from the motorway to within a few hundred yards of his street. He stared at the photograph and examined the centimetres between his terrace and the red line. He supposed they would use the new road to visit more often. Sighing heavily, he stepped inside the screens.

In reply to a question the naturalist was saying, 'They really couldn't be transplanted to the coppice reserve. It's out of the question. That's a totally different habitat. . .' He was not much older than Ashley, lank-haired and dressed in combat fatigues. He pushed his sleeves up his forearms, repeatedly jerked his head to disturb his fringe. Facing him there were seats for perhaps 120 people, enough to fill four classrooms, but only half a dozen were occupied. Isolated at the back, Hazel sat in a posture of conscientious attention, her elbows on her knees, fingers pressed to her temples. A thin dreadlock fell between her eyes; a tangle of longer locks sprouted from her crown. Ashley recognized the coat draped over the back of her chair as his own. The striped leggings she wore had been Jay's. He edged between two rows of chairs and sat with her.

'Going well?' he whispered.

Hazel waved an exasperated hand at the Inspector. 'It's a *farce*,' she complained. 'It's a total fucking stitch-up. *He*'s not remotely fucking interested.'

The Inspector, a bald, compact man in a tweed jacket, sat alone at a wide table, a vacuum flask at his elbow. He was listening to the naturalist with arms folded, his chin drawn in and gaze lowered as if contemplating some other, more personal matter. Reaching now for a pair of spectacles, he raised a hand to halt the proceedings and indicated an usher to come forward. There was a long murmured conversation. The naturalist flipped through his notes. A young woman leafed through a ring-binder. Then the usher advanced on Ashley and Hazel. The naturalist said, 'I'll just wind up by reading this supporting statement from English Heritage. There should be photocopies . . .'

Anticipating a confrontation, Hazel became agitated in her seat, but the usher's face was apologetic and his smile directed at Ashley. 'You're welcome to chat behind the screens if you wish, but the session will be closing quite shortly. Only a few minutes more.'

'No, that's fine,' Ashley said. 'Thanks.'

Hazel glowered as the usher backed off. 'Not real,' she murmured. 'This is not fucking real.' She sat upright in her seat, then sighed and slumped back. She braced her feet against the chair in front. Moments later she began to speak out, addressing no one in particular. 'The trouble is they don't realize how lucky they are to have the privilege of living on this planet. She's our source – Mother Earth, that's why she's called Mother fucking Earth – but they just keep carving her up, they just keep sawing off the branches we're sitting on . . .'

Without acknowledging Hazel, the Inspector raised his eyebrows to the naturalist, and the younger man faltered, then shrugged. 'That's it,' he conceded, briefly displaying the last of his notes as Hazel's voice trailed off. 'I'll leave it there.'

'Thank you,' the Inspector said flatly, and rose from his chair. 'A rebuttal to this evidence tomorrow?' His clerk emerged from the room behind him and nodded. 'Then we shall adjourn, with a brief word to our two friends at the back, that if either of you should return here in the morning you shall be barred from entry. The police will be informed.' He fastened a button of his jacket as if to signal the end of proceedings and retired to the photocopying room. The usher followed with his flask. Various other officials began to pack away their documents.

With a hand on her elbow Ashley encouraged Hazel to stand. Her face was pale and her mouth tightly drawn. As he helped her into his coat Ashley realized she was trembling and tightened his arm round her shoulders. The few remaining spectators were pulling on hats and scarves and filing from the enclosure, none looking in their direction. Ashley tugged Hazel to follow, and she nodded but shrugged herself free of his arm. In the area outside the enclosure the naturalist saw them. He hesitated, then came forward, diffidently offered a hand. 'Owen,' he said.

Hazel pressed her name-sticker to one of the display screens, and said, 'Want some tea?'

There are moments reading your account of your wanderings, Douglas, when I'm gripped by a positively Mum-like enviousness. It's not so bad now, in the holidays, but my career is snail-backed and gutter-bound and I never feel so misplaced in the world as in the company of the people I work with. Last Thursday was the end of term, which means Santa's Grotto, where each member of staff receives a saucy (and anonymous) present from some other member of staff, and several of the teachers dress up in the saucy undies they received last year and perform a saucy cabaret for the great amusement of the rest. Photographs are taken, embarrassments remembered. The event looms large in the staff social calendar and there's much peer pressure to take part, as we educationists say. But I refused. Me and Miserable Mike, the mad maths teacher, refused. I left at lunchtime with the kids. What a relief or what! So how come I felt so miserable? I suppose because it's Christmas and I shan't be going to Goa . . .

Not that I don't know how to be festive when I want to. The Friday before Santa's Grotto was the annual Prefects' Dinner & Dance, where I got pleasantly drunk and displayed, I'm told, 'another side of Mr B.' — ie, cheerful, ie, festive (ie, I'm afraid, amorous – I pecked every pair of prefect's lips offered to me). The majority of the sixth-form boys got very unpleasantly drunk very quickly, however, and displayed another side of themselves – ie, seamy – and lowered the tone even further than the depths already plumbed by the head boy's speech. The retiring headmaster himself recited Shakespeare – a playwright – and compared the upper sixth to saplings and seedlings, soon to branch into adulthood, whilst the head girl's contribution was a model of its kind, short and sweet – as is she. But then the head boy took half an hour to embarrass, individually, every person present, recalling Christobel Mimms's dirty underwear, Mrs Miller's boast that she could toss off Coleridge, Anna Peterson's claim to have ATTRACTIVE stamped on her forehead, Mr Brook's famous fits of blushing . . . After which Euan Eliott won a pair of plastic tits in the raffle, strapped them on, and invited each female member of staff to give him a shag . . . This is what babies turn into.

Boy babies.

Actually, having pretty much settled on Maggie for a girl, we're having real difficulty coming up with an even half-decent or acceptable name for a boy. This is a game you might like to play on your travels. Think of a boy's name. Think of a girl's name. Now doesn't the boy's name always recall its own worst example, and the girl's name its own best example? If I think of Andrew, for instance, I remember shady Uncle Andy the religious nut, next-door Andrew with the air rifle, Andrew the opinionated bastard in our staffroom, several Andrews of dubious intelligence, and Andrew (what else?) our head boy. But not a decent Andrew ever. Yet if I think of Angela I never recall (or at least not immediately) the girl from across the street who split my head open with a half-brick when we were playing doctors and nurses, but always that girl with sea-green eyes who worked in the chippy and caressed my hand when she returned my change. (We never actually ever spoke, and the last time I saw her she was going out with that no-brain Andy who fought in the Gulf War and once jacked himself off for a bet in the PE showers.)

Our own Maggie-not-Andy is becoming a quite prominent feature these days, enormous really, and has long since started to wriggle. It kicks furiously at regular intervals throughout the day and well into the night. When it first began to get restless ('a little ping', said Jay) I closed my eyes and held my hand over the bulge and gave it my best shot, but I couldn't tell baby's toe prod from Jay's digestion. Since then it has developed thighs and calves in the true Brookian mould and it's now possible to watch the assault on Jay's innards from a distance of several yards, though I still can't seem to place my mitts in quite the right place. The midwife says it's a good sign anyway, the hyperactivity. And the fact that we didn't get a result from our spina bifida test was also a good sign, apparently, as I told Mum on the phone. 'Well, I know what I would've done if one of mine had had spina bifida,' she said. 'What's that then, Mum?' I asked. 'Abortion,' she hissed. This was on Christmas Day.

The ground on the incline was frozen hard, in patches thawed to a skim of fibrous mud that made walking precarious and strenuous. Shallow ribbons and lenses of ice had formed in the ruts and hollows, frozen pools in the crotches between the roots of the trees. Ashley gripped Jay's gloved hand and walked unsteadily sideways, his feet slipping with each step. Her cheeks were blotched pink, and at the top of the rise she was panting. 'Okay?' he said, and she nodded distractedly, turning a slow circle as she gathered her breath. She wore a baggy hat that her sister had knitted for Christmas, and a raincoat plumped out with woollens. 'Which way now?' he asked, and she tugged off the hat, flipped her hair free of her collar.

'Through there,' she decided, and led him towards a thicket of spindly trees. They entered with hunched shoulders, arms raised against the straggling branches. Above them the tangled basket of the canopy creaked on the breeze. A litter of frosted leaves crunched underfoot; birds rustled in the denser shade of the shrubs. In the half-light of the interior Ashley paused to pull down a branch, and said, 'I think these might be hazel. Or aspen maybe.' He opened a pocket guide and compared a twig in the gloom with its illustration. 'Would you get aspen here, Jay?'

'Dunno,' she said from the distance.

Where the light brightened the trees became taller and sparser and they walked upright several yards apart, following a route suggested by the pattern of the trunks and shrubs, dead wood and ditches. All around there was a constant fire-like crackling of ice as it thawed. A crust of blue-tinted snow lay over the unsheltered ground, its surface pitted with droplets of water and broken by the shoots of young trees. Ashley watched the overarching branches and registered the transition of one group of trees into another. Holly was frequent and obvious, and he recognized birch by its bark, oak by the crookedness of its limbs. But he soon tired of trying to identify the others, frustrated by the absence of leaves, the sleeves of moss over the trunks. He pushed the book into his pocket. Ahead of him Jay walked with eyes lowered, her pace seeming to quicken or slow as the woods closed and opened around her. When finally she disappeared from view he hurried to catch her.

Her raincoat was unbuttoned and she was walking with her hands tucked under her jumpers, cupping the sides of her belly. 'What's up?' he asked, and she shook her head, smiling. They passed into a corridor of bent trees, trunks rising from banks on each side of them, bare branches linking overhead. She made him stand close behind her and gathered his arms round her waist, placed his hands flat to her abdomen. Ashley felt the warmth through her vest and rested his chin on her shoulder. The mustiness of the perfume in her clothes was the smell of their bedroom. He raised his hands to her breasts. It was dark and the surrounding trees appeared black. Ashley listened for the sounds of the town and heard only bird-calls.

At last Jay repositioned his hands on her belly, and said, 'Ready? The baby walks when I do.' A patch of snow gleamed from the clearing ahead of them, and she led him clumsily, almost tripping, towards it. They stopped in the open, a fallen bough blocking their path. 'Did you feel it?' she asked, then flinched as if from a blow. An aircraft ripped out of the silence above them, whipped low across the treetops. The birds scattered, screeching, and Ashley tightened his arms around Jay. He felt a movement, a ripple under his palm, and started to smile, his face pressed to her back. Releasing herself slowly, Jay buttoned her raincoat and used her hat to brush some frost from the bough. She sat beside a clump of fresh sprigs. The branch was not detached but part of a living tree that had overbalanced, still rooted. She tugged him to sit with her, and said, 'Well?'

Ashley leaned against her, as the encircling trees leant into each other. 'Yes.' He nodded. 'I felt it this time.' The sun came low through the curtain of birches behind them, casting pale shadows on the carpet of snow. Soon they would have to return, but they delayed and didn't speak. The quiet that descended seemed deeper than before. Ashley looked to where their footprints emerged from the wood, and realized the snow was falling again. His gaze came to rest on a clutch of tiny green blades, the first shoots of spring in the husk of winter. It was the last day of the year. 'Where are we anyway?' he asked finally.

'No idea,' she replied, and they rose as the snowflakes began to thicken around them.

JANUARY

THERE WERE times when she'd enter a room and her shape would surprise him. He would have to look twice, to remember the reason. She ate more than she used to, and sometimes he forgot why and her appetite disturbed him. Occasionally the other teachers at school would ask after her health and he wouldn't always know what to answer, for a moment confused by their interest. Then he'd say, 'Fine,' and resent the intrusion. But for Jay there were few moments of forgetting and she felt little relief from the weight of her symptoms, or the attention her body attracted. Returning from the city centre one Saturday she found Ashley stripping a wall in the bedroom, and suddenly started to cry.

'I am so *sick* of being stared at,' she said. 'I'm out to here and I can't walk down the street without getting wolf-whistled or flashed by car headlights and practically every man who goes by me stares at my *tits*. It's so fucking outrageous!' She pulled off her sweatshirt and slumped on the bed, angrily plumped up some pillows.

Ashley sat at his desk near the window. There was a half-written letter to his brother in the typewriter, a roll of toilet paper by his elbow. When Jay held out her hand he tossed the roll towards her. 'Your tits are nice, Jay,' he said.

'Fuck off, Ashley.' She blew her nose and quickly unwound some more tissue. 'The women are nearly as bad. Soon as I get on the bus I can feel them all looking at my belly, then another sly glance to see if I'm wearing a ring. Every fucking time!' She groaned and leant into her pillows, turned her face to the newly bared patch of wall. Like most of the rooms in their house the wallpaper was old and already partially stripped. They had begun the job soon after moving in, but found the coverings went back in layers, each one firmly stuck to the next and impossible to remove without effort. The plaster beneath was unstable and often tore away with the paper, causing sudden sootfalls of rubble and leaving hollows too wide or deep for patching. Jay had wanted to paint over the existing coverings, but then claimed she preferred the pattern of ripped paper and gouges, the differing colours and textures. For nearly two years Ashley had lost interest. Now Jay said, 'What started this off again?'

'Something to do,' he shrugged, and swivelled in his chair, suddenly embarrassed. He clambered on to the bed and sat across her shins, a hand to either side of her knees. 'Nest-building you know. Makes a difference, huh?'

'Not really,' she replied.

'Hard work anyway,' he said, and showed her a blister caused by the scraper.

At his parents' home in Ravensby the paper had peeled away in long sheets, revealing walls of smooth grey. Only on closer inspection did the cracks become visible, tight and jagged on every surface. The house had been built two years before Ashley was born, and theirs was the only family to have lived there. In his first week of primary school he had returned one day to find his father redecorating the living room. Where previously there had always been wallpaper, now there was a painted inscription on the blank plaster, his and Douglas's names and birth dates. It was as if the words had also always been there; as if he was meant to live in that house, and with that family. At that time he had felt only contentment, and wonder, and imagined that every other home must somewhere conceal the names of the children who lived there. He could not remember when his wonder had turned to puzzlement; or later to disappointment.

Sitting by Jay's feet, he said, 'I might phone Dad later – see if he's got any ideas about these walls. Before they cave in completely.'

'He'll die of shock,' she said. 'When did you last ask him anything?'

'Last New Year. I asked if he wanted another beer.' Ashley unknotted her laces and dropped her boots with a clump to the floorboards. He pulled off her socks, then helped with her leggings and pants. 'It's pointless anyway,' he sighed. 'He's okay on painting or papering, but anything else, he just gives Mum the *Yellow Pages* and tells her to call out a tradesman.'

'Look at my ankles. They're so puffy.'

'They're fine,' Ashley said. 'Same as normal.' He tugged the sheets and blankets from beneath her, then swept the covers back over her legs. The calor heater spluttered in the draught.

'I am so sick of being *fat*,' she complained. 'I want to be thin again. I want to fit my clothes again.'

'You haven't got any thin clothes,' he told her. 'Hazel took them.'

Jay's sister had departed a few days after Christmas, hitching a lift in the lorry which had brought her two months before. She was going to spend the rest of the winter in a cottage in the Black Mountains, helping to nanny some friends' children. She would write lots of letters, send photographs; and perhaps she would return for the birth. Her caravan was again parked at their kerbside. She had sold it to a friend, she'd said, who would be arriving the next day to collect it. But four weeks later they had still to receive their first letter, and the caravan was becoming muddied by footballs, a target for the kids in the street.

Ashley slipped off his trainers and jeans and got under the bedclothes. In the weeks before Christmas Hazel had helped him to clear the clutter from the back bedroom. It was the only room in the house with sound walls, and together they'd laid two coats of yellow emulsion over the paper, then glossed the woodwork and washed the curtains and carpet. Amongst the boxes and bin-bags Hazel had found a child's mobile, and this now hung from the ceiling. But the baby would not be sleeping in that room. There had been no discussion, no argument. At Jay's insistence everything they'd removed was returned – all the bags and boxes and pieces of furniture – because the baby was going to sleep between Ashley and her. It wasn't natural, she'd said, for a child to be isolated at night. It happened in no other culture.

Lying beside her now, Ashley cupped his hand under her bulge and pressed his face to her breast, the stiff contour of her maternity bra. He closed his eyes. From the house next door there came the noise of voices shouting over the television, and a smell of cooking, as if this were seeping out through the bared walls. He tucked his hand inside Jay's top and rested his palm on the raised knot of her navel. Their bodies were touching along their full length, and he could hear her breathing, his own pulse in his temples. But he was conscious also of a distance between them, a yearning to be nearer. He hooked one leg over hers, and she said, 'You're pressing my bladder, Ash.'

'Sorry.'

She gathered up her shirt and pulled it over her head, tugged the sleeves from her arms. 'I feel like I've got a boiler inside me. Everyone in town was wrapped in scarves and winter woollies and I was tramping around with my coat flapping open. It was freezing out there, Ashley, and I just thought, *brilliant, fresh air!*' Sitting upright she turned and indicated the clasp of her bra and he helped her remove it. The straps left red grooves on her back and under the loll of her breasts, and he noticed the plumpness of her skin where her ribs used to show.

As she eased back to her pillows Ashley lay inside her arm and closed his mouth over her nipple. It was firmer and fuller than it used to be, and more ticklish. Jay squirmed a little, but held her hand to the back of his head, wouldn't let him pull away. After a while she said, 'Wilma from the management committee is pregnant again, Ashley. She had her first in the Western and she was telling me – she went into labour a month early and her consultant immediately wanted to do a Caesarean. No discussion or anything. Caesarean. But she just refused, so they dragged in all these other doctors to put pressure on her, only she wouldn't listen to them either and the baby was born without any complications, just like she said it would be.' Her fingers caressed the back of his neck; she took a long breath. 'So then it was taken away to intensive care for observation – before she could even object – and her last words were they mustn't feed it, not till she'd had a chance to try it on the breast, only it came back with a bottle in its mouth – the *sister* was feeding it. Wilma was furious, really pissed off. So this time she's put in for a home birth, and they can't say no, they have to provide a midwife.' She tapped his neck with her fingertips. 'Ashley?'

'What?' He looked up to her face. Then, 'No way, Jay! No way are you having it at home, not the first, not in all this mess.'

'It's my body,' she said, 'my hole it has to come out of.'

'You can't! You might as well have it on a building site, or some junk shop. What if anything went wrong?'

'It won't,' she said. 'Why should it?' But her tone was

sulky, without conviction, and he supposed she was not serious. She dragged down a pillow and rolled away from him, on to her side. Ashley curled against her. 'I just can't handle hospitals,' she said. 'It's that smell, and all those people shuffling around in their slippers and pyjamas. It's like Hazel says about schools, you just become part of the process, only it's worse. It's humiliating.' She raised her head and squinted at him. 'And hospitals are full of germs, Ashley, more than this place will ever be.'

'Full of medicines too,' he murmured.

He gnawed gently on her shoulder, caressing the swell of her hip, the heavy crease at her waist. She was broader than she had been, or seemed so. His cock twitched in the cleft of her buttocks, and she eased back to meet him. Quietly she said, 'Put it in me, Ashley,' and he entered her slowly, arching his body from hers. Naked she appeared to him without edge or blemish, roundly desirable in a way she had not been when thinner. Her shape was something private between them. He pushed away the bedclothes and smoothed his hand over her arm, her head, across the curve of her back. Often when they made love it was her size that he'd cling to, which most excited him. Pressing deep inside her now he ached to draw closer still and he moulded his body to hers, smelling the damp in her hair, the sharpness of her sweat. She sought out his hand and guided him downwards, parting her thighs. He moved his fingers under hers. Then her breath came in quickening gasps, and he felt himself like a child, holding tightly against her, barely moving as slowly her contractions unfurled and intensified and gradually, eventually weakened. She clutched his hand to her belly and he came without warning.

An hour later they woke to find the gas fire guttering, about to expire, and the bedclothes in a heap on the floor. It was as dark as early evening but the clock showed half past one.

They could hear a boxing commentary from next door. Rolling on to his back Ashley said, 'I had another one of those dreams, Jay,' and watched as she pulled on a dressing gown and switched off the heater. A belt of hailstones hit their window. She crossed to look out. 'You were whispering to someone in the kitchen,' he said, 'but when I asked who, you just gave out this huge sigh, like *Fuck off, Ashley*. You were really foul, so I lost my rag and started shouting, *You're such a fat cow, Jay, you really make me sick – just look at your ankles*. Then that guy Owen turned up, your beetle man, and I punched him on the nose. I broke it, there was blood everywhere, but you just looked so unimpressed, really aloof. I felt like a total prick.'

'You are,' she said, and patted his knee. 'That's your mum at the door.'

'What?' There was a rap on their letterbox, and he rose from the bed. 'I don't believe it.'

'Your dad as well,' she added.

The hail was as fine and dense as a mist. Ashley saw two boys sprinting to the top of the street, and a young woman in high heels pushing a pram down the centre of the road, cringing inside her jacket. His father watched her go by, then ducked into the boot of his car. He unloaded some boards and leant them against the rear wheel. Drifts of hail like blown sand swept along the pavement, and Ashley heard his mother saying. 'Will you just wait a minute, Ken. They might not be in.' The letterbox clattered again, and with a loud sigh Jay descended the stairs. Ashley felt the chill from the window and covered his groin. It was still clammy from sex. He looked round for his jeans and noticed his letter to Douglas in the typewriter. He pulled the sheet from the roller and slipped it under some files, then heard his mother speaking rapidly to Jay in the hallway, upset by the weather, angry at his father. He sat on the edge of the bed and listened with his head propped on his fists.

'Ashley!' Jay called, and laboured back up the stairs to find him.

Do you remember the Begley bitches, Douglas? Do you even remember the Begleys? They lived in one of the houses across the green at the back of us and they owned at least twelve super-prolific mongrel bitches, none more than six inches high. Very small animals. They were Catholics, the Begleys. The mutts were all sorts. Perhaps they'd moved on before you were old enough to notice, but it was the bit in your letter from Panaji about seeing two dogs joined at right angles that made me remember them – I saw the very same dog-thing in our own back yard (almost). It was a sunny day – there may even have been widespread dust in suspension in the air at the time – and we were playing football on the green (us big boys, not you baby ones) when the smallest of the Begley bitches got entangled with PC Beaver's newest Alsatian, which was very possibly a virgin until that afternoon, and which got stuck inside her. In trying to get himself unstuck PC Beaver's Alsatian stepped over his own willy and found himself facing in the opposite direction to the Begley bitch, who then also stepped over his willy so that they ended up at right angles, the police hound's willy being very long and pink and slimy, pretty much like his tongue, pretty much like his facial expression, and hers, so I went and knocked on the door of the Begleys', who all piled out to watch but didn't intervene, and then our mum came charging out with a bucket of cold water, and another, and a third, until the beasts were separated. I didn't realize until that time that that was how it was done (sexual congress, not canine coitus interruptus), and I didn't realize that dogs had a pink retractable willy inside the hard hairy one. Many years later Sue-from-school demonstrated the very same thing by masturbating her own much bigger mongrel until his own slithery pink thingy poked out; and some time after that I saw an off-duty circus horse get a stiffy for no reason at all, his willy extending like a telescope, one section after another, until the organ almost thwacked in the mud. He was tethered to a peg on a piece of waste ground in the lee of the dark satanic steelworks, and reclining beside him were a llama and a giraffe. And I only went for a walk that afternoon to clear my head. It was the occasion of my first ever spliff.

And the moral of all this penile reminiscence? Why travel half way round the globe for experiences readily available in your own back yard (almost)? In addition to which, why blow every last penny of your redundancy to finance the trip when you can glean all the information you shall ever need about anywhere in the world by regular subscription to a Sunday newspaper, price £1 per week? By happy chance, the account of your Goan misadventures coincided with another full-colour feature in the Sunday travel pages. So there you were, stoned out of your bonce on Benaulim beach, pissing all over your sandals, without a clue to your whereabouts, and here was I, homebound and fully informed – to wit: that tourists like you are lowering the Goan water table and overstretching the Goan electricity grid, and if any more of you arrive, the resident hippies will lose their Goan tempers, they will positively freak.

And the real reason for this sourness? Envy of course. I don't believe I have a single interesting thing to tell you, no incident of any significance, no misadventures, no beach parties, no nothing. Except! Of Course! The Bulge! Which continues to grow at a truly interesting and significant rate, although Jay refuses to share my excitement as her burden is beginning to weigh – she's gained a stone in a mere five weeks. And her fingers are swollen (that's called oedema), her sinuses are blocked (which means she can smell nothing, and snores like a hammer drill), her back is sore almost constantly, and she has a pain in her left leg, which the doctor says might be cramp, or possibly a varicose vein, or possibly even thrombosis, which may cause blood clotting and would require surgery, which can't be performed until the baby is out. The snoring is a cause of much unhappiness, not to say anger and bitterness, and may also, eventually, require surgery to remove Jay's adenoids, or so says the doctor. The baby at *any rate is happy, with a good sturdy heartbeat, and is the proper way up.*

One thing about the road campaign (of which I shall say nothing as there is currently nothing to say; the Inquiry Inspector is no doubt washing his hands before he hands down his judgment; the Objectors have gone into hibernation) is that practically every other person I met at the few meetings I tagged along to was a real-life parent, so I become acquainted with practically every variety of infant between the ages of six days and six years, from the wailers to the whingers, and it occurs to me on reflection that either a child cries all the time, or else it cries just some of the time. An important lesson. Also, babies have a mood cycle of approximately twenty seconds – chuckles now are tears in a trice – which is slightly worse than Jay's present average, and slightly better than mine. It's hormones, no doubt, but I seem to swing manically between extremes – either I'm swimming in my own murky element (morose, maudlin, miserable, full of the usual millennial misgivings) or else I'm frighteningly euphoric – I feel like someone is tickling my gills and I can't help smiling because baby is on its way and all is for the best in the worst of all possible worlds. Which would be okay, except I know I'll plunge back into all the murky m-words at the merest excuse. Sun-, beach- and drug-deprivation may also be factors, of course.

'Is he coming in?'

'He's worried something will happen to his car.'

Ashley stood at the living-room window. Across the street the flats were splashed with watery sunlight and the damp on the pavements was starting to dry, but on this side there was shade and a carpet of hail. It had settled as a crust on the roof and bonnet of his father's car. The motor was still running, sending out a long cloud of exhaust whilst his father sat reading the newspaper, already strapped into his seatbelt. When he realized Ashley was watching he gave a slight nod and reached a hand to the dashboard as though for his keys, as if about to come in, but then he squirted some water at the windscreen and switched on the wipers. He reopened his paper. Ashley shook his head and retreated to sit beside Jay on the sofa.

His mother said, 'He's sulking because we got lost again, he wanted to come a short cut, but I told him, that's one-way, Ken, you'll see.' She was perched on the seat of the rocking-chair, balancing a mug on her knee. She was thin and tall, but her posture made her seem frail, much smaller. She still hadn't unzipped her coat.

Ashley said, 'You should've told us you were coming.'

His mother sipped some tea. After a long pause she said, 'I saw some lovely second-hand prams in a shop near work, good sturdy ones. I suppose you'll be needing a pram?'

'We're getting a sling,' Ashley told her, and picked at the wallpaper beside him.

She blew on her tea. 'I shan' t stop long,' she said. 'I'll just finish this and I'll be gone.'

Ashley looked at the boards his father had unloaded from the car, now stacked against the bookshelves. On the curved surface of the facing board there was a picture of an apple, a bird and a cat, with the letters ABC entwined in a tree. The other end-board had numbers, and the parts would assemble as a cot. It had been Ashley's, later passed on to Douglas. He wasn't surprised that his mother had kept it – like Jay she hoarded many things, although she stored them more neatly – but he could not remember having seen it in their house. 'Where was that hidden?' he said.

'Your grandma's attic,' she said promptly. 'You'd be surprised what's up there. Your father was surprised – he reckoned this had gone to the dump years ago. He wouldn't be told different. That's why he wouldn't go up for it – he said it'd be a waste of time, so I had to go up myself. But he's just lazy, and he's getting worse because he doesn't work. He won't get off his backside for anything, not even your grandma – he leaves all that to me now, but I keep telling him, *She's not mine, Ken, she's yours, you can't just wish her away.*'

She was becoming angry, the words tightening her throat, and Jay said, 'It's a lovely cot. It's kept very well.'

His mother swallowed the last of her tea and stood up, looked around for somewhere to deposit the mug. 'I'll be glad when that new road is built, won't you? That'll make life a lot simpler. Getting here, I mean.' She placed the mug on a pile of campaign leaflets and papers and waited to see if it would topple, one hand poised to catch it. 'Because the city centre's hopeless. It has been for years – the queue of buses waiting to get over those bridges. I reckon they need a new road just for the buses, don't you?'

Jay took a sharp breath, and Ashley tensed at her side. He glanced around quickly. Unlike her sister, Jay rarely betrayed her feelings to people she disliked or did not know, and she was always polite to his parents. But when she did become angry her fury was startling, uncontrollable and spiteful. She gasped again now, and he realized she was not annoyed, not even listening. 'What is it?' he said, and she gripped his arm tightly, carefully lowered herself to her knees. With both hands under her belly she pressed her forehead to the floor. He got down beside her. 'Jay? What is it?'

She didn't reply, and his mother said, 'It'll be cramp probably. I expect she'll be all right.' Then, 'I suppose really I ought to wash these cups, shouldn't I? Before I rush off. Is the water on, or shall I boil a kettle?'

Ashley circled his hand on Jay's back, heard his mother collecting the cups, quietly leaving the room. There was a full sink of crockery in the kitchen, and no hot running water. But he knew she would not return until she had completed the washing-up, wiped down all the surfaces, rearranged the work-tops to resemble her own kitchen. It was how she was bound to behave, as if nothing unusual was happening. And he found himself shouting, 'Would you just leave that for now, Mum? There's no need!'

With an effort, he concentrated on Jay as she brought herself upright. Her face was pale and frightened, her mouth open. She steadied herself with a hand on his shoulder, cautiously got to her feet. Her legs were shaking, he could feel it. After a few moments she murmured, 'I'd better go to bed,' and allowed him to guide her to the foot of the stairs. She nodded to the kitchen. 'Make her stop that,' she said.

'What's your father up to?' his mother asked when he went through. 'Getting impatient, I expect. I'd better be going, Ashley, before he starts moaning. I'll leave the cups on the table, all right?' They heard the bedroom door closing. His mother glanced up and said, 'I ought to have phoned first, but you know what he's like – once he's ready, that's it, everybody out.' She pulled a face of resignation and went towards the front door. 'But I'm sure Jay will be fine. These things pass, you'll see.'

She fumbled with the locks, as she always did, and then waited for Ashley to help her. He reached around her, raising himself on his toes, and she quickly ducked under his arm. They did not touch, and he caught a faint smell of soap, their bathroom at home. 'You'll let me know if you do want a pram?' she said, and he nodded without looking at her. In the car his father was folding his newspaper, already indicating to pull out. He began to move off before his mother had fastened her seatbelt. She waved towards Ashley, not quite meeting his eye, and he made a gesture in return, shivering on the doorstep until they had gone. The kettle started to whistle in the kitchen. He turned it off and hurried upstairs to find Jay.

FEBRUARY

*B*EACHES, WE *know all about beaches. Jay officially became a* BEACHED WHALE *whilst you were resting up on the sands of Kovalam, Douglas. This is the title of chapter six in her guidebook and describes the period from twenty-eight weeks to childbirth. There are no palm trees or pineapples unfortunately, but thankfully no sweating eyeballs either. Our weather continues to run the precipitational gamut, and if India really does boil your brains to slurry, then I'm glad. Jay hasn't an opinion either way, meteorologically speaking, as she has too much else on her plate, including all of the following:*

CRIPPLING PAINS IN THE PELVIS *(baby's big head squashing a nerve on her pubic bone)*

CONSTANT PEEING *(baby's big head squashing her bladder)*

CONSTIPATION *(baby's big head squashing her bowels)*

BREATHLESSNESS *(baby's big bum squashing her diaphragm)*

BACKACHE *(baby's big everything)*

BRAXTON HICKS CONTRACTIONS *(caused by Braxton Hicks)*

CARPAL TUNNEL SYNDROME (or 'tingly fingers', caused by fluid retention)

SWOLLEN ANKLES (caused by a gloomy outlook, the result of all of the above)

And AMNESIA ('Some women find their memory is never quite the same again')

But not PILES ('Yet')

Or SUNBURN (Ha!)

Apparently it can only get worse. But, as the book also says, 'Pregnancy is not an illness but a natural life transition with important holistic and spiritual dimensions.' Rather like South-East Asia, I suppose.

Jay lay on her side, facing away from him. It was dark outside but not yet late. Cars passed at intervals beneath their window; a black cab thrummed to a halt, doors slammed and a man began shouting. Ashley extended a hand to Jay's hip. The wind soughed through the sycamores. A wheelie-bin was blown the length of the street, colliding with parked cars and setting off their alarms. Jay sighed and pushed his hand away. As the alarms began to expire she turned laboriously towards him, dragging her pillow with her, but almost immediately went back again. Ashley lay close to his edge of the bed, afraid to move in case he disturbed her. She tugged the bed-clothes and left him uncovered.

He stared at the twitching curtains, felt the cold of the draught from the window. His fists were clenched. He splayed his fingers until he felt the stretch in the tendons, then laid his hands flat to his stomach. A bus moved off in the distance and his mind returned to his journey from school that evening, some boys at a shopping parade hurling stones at the traffic. They had shattered the window immediately behind him, another in front, and the driver had accelerated beyond the next stop to the nearest depot, from where he'd refused to continue. The following bus was twenty minutes behind. Too weary to argue, Ashley had walked half a mile to a windowless shelter beside a dual-carriageway, hoping to catch a bus on a different route. But nothing had appeared for nearly an hour. A skim of icy cold had remained on his face until he arrived home; his throat was too raw to speak and he had barely listened as Jay described the events of her own day. She later accused him of being this sullen every evening, whatever his reason, and then they had bickered till bedtime. He swallowed painfully now, and realized his hands were clenched as tightly as before.

He closed his eyes and rolled on to his side, pulled the bedspread across him. Jay was starting to snore. For several minutes he tried to ignore her, then reached to the floor for his alarm clock. He held the dial close to his face. It was a quarter past ten. He turned on to his front and wondered if he could afford another day's sick leave, and what symptoms he might use. On his previous sick-line he'd claimed migraine, double-vision and nausea, all stress-related, and all invented, as his head of department surely knew. In their monthly meeting she had queried his performance in class, his attendance and timekeeping, even his standard of dress. He wasn't delivering the curriculum, wasn't managing his workload or controlling his pupils. He pictured her now as she had appeared at her desk, her soft pink jersey sagging where she sagged, a hanky tucked into each sleeve, another crumpled into her fist. Her complexion was grey and there were pouches under her eyes. She had a bronchial wheeze, and coughed and sniffed constantly, but she worked late every evening and he had never known her to be absent. Sore throats, she had told him on another occasion, were an occupational hazard.

Jay's snoring rasped louder. Ashley nudged her foot with his and for a brief moment she faltered. Outside the wind blustered; his clock gave a smart click with every second. He twisted onto his back and stared at the ceiling, clenched his jaw and relaxed. He tightened and loosened the muscles of arms, his buttocks and legs, turned his feet inwards and out. Before she was pregnant Jay had sometimes massaged him to sleep. He tried to knead his own shoulders now, but could only pinch with his fingertips. Somewhere along their terrace a drainpipe was rattling. A tin can clattered over the pavement, and he thought of the beer in their fridge. He raised his eyebrows as high as they would go, and then frowned. He did have a headache. He would take some aspirin with his beer. As he rose from the bed he looked at Jay and gave a loud sigh, then trod heavily round the bed to the door. The sound of her snoring followed him downstairs.

To get her revenge Jay has enrolled us for classes with the National Childbirth Trust, eight of them, every Wednesday evening from 8 till 10, and so far we've done three. We were expecting a room in a public hall or a health centre with an assembly of couples in Seventies tee-shirts and sideburns all breathing vigorously and smelling of socks, but instead we got a private apartment in the posh North Side, twelve stripped-timber doors leading off a huge central hallway, the original wood panelling and moulding intact, ornate ceiling roses, varnished floorboards, but nearly as scruffy as our place, and nearly as cluttered, the walls all covered in 'Stop the Road' and 'Save the Earth' posters, cobwebs in every corner. And there was an assembly of couples in Seventies tee-shirts and sideburns all smelling of socks. The heavy breathing comes later it seems, lesson five.

Being the only pedestrians and bus-users, we're always the last to arrive. The first time we found seven other couples sitting in a circle on chairs and cushions, the women all squatting in front of their partners and taking it in turns to introduce themselves, the first amongst them being Alana Bishop (her real name), who is terribly posh and was on my teacher-training course and who I remember chiefly for snogging undergraduates in the Union bar ('such a divine kisser, such beautiful lips!'). She had moved here, she said, because her husband had been relocated through work ('He works in the Media, I don't know what exactly') but she herself had given up teaching and didn't ever intend to go back ('He's terribly well paid, shocking really'). She was, she said, 'awfully excited' to be having a baby. I said I was awfully excited also.

The actual session was all right, if embarrassing, and near the end we did just a little bit of breathing, a warm-up for later – our 'facilitator' (whose home it is) dimmed the lights, we all closed our eyes, allowed our jaws to hang open, hands loose in our laps, and then she intoned, 'Breathe in the joy . . . breathe out the negativity.' Whereupon I became rather tense again.

Next session we arrived to find the women all clutching their bums and privates and rocking gently backwards and forwards. Interesting, I thought, but it turned out to be an exercise in getting to know your pelvis. Us chaps got to look at some diagrams, and then we all watched our facilitator passing a plastic dolly through a plastic pelvis from various angles, thus demonstrating that a standing or squatting position allows more room for the dolly to pass through, whilst a prone or supine position is somewhat less helpful. Quite instructive, obstetrically speaking, and I suppose by the end of the course I might just make a semi-competent labour partner, but Jay isn't so sure. In this week's session I had to ask, 'What is an epidural, exactly?' Which seems to be a fairly major confession of ignorance at this level of committed parenting.

At ten to midnight Ashley heard shouting and switched off the table-lamp. The voices were male and pitched almost to screaming. He swallowed the last of his beer and stepped across to the living-room window. The nearest street lamp was faulty, flickering orange in the darkness, and for a moment he couldn't see anyone. Then a boy ran past wielding a bike chain, and Ashley realized two others were standing on the bonnet of a car on the opposite kerb, almost hidden by Hazel's caravan. Their necks and faces were taut, bodies straining into the wind as if on a leash, arrested and furious. When they leapt down Ashley drew backwards, watched as they advanced along the centre of the road, a yard apart and poised to run on. He loosened the bolt on the window and pulled the sash upwards.

The other street lamps cast long fractured shadows through the branches of sycamores and it was impossible to tell who was fighting who. There were perhaps twenty boys at the junction to the next road, and although some were black and some Asian, this did not seem to be the division between them. Ashley felt a stir of excitement and leant further into the cold. The way the crowd moved resembled the fish in his aquarium at school. Each individual seemed pulled by the rest; there were sudden scatterings within, abrupt changes in direction. Often in the local park he had seen confrontations between gangs of much younger boys. They faced each other across a distance of lawns and flowerbeds, hurling threats and sticks, advancing and retreating. But he had never seen a blow landed. And here too, as he watched their older brothers from his window, the violence seemed merely threatened. One boy was striking a bottle repeatedly against the top of some railings, unable to break it, but when the crowd spilled towards him he tossed it over his shoulder and saw it smash where it landed. Ashley smiled. Then the boy stumbled and was beaten to the ground.

The attack was fierce and concentrated. Four or five young men jostled to aim kicks at the boy's face, the small of his back, his groin. He struggled briefly to stand and was rammed to the pavement. He lay in a foetal curl, both hands protecting his head. His body was tight and resisting, took several blows with slight shifts and turns, then became very still. The frenzy of his assailants cooled and they kicked with more deliberation. One collapsed his weight on to the boy's back, landing with his knees, and another copied him, launching himself with a jump. Ashley murmured, 'Oh no,' and felt a rush of adrenalin, a sudden urge to run out. But he knew he could not fight, had not thrown a punch since he was a schoolboy. Further along the terrace there were spectators in most of the doorways, heads leaning from windows, faces watching from every floor of the flats. Ashley started to shiver, felt his adrenalin sink to nausea.

To supplement our weekly sessions with the NCT I've been working my way steadily through a massive manual of pregnancy and parenthood, making notes under the appropriate headings for every stage of the process, and soon I shall be supplementing these notes with snippets from our many other guides and manuals, and then trying to condense everything I need to know on any aspect of labour and delivery into one 6 × 4 index card per topic. I'm nowhere near organized yet, and I've a feeling I'll still be several chapters short of full preparedness when the waters break and the first contractions begin, in which case I shall have to ask the midwife for a twenty-four-hour extension.

For fieldwork, we went to meet the chief midwife at the maternity hospital last weekend, and had a guided tour of the building, which is 150 years old and positively the shabbiest, most decrepit edifice in the entire National Health Service, on top of which the 'birthing rooms' look like dental surgeries, but the midwife is very progressive, which is to say very old-fashioned, a non-interventionist, strong on Nature's Course and down on scalpels and drips and enemas. She even has grey hair and a wart on her chin. Just the job. We're having a sort of almost-home-birth called a 'domino' (standing for 'domiciliary midwife in and out'), which means we're assigned our own midwife (actually a team of four) for the rest of Jay's pregnancy, and will stay here in the comfort of our own squalor until Jay is 'six centimetres dilated', or 'almost ready to drop it', whereupon one of the midwives will come and whip us off to the maternity hospital for the actual birth, after which we'll hang out for six hours or so, make sure everything is okay, then catch a taxi back for the first big bawls.

Whilst she's incarcerated Jay will be able to wear her own togs, get up and wander about, choose her own birthing position, play what she likes on the tape machine, stay longer if she feels like it, and go home as soon as she's ready – unless anything goes wrong, of course, in which case the obstetrician is hauled in and all the machines are switched on. As the Primary Birth Partner I get to share everything but the pain and discomfort, and afterwards cut the cord to inaugurate the arrival. Which is a big responsibility, I do realize.

Actually we're getting very impatient to get 'hands-on', and to know that everything will be all right. I continue to have flutterings of excitement, sometimes genuine surges, but equally often I have deep terrors and anxieties. Other times I just about remember to step around the bits of cot as I come in and out of the bedroom. I can't really imagine what it'll be like. With seven or eight months to think about it you have plenty of time to invent your perfect child and you even sometimes find yourself talking to it as it peers up from the side of your leg, but this close to the actual thing it starts to invent its own alter ego, and at the back of my mind there's another baby entirely, which is always sick, always crying, all-consuming, and destined for delinquency. It's a worry, and I've a feeling that if anything went wrong now, our lives would still be totally changed and we'd never be able to fill the space left by all this preparation and expectation. But at least we'd have an excuse to return Mum's cot.

Jay said, 'What are you doing?'

He drew down the window and locked it and retreated into the room. 'You were snoring,' he said. Police cars were arriving at speed from the top and bottom of the street, doors urgently slamming. A wagon had stopped beside Hazel's caravan, its light flashing through the gap in their curtains, a strip of blue on Jay's face, the thin white of her nightshirt.

'It's not my fault,' she told him. 'I can't help it, Ashley.'

'No.' He nodded. 'I know.' Some women were yelling at

the police, the wind howling around them. An ambulance was coming. There were dogs, too. 'But it's every night,' he said.

'What do you expect me to do!'

He shrugged, and tried to smile. His heart was slowly pounding. He pointed a thumb at the window. 'There was a fight,' he said.

'I heard it,' she said. Then after a pause, 'Why don't you make up a bed down here?'

'Could do,' he murmured.

'Or the back room upstairs. Just till the baby is born.'

He nodded very slowly, didn't know what to do with his hands. He hooked them behind his head. For some moments they faced each other across the room. It was cold and Jay shivered. Suddenly there were too many things he wanted to say, about the baby, his day in the classroom, the boy being beaten outside. He swallowed, and felt the words welling inside, but she was too far away. She looked at him quizzically. Seconds passed before she reached him.

'Don't cry,' she said then. 'For fuck's sake, Ashley. Not that.'

MARCH

T HE WEATHER map showed a swirl of cloud completely covering the British Isles. Ashley switched off the set and pulled on his coat. He glanced at the clock and blew on his tea, took a single gulp and abandoned it. He left his mattress where it lay on the carpet. In the hallway he stumbled over a pile of clothes and cursed, checking an impulse to shout, 'Bye!' as he opened the door. Outside the wind whipped back his hood. He sank his hands in his pockets and bent into the breeze, a plastic carrier slung from one wrist. On the other side of the street the pavement was lined with green wheelie-bins left out overnight for emptying. Litter spilled into the road and swirled in the mouths of the doorways. He watched a white paper bag ballooning over the rooftops, saw it collapse in a crosswind as though punctured. The sky above was a luminous grey, much brighter than the buildings and trees.

At the far junction the bus stop also appeared to lean with the wind. The pole was concrete and buckled, the rusting rods through its middle exposed like a tangle of arteries. A lorry had once run into it and a child had been killed. Periodically small bunches of flowers would be left there to wither, and once Ashley had seen a cross made of lolly sticks, tied to the pole and wound with dandelions and daisies. There was a patch of waste ground beyond, derelict factories blocking the view to the river. A huddle of people were sheltering in the angle of a broken fence and when they began to step forwards Ashley started to run. The bus was a single-decker, a converted coach, already indicating to pull out when he reached it. The doors flipped open and the driver scowled but didn't look at Ashley's pass. As he edged along the aisle, bumping into the other travellers and murmuring apologies, familiar faces ignored him. He trod on someone's toe and then the bus lurched and he hit a woman's arm with his bag. She stiffened away from him. In the fug of smoke at the rear he found two empty seats and knocked his head on the luggage rack sitting down. The window was too dirty to see through and there was no heat from the radiators. He pulled up his hood and folded his arms. After the next stop he closed his eyes.

I'm writing this as my head rattles in its socket, so at times the words may be a little indistinct. This is caused entirely by the motion of my humours and not by any attempt to recreate one of your train journeys. On Saturday we received from Sang Khom one postcard and from Langkawi (I think) one letter, but it seems you didn't receive my letter addressed to you in Penang, written when you were in Madras, and now as I write you are back in Bangkok, but in Singapore as you read this. I feel as if I'm speaking to my own echo.

Of course, reading your traveller's tales we often wonder if we're becoming just a little homespun and housebound, when in truth we're already very homespun and housebound indeed, and about to become even more so. Our response to your latest news was to lock the front door and close the curtains and not venture out for the rest of the weekend – Jay retreated to bed and I retreated with her but soon found myself trapped in the throes of an attack of nest-building mania. So whilst you continued your amble along the banks of the Maekhong I finished painting over the cracks in our kitchen ceiling and screwed the fire extinguisher to the wall, I glossed some door-frames which didn't need it, I built and unbuilt the cot we probably shan't use, I sorted the baby's bedclothes into sheets and blankets and miscellaneous padded things, and reshelved them exactly as they were before, I tore the heads off all our stuffed toys and tested them against naked flames, I wrote lists of things-to-buy and things-to-ask-the-midwife and found they corresponded exactly with Jay's lists of things-to-buy and things-to-ask-the-midwife, I packed and unpacked our maternity holdall, I washed and ironed every stitch we own, and finally, at ten o'clock on Sunday evening, I began to fix the new ceramic tiles to our front-room fireplace, hideously and outrageously red as they are. They are far too RED. An eyesore, and still barely half done. You will have to remind me to point them out when next you visit. I might even describe how I envisage their completion.

All of which meant I stayed up far too late again, hoping to delay the arrival of yet another Monday, but that chugged along anyway, bang on time and three hours before I was ready. Work is grim, since you never tire of asking. Several times every day I find myself arrested in mid-stride, mid-sentence or mid-thought, poised between staying and leaving immediately, walking out and never returning. I can't be arsed to care if the kids I'm teaching are uninterested, and I've run right out of sympathy for the dimwits. I've also just about given up on the staffroom at lunchtimes and intervals, whatever the cost to my retirement whip-round thirty years hence, and I daren't look to my fish tank for consolation because whenever I do I find some fresh outrage has occurred, some hapless guppy is being eaten half-alive or some black widow is beating herself senseless on the glass. The fishes are overbreeding *and getting mad at each other and cannibalizing their own flesh and blood. It is very grim indeed.*

Jay, however, hates being at home. She has now entered her period of maximum immobility, is barely two weeks into her six months of maternity leave, and is already itching, or twitching, to get back to work. I have every sympathy. In fact, I've volunteered to sacrifice my own career to hers, to yoke myself to the kitchen sink and changing mat, to happily keep house whilst she cheerfully toils to keep us. But Jay's not so sure, she also wants her fair share of the cuddles and gurgles and sundry other joys of parenthood, so she's suggested a compromise, that we each throw in half a towel – ie, she returns to half her job, I escape from half of mine, we job-share alternate halves of the week. Jay's reputedly socialist-feminist cooperative could hardly object, particularly as all concerned are also her personal friends. And, so far as I know, my school couldn't object either because it's my contractual right as a County Council Southern Subdivision Education Department employee to be half the man I was if I so choose to be. There just remains the problem of approaching our new headmaster, Mr Kirk, who is Scottish and brusque and extremely intimidating, a masculine man, and no doubt already looking for the merest excuse to ditch me entirely.

In the staffroom the windows were open against the stifling heat of the boilers, but the breeze from outside was harsh and disruptive, whipping at the plants and stacks of forms on the window ledge. Standing next to a radiator, Ashley felt the warmth prickling his face and reddened further as he scanned the room for the headmaster. The teachers sat in clusters of a dozen or more, and some were staring back at him, detached from the conversations around them. Their gaze had the unsettling effect of a classroom of pupils. Resisting the urge to leave, he picked up a copy of that day's information sheet and joined the queue for the tea bar. He noticed there was a poem and read it conscientiously.

CASUAL DRESS DAY THIS FRIDAY!
Be environmentally friendly
And make everyone GREEN *with envy*
At the amount we can levy!
£728 is the total to beat
So look out your green gear
Be it fancy or plain
And recycle it again
So our efforts won't be in vain.
We appeal to your sense of fun
To make our highest total this one!

'New teacher?'

The woman was young and hesitantly smiling. Ashley shook his head. 'No,' he replied, 'well-worn, actually.' He folded the sheet into his shirt pocket. She edged a few inches along, her eyes drifting to the table of sweets and biscuits beside them. 'You?' he asked, and she gave a sharp click of her tongue, seemingly frustrated by the difficulty of choosing. She snatched at a chocolate bar, then cautiously replaced it.

'No,' she said distractedly. 'No, I'm not.'

Ashley waited for more, but she turned back into the queue. He stared at the nape of her neck, then heard the door opening behind him, a sudden in-rush of noise from the corridor.

The latecomers had taught in the school since it became a comprehensive, one history, the other domestic science, and were soon to retire. They lived locally and were dropped off most mornings by their husbands, walked home together in the evenings. Sometimes Ashley would pass them on the way to his bus stop, and exchange greetings, but he never slowed to join them. He didn't suppose he'd be welcome. On seeing him now the smaller of the two widened her eyes in pretended surprise, briefly laid her hand on his forearm. 'Oh,

Ashley!' she exclaimed. 'There you are. We thought you'd gone into hiding.'

'I had, Mrs Burrell.'

Her companion watched him through brown-tinted spectacles, and drily remarked, 'I'm not surprised.'

'Mrs Marnie?'

'Apparently you've abandoned your curriculum,' confided Mrs Burrell, now touching his hand. 'Declared your independence. Not that we mind, of course, it's none of our concern.'

She was smiling. Mrs Marnie was not. 'I hadn't realized,' he said cautiously. 'When did I do that?'

'Last Friday,' Mrs Marnie told him. She spoke crisply, as if to a classroom. 'I took your second-years after they'd left you and I couldn't do a damn thing with them. It seems you'd spent the previous hour discussing the wonders of human reproduction. Is your wife's pregnancy an appropriate topic for geography?'

'She's not my wife,' Ashley said coolly. 'But it is geography. We're doing population.'

'You're *doing* population,' Mrs Marnie repeated, surveying the room. 'I see.'

They had reached the hot-water urns, a long counter of cups in matching saucers, two prefects holding pots of coffee and tea. Ashley watched his cup being filled and dropped a few coins in a tray. 'So how is the father-to-be?' Mrs Burrell asked then. 'Excited?'

'I will be when I've finished reading up on it. But I don't think I'm going to meet my deadline.'

'That'll all go out the window,' declared Mrs Marnie. 'You needn't bother with that.'

'Babies all have their own personality,' Mrs Burrell smiled. 'They each come out differently, all in their own good time.'

The women turned their attention to the tea bar, and Ashley took a tentative sip from his cup, unsure whether their conversation was over, if he should wait or find a seat. Mr Kirk was sitting beyond the toilets in the farthest corner of the room, a couple of empty armchairs nearby. Ashley said, 'I'd better go and have a word with the boss then,' and paused a moment longer. Mrs Marnie asked one of the prefects to refill a milk jug. Mrs Burrell searched her handbag for a capsule of sweeteners. He nodded and left them.

The staffroom was the length of three classrooms but not much wider and it backed on to the school playground. Footballs thudded repeatedly against the far wall; children's yells regularly pierced the hubbub inside. Ashley crossed the carpeted floor with eyes lowered and almost didn't notice Robin Crawley coming out from the Gents. They each rose on to their toes to avoid a collision, and Robin said, 'Mr B.! How's it going?' There was a penny-sized patch of damp on his crotch. His hair was pulled back in a pony tail.

'Fine,' Ashley shrugged, and then added, 'not bad.'

'Nice one,' said Robin, and nodded. He taught in the classroom below Ashley's and they were much the same age, often presumed to be friends although they spoke only rarely. It was Robin who organized casual-dress days, placed poems in the information sheet. As Ashley edged around him he asked, 'So how's the girlfriend doing? Getting big now, yeah?'

'Quite big,' Ashley agreed.

'Still painting the old murals?'

He drew an imaginary shape in the air. Ashley backed into a coffee table. 'No,' he said. 'She's too big.'

'Right,' Robin grinned, and pointed two fingers at his own head, pretending to shoot himself.

Ashley watched as the tracksuited head of PE entered the room and strode to the tea bar. He was smiling, looking towards them. With one hand cupped to his mouth, he shouted, 'Mr Crawley. Chrissie Mimms is outside. She wants you, now!'

Several teachers began laughing, a few whistled. Robin

quickly checked the top of his flies, his shirt buttons, and said to Ashley, 'Well, best of luck, Mr B. And wish the mum-to-be all the best, yeah?' Then he departed, tucking the tail of his shirt into his waistband and tugging his pony tail as if to lengthen it. 'What does she want?' he called. 'Did she say?'

'Punishment exercise!' a voice answered and there was more laughter, other comments. Ashley blew on his tea and sat down.

The headmaster was talking intently to another senior teacher, a pile of documents on his lap, an open briefcase beside him. Ashley carefully unfolded his information sheet. Beside him the school's librarian was browsing through a catalogue of computing supplies, his feet on the rim of the table. Opposite sat the elderly head of biology, her legs planted firmly apart and her skirt pulled taut by her knees. Ashley glimpsed the top of her thighs and quickly looked down, pretended to re-read the day's notices. After a moment she said, 'Who would have daughters? If that girl's father knew how they talked about her . . .' Seconds passed and no one spoke. Ashley realized she was addressing him. He looked up. 'What are you hoping for, Ashley?' she demanded. 'A boy or a girl?'

'A girl?' he offered, and lifted his cup, then replaced it without drinking. 'Usually a girl anyway.'

There was silence. The headmaster fastened his briefcase and said, 'When's it due?'

'Four weeks.'

'Where at?'

'Home. Well, partly . . .'

'Hospital,' snapped the headmaster. 'Have the baby in hospital. You've got all the machinery there, doctors, midwives. Anything goes wrong, no problem.'

Ashley realized he was expected to reply, and tentatively said, 'Hospitals aren't necessarily safer though.'

'How?' The headmaster's gaze was direct and unblinking.

He stretched an arm along the back of a chair, rested one foot on his knee.

Ashley concentrated to recall a passage from one of Jay's books. 'Well,' he began, 'if you're in hospital, you have to fit in with the hospital's own procedures and protocols. They might just decide to induce the birth, for instance . . .'

Mr Kirk was dismissive. 'Say no. If you don't want anything, just say no.'

'But you can't. If you're in a big institution like that, you get put under a lot of pressure to do things you might not want to do. Like pain control – the easiest thing is just to whack the woman with some drug or other, give her an epidural, say. Which is quite hard to resist if you're in pain and surrounded by all these machines and doctors and stuff.' The headmaster stared back but didn't reply. Ashley went on, speaking rapidly as if reciting his tables, 'But then with the epidural the woman can't feel anything from the waist down, which means she doesn't know when to push, or whether she's pushing hard enough, so the birth takes longer, and the baby gets distressed, so they end up using callipers, or suction, or whatever, to get the baby out, which probably involves having to do an episiotomy . . .'

'You're a Luddite, Mr Brook,' said the headmaster. 'But clearly well briefed. Let me know if you need any time off.'

Ashley drew back his legs as Mr Kirk stepped across them. 'Actually, I was wanting to have a word with you . . .'

'In my office,' breezed Mr Kirk. 'Mrs Poole will arrange it.'

As the teachers ebbed from the room Ashley remained in his seat, gazing up at the ceiling. Footsteps tramped along the corridor above, surged past the windows. Beside him the librarian tossed his brochure on to the table. He cracked his knuckles, and sighed, and finally said, 'My wife went into labour when I was on a conference, Ash. Three in the morning it started. I didn't get to the hospital till after twelve. I went home first, had a shower, quick brush-up, couple of slices of toast. The labour went on all day – didn't end till breakfast the next morning. And I loved every minute of it. Brilliant experience.'

Ashley turned to face him and said, 'Not so great for your wife though.'

'No. Maybe. I took loads of photos actually – and you should see her in these, she looks rotten, totally bushed. I wish now I'd taken one of those Camcorders, to capture the way it really was.'

He mimed filming the birth, and Ashley rose to leave, mentally calculating the hours remaining till home-time, the days left in the term.

I ought not to be so downbeat. There's a warning in the latest issue of Planet News that 'negative news creation creates an inward spiral within the reader leading to congestion and depression'. And naturally I would hate to be the cause of any such symptoms in you, especially when you're vulnerable to so many far uglier lurgies: malaria, for instance, or typhoid, not to mention cholera, dysentery, hepatitis, kwashiorkor, beriberi . . . even 'subfertility', which you won't be aware of and against which you won't have been innoculated. This one applies to me too, as my second-years explained to me last week. Great Spermy One I'm not. In fact, there's every chance my fertility is on the slide. It could be that my pants are too tight, my testicles a little hot under the scrotum, or that I eat too much fish from waters polluted by sewage containing the oestrogen-rich excrement of women using oral contraceptives. Neither of these factors will affect you, with your new baggy pants and dietary prejudices, but another possible cause is contamination from the 'highly toxic and persistent chemicals used as insulators in electrical equipment', as described in my Sunday newspaper. In other words, ditch your Walkman.

All of which means our baby was just a lucky shot. Or not . . . Lucky? How can this be when we're so often in the doldrums and Jay is so completely incapacitated? Her carpal tunnel syndrome is now becoming chronic and her right hand in particular is particularly chronic, painful and puffy, practically useless (seem to have the alliteration key here . . .). In fact, it looks like one of mine, a goalkeeping spatula special. However, as partner-in-pregnancy it's my duty to provide massage on demand, which is a real pain in my thumbs, but something I've become quite adept at. Massage was a Big Thing at our NCT classes, ying to discomfort's yang, a caring and committed expression of positivity (breathe in the joy!). And I say 'was' with great positivity and joy because we finally jacked in the course, it was making us narky. We've absconded to the hospital-organized antenatals instead – two so far – which are pretty much a repetition of what we learned at the NCT, but without the baubles and bangles. There are plastic seats rather than bean bags, videos rather than charts, instruction not discussion, an instant-drinks trolley where the NCT had an upright piano. Every couple is unlike every other, they all sit in rows facing the midwife, and no one speaks or asks questions. Dead on.

This week our video was a demonstration of the would-be father's supporting role in labour, which entailed the inevitable Seventies Man in spangly tee-shirt and hipster denims standing limply at the side of the birthing bed, one hand on his hip, the other dabbing a flannel on his wife's brow. He barely altered his stance when the baby was born and said not one word throughout the entire process. An admirable role model, I thought. But really I don't see why these lessons must go on for weeks and weeks. Why can't it all be crammed into a single session? And why, wonders Jay, must her pregnancy drag on for nine months, why can't it all be over in one, or at the very most eight? She's ready now. I doubt I ever will be, however many classes I go to.

The mattress on the living-room floor was stripped of bed-clothes, its blue and yellow stripes blotched with blood and sweat stains. The gas fire was full on. The wind gusted in the chimney breast and troubled the flames and Jay sat upright against the sofa with several pillows for support. The bib of her dungarees was turned down and her tee-shirt raised to expose the hard smooth globe of her belly. Her cheeks burned red like tomatoes. She was reading a document. It was open on her lap. There was a pot of tea on a tray at her side and a small bottle of medicine.

'What's this?' Ashley asked.

'The midwife gave it me. It's supposed to pick me up.'

He read the label aloud. '*Niffrex Elixir. This medicine may colour urine or stools*,' but Jay didn't smile. He said, 'I fetched the photos. They're really badly printed, there's no contrast.'

She accepted them listlessly, dutifully glanced through them. She'd posed naked in the bedroom a fortnight before, and her reluctance showed in her posture, her facial expression. The room had been too cold; she'd got cramp in her legs. 'I can't believe I'm so big,' she murmured. 'It's weird.'

'I shouldn't have done them against a white wall,' he said.

'You can see all the veins in my tits.' She returned the photographs to their envelope, handed them back to him. 'They're quite disturbing,' she said.

'Shame they're not in focus, though.' Ashley slumped on the sofa beside her, still wearing his coat, his work shoes. He loosened the laces but felt too weary to kick off the shoes. 'What are you reading?' he asked.

'It's the Inspector's report,' she said.

'And?' He sat upright.

Jay turned a few pages, read out in a monotone: '*Having considered all relevant matters and having taken into account the objections, counter-objections and representations, I recommend that the . . .* blah, blah . . . *Draft Orders be made.* In other words, build the road.'

'Let's see.'

Jay lifted the document with two hands, passed it over her shoulder. The cover was pink, the binding plastic, the contents typewritten. Ashley glanced towards the back. There were almost 500 pages, it was an inch and a half thick.

'All this to say that?'

'Yes,' said Jay, and with an effort she raised herself to her feet. She gathered her dungarees to stop them from falling and shuffled across to the rocking-chair. She sat facing the fire.

Ashley held the report in one hand, allowed it to flop over. The bulk was surprising, though the judgment was not. It was the third time the bypass had been to an Inquiry and this route was designed with previous objections in mind. The Inspector was known to have approved schemes elsewhere. Ashley laid the document beside him, on top of his photographs. He would not read it. 'So what happens now?' he said.

Jay contemplated the flames and didn't immediately reply, didn't appear to have heard him. He waited, then asked again, and she said dully, 'What does it matter? I can't do anything anyway. I'm physically incapable. I can't even write letters.' She looked at him as if in accusation, displaying her fingers. 'I'm lumbered, aren't I?' Her mouth tightened, began to tremble. Heavy tears rolled over her cheeks and she brushed at them angrily. 'I'm shit-scared about this, Ashley,' she said. 'I know you're thinking it'll all be over in a few weeks, and then we'll be back to normal and everything will be nice, but I've still got to *have* the fucking thing, it's still got to come out of me. Look at those photos, for fuck's sake. Look at the size of it. I'm going to give birth to that *lump* and then somehow I'm supposed to know what to do with it. I'll be stuck in this house in this fucking street for twenty-four hours a day and I don't even know how to change a fucking nappy!'

'I'll be helping,' he said quietly.

'Big deal!' she shouted. 'Big fucking deal!'

With a long sigh Ashley sank back on the sofa. He tucked his chin inside the neck of his coat. Jay stared into the fire, breathing heavily, and he pushed at the Inspector's report with his finger, caused it to slip to the floor. It landed heavily and his photographs followed, splaying over the mattress. Jay didn't look round. He retrieved one of the pictures and examined her face looking out, the pudginess of her features. This image, he realized, was in focus. 'You're not looking forward to it then,' he said finally.

'No,' she replied. 'I'm not looking forward to it.'

'I'm sorry,' he said.

She glanced up, briefly held his gaze and looked down. 'Don't be,' she said.

Ashley removed his shoes, slowly unbuttoned his coat. He held out an arm for Jay to sit with him, but didn't know how to ask her. She didn't move, and he didn't speak. When the telephone rang neither answered it, and they were sitting in darkness when the day's first rain struck the window.

APRIL

T HE ICE was too large for the neck of the flask. Steam began to spout from the kettle and then the whistle started, a sudden shrilling beside him. Ashley dropped the ice and turned off the gas. He stepped in a puddle of water. Jay was sobbing, gasping in the bathroom. 'You okay?' he shouted, and emptied the kettle to a second flask. But he'd forgotten to spoon in the coffee. He slammed the kettle on the stove and hurried to the bathroom, found her leaning with her head to the wall, half-way between sitting and standing. 'Jay?' Her trousers were bunched round her ankles and her knickers were at her knees. With one hand she clutched the towel rail, the other her belly, and when he touched her shoulder she turned and spewed in the toilet. He said, 'What did the midwife say, exactly?' Then, 'Jay, what did she say?'

'It wasn't her. Ella wasn't there.' She ran the cold tap, allowed him to pull up her clothes. 'It was a receptionist or something, I don't know. She said it might be a urinary infection. I'm not doing this again, Ashley.'

'Is it a urinary infection?' he asked.

'Like fuck.'

'Shall I phone again?'

'No, not yet.' She swilled her mouth and picked her way through the towels and wet clothes on the floor. 'Just finish the packing,' she said. 'I'm going for a walk.'

'Where?'

'The front room.'

Ashley stood in the kitchen and looked at his study cards. At the top of the stack was a list of things for their holdall. *Ice pack for J; coffee for A* . . . He re-lit the gas and emptied the flask into the kettle, then spooned out a rough measure of coffee. His hands were trembling. As he searched for something to break up the ice-cubes he caught his reflection in the window – a black jumper – and reminded himself not to wear black; Jay said it meant funerals. They were both to wear yellow for sunshine. But his yellow jumper was damp, it would have to be ironed. He found the iron in a cupboard of sauces and pickles. Jay was calling him now. Before he ran to the living room he struck an ice-cube with the heel of the iron and saw the pieces skate to the floor.

The tea-time news had just ended. Jay was kneeling on a rug by the fire and Ashley knelt with her, his knees between hers. She was trying to regulate her breathing, deep inhalations, lengthy exhalations, but she was losing control. She started to pant, gasping for air. Then she screamed. Her hands flailed and Ashley grabbed hold of her wrists, looped her arms round his neck. He chanted, 'Puff, puff, blow! Puff, puff, blow!' suddenly unsure if this was what they had practised, or something they'd been told to avoid. But Jay held his gaze and matched her breathing to his. The intensity of her attention made him self-conscious; his voice trailed away. 'That's it,' he murmured, 'that's good.' Their foreheads met. In the kitchen the kettle was shrieking.

'That was the worst,' she said finally. 'That was definitely the worst.'

'Why didn't you wake me?' Ashley said. He had fallen asleep on the sofa after work; Jay had told him he would need his energy for later.

'It wasn't so bad then, I didn't realize it would come on like this.'

'They shouldn't be this close together,' he told her. 'Twenty minutes to start with. If they're this close we ought to have a midwife.'

'I'll phone,' she said irritably, 'I'll phone in a minute.' Ashley helped her to stand and watched as she paced across the living room. 'But find my TeNS,' she said then. 'It's in the bedroom somewhere. And tidy up – I promised her it would be tidier. Everything's a mess.'

'That's none of her business, Jay.'

'Ashley!' she shouted. 'Just do it!'

The TeNS machine resembled a Walkman. Twin wires led not to earphones but to pads the size of plasters, and a solitary dial controlled the current between the pads. The pulse was supposed to distract Jay from her pain. Ashley found it in a tangle of bedclothes, the adhesive ends stuck to the sheets, caught up in Jay's nightgown. A grubbied sticker said it belonged to the maternity hospital. He lay it on the desk and took a deep breath, tried to think what to do next. Although swept and dusted, and the wallpapering recently completed, the room retained the fustiness of the hours Jay spent resting in bed. Ashley stripped back the blankets and opened a window. Outside the mist of the afternoon had thickened to fog and the air smelled coolly of trees and damp pavements. Downstairs Jay was puffing and blowing through another contraction. Hastily undressing, he noticed a workshirt on the rail, white with yellow stripes, and tore it from the hanger. He hurried back down wearing only his underpants.

'Here's the TeNS', he said, and dropped his bundle of clothes to the floor. 'What now?' Jay closed her eyes, loosely clasped her hands in her lap. The pain was subsiding. With each inhalation her nose narrowed, flared on the exhalation. Finally she looked at him, and he asked, 'Shall I put it on for you?' There was a pause before she nodded, another few seconds before she threw up. The vomit spattered his clean shirt. 'You'd better show me where the pads go,' he said.

Packed and zipped by the living-room door, their maternity bag looked as though it might burst. Ashley stood close beside Jay and watched it uncertainly. He strained to hear what the midwife was saying. 'Is she coming or not?' he whispered, but Jay flapped him to be quiet. Then she winced and let go of the phone, fumbled to turn up her TeNS. She dropped down on her haunches. Ashley picked up the receiver. 'Sorry, Ella,' he said, 'but that's another one starting. Is someone coming out here? I thought someone was coming.'

The voice said, 'It's just so foggy, you see. We can't find our map.'

'Do you want directions?' he asked.

'I'll have to find a pen . . .'

'Or shall we come in?'

'What does Jay want?'

'Jay, do you want to go straight in?'

'No!' she cried. Then 'Maybe . . . I don't know.'

'Which?'

'We'll go in. Say we'll go in.'

'We'll come in,' he said.

'Will you get a taxi?' asked the midwife.

'Could we have an ambulance?'

'I don't know if there is one.'

'I don't think we'd cope in a taxi.'

'I'll tell them you want an ambulance.'

'How long will it be?'

'An hour maybe. It's an emergency service, you see – they only allocate so many.'

'Right,' he said.

'And then there's the fog.'

'Maybe we will get a cab.'

'It's up to you.'

Ashley hesitated, and Jay gave out a yell, furiously twisting the dial on her TeNS. '*Shit!*' she shouted, and ripped the pads from her back, hurling the machine at the sofa. 'Fuck!'

'An ambulance might be better,' he said.

'That's fine,' said the midwife. 'Whatever you want.'

'It's just we don't know whether we're coming or going,' he said.

'Same here!' The midwife laughed.

In the back of the ambulance they sat side by side and hoped the medic would not speak to them. Three hours since her first spasms, Jay now lapsed almost to sleep between crises and breathed to a rhythm when the pain gripped her, to the drill they had learned in their classes. With one arm around her shoulder, Ashley looked through the darkened rear window at the glow of the following car's headlamps. He wished he could see more, the direction they were taking and what they were leaving behind them. He thought he recognized a street corner, a building and hoarding, and tried to form in his mind a map of their route, where they were in the city. But then another contraction began and he sought Jay's hands, returned his attention to her. The paramedic crouched before them with a cylinder of gas. 'Will you take a blast of this, pet?' he said, but Jay shook her head in annoyance.

'We're trying to do without,' Ashley apologized.

'Fair enough,' said the man, and returned to his corner, seeming disappointed, a little sceptical. In the silence which followed he said, 'This'll be your first then?'

Ashley nodded. After a long pause he asked, 'How about you?'

'A few,' the medic replied. He folded his arms and casually said, 'Couldn't tell you the number we've taken in, but I've delivered fifteen. Works out about one a year.' He indicated Jay, now slumped against Ashley. 'The last one, she wouldn't take anything either. She was only young. Younger actually – she lived with her mum – and when we got there she was hiding under the sideboard. Bum in the air. She wouldn't come out. I had to deliver the baby like that, with this girl holding on to the legs of the sideboard and calling me all the f's and c's under the sun, and her mum yelling at her to stop the bloody swearing. She left the room in the end, the mum – she couldn't stand the language. Baby popped out five minutes later.'

The ambulance slowed and sounded its siren, then began to accelerate. Ashley said, 'Was it a boy or a girl?' but the medic nodded routinely, already turning to speak to the driver. With a restless sigh, Jay released herself from her seatbelt and curled up on the bench. Ashley drummed his fingers on its polythene cover. He felt for his study cards and wound the elastic band onto his wrist, cupped the stack close to his body. He tried to read through his notes, but the words had become too familiar to register. Beside him Jay took a sharp breath and sat upright. Ashley returned the cards to his pocket as the medic released the gas cylinder from its carrybag. Ten minutes and two contractions later the ambulance took a tight bend, ascended a ramp and swung right. The lights of the road disappeared and they came to a halt.

'That's you!' called the driver.

'In your own time, pet,' said the medic.

There was no exchange of thanks and good luck, and although Ashley readied himself to shake hands with the crew, the paramedic left with a cursory tap on his arm and the driver remained in his cab. A burly, brown-coated porter helped Jay to a wheelchair and swung her around, pushed off without a word or glance backwards. They passed quickly through a stone-floored succession of echoing lobbies and glass-sided corridors, lifts and tight corners, Ashley trailing several paces behind, struggling with the bulk of his holdall. White- and green-coated staff stepped by them, ignored them; new mothers glanced out from the wards. A television in a deserted dayroom was showing the start of the nine o'clock news, and beyond this they came to a door marked *Inspection Room 2*. The porter stationed the wheelchair and turned to leave them. Ashley put down his bag. 'Is that us then?' he said. 'This is where we're supposed to be?'

'Think so,' said the porter. 'I'll send someone, shall I?'

'If you wouldn't mind.'

'Wilco,' said the porter.

The door was unlocked – Ashley tried it – but they did not immediately enter. There ought to have been someone to guide them; a sign somewhere to identify this room as theirs. But the interior was as blank as the corridor; the lights were switched off and the curtains were open. It wasn't a part of hospital they had seen on their visits. Ashley could not think how it connected to the rest of the building; everything appeared as if wrongly arranged. He crouched beside Jay and linked his fingers through hers, puffed out his cheeks and goggled his eyes. She forced her mouth to a smile. Then a shadow of pain passed over her. 'Come on,' he said quickly, 'we'd better go in,' but Jay suddenly grabbed for his arms, gripped him so tightly he almost cried out, nearly jerked himself free. Jay's eyes were wide with alarm, and he shouted in panic, 'Big breaths, Jay, breathe in slowly, breathe out, like me . . .' But this time he could not coach her. As Jay's breath quickened so did his own, and when Ella finally found them they were both panting, clutching each other tightly in the corridor.

'Oh, yes,' she said brightly, 'this looks like labour to me.'

★

They had entered the building from the rear, risen four flights from the basement. The delivery rooms were on the top storey, facing across the fog-bound city to the river, a bank of lawns and rosebeds somewhere below them. Before they'd left the inspection room Jay had surrendered her clothes and changed to a white hospital gown, willingly agreed to a pain-killer, an injection of diamorphine. Their midwife said that was the sensible thing. Disposing of her plastic gloves to a pedal bin, she told them Jay was four centimetres dilated and doing very well, but the baby would now need to be monitored; it might also become drowsy, forget to breathe when it was born. Jay made no objections, and so Ashley said nothing, didn't offer their *Birthplan* until Ella remembered to ask for it. The leaflet was frayed at the corners and torn down the folds, coloured pink and blue like the delivery-room curtains, the floral border round the power points. Ella laid it flat to the bed. She drew up a chair and sat down, scanned the ticked boxes and turned it about, frowned as she deciphered Jay's handwriting. Then she nodded and smiled. 'You're going to cut the cord, Ashley?'

'If that's okay.'

'Sure, there's nothing to it.' She secured the form to a clipboard, and mimed a pair of scissors, a single snip. 'It's like opening a supermarket.'

'He's never opened a supermarket,' Jay said.

'This'll be good practice then,' replied Ella, and gently smoothed Jay's fringe from her eyes. 'How're you feeling now? A bit woozy?'

'Travel-sick.'

'But it's helping?'

'Yes.'

'They'd pay twenty-five quid for a shot of this on the streets, Jay. You're lucky.' Ella included Ashley in her smile, and rose from her chair. 'But I'll get you something for the nausea.'

The room was very warm. Ashley lifted the sash window and leaned out. He listened to the traffic in the city centre. There were buses and taxis on the nearest main road, footsteps hurrying through the hospital grounds. Every sound seemed distinct from every other, amplified in the mist, and for a moment he imagined the city revolving around the fixed point of their room. An aeroplane passed overhead. A lorry ascended the hill from the river. Everywhere people were crossing and winding towards the end of their day, and tomorrow they would begin again, oblivious, unaltered, whilst for him and Jay everything would be different. He tried to picture what lay ahead, but couldn't see beyond the room as it was now, the lights dimmed and Jay half-asleep on the bed, paper quietly feeding through the machine at her side. He glanced up at the clock. It wasn't yet ten. He lowered the window and looked restlessly about him for something to do.

There had been no obvious place to empty the contents of their holdall, and no shelf or drawer for Jay's clothes. Their belongings now lay at the foot of the bed. He moved the pile closer to the wall and kicked off his shoes, pulled on some plimsolls. He poured himself a coffee, a cup of iced water for Jay, and placed their flasks either side of the sink. They had also brought tapes and paperbacks, a camera and flashgun, rolls of soft toilet paper, a child's rubber ring for Jay to sit on, fruit and sandwiches, a sponge and a hot water bottle. He lined these along the skirting board but left the baby's new blankets and clothes inside the bag, still in their cellophane wrappings. Hearing the zip, Jay opened her eyes and drowsily said, 'It looks more like home now.'

'That's something anyway,' he replied.

Already very little had happened as they'd hoped or expected. The strap which girdled Jay's middle was tracking the baby's heartbeat and the peaks of her contractions. Ashley glanced at the printout, watched as the display changed from

128 to 140 to 110, a heart-shaped symbol flashing next to the digits. He did not know if this was normal or not, and realized he did not want to know. He stood close to Ella's clipboard and read through their *Birthplan*. There was to have been no medication, and no technology; Jay was to be free to move around, unattached to any machine. He recalled the evening they had spent completing the leaflet, selecting their options, ticking boxes. In each case Jay had asked what he thought, then marked her response before he could finish his answer. At last he'd complained, and they'd argued, but really there had been no need for discussion. He had wanted every choice to be hers, for Jay to choose for him.

'Here's some water,' he said, and Jay smiled but didn't open her eyes. He sipped from his coffee. In most cases she had opted for whatever seemed closest to a natural birth, saying she preferred to trust in fate and spontaneity, her own instincts. And Ashley had conceded, for nothing else between them had ever been planned. They had lived together for five years, and now owned the house that they shared, but this too had occurred without much thought or discussion. They had made no promises to each other, and Ashley had never assumed they would stay together, nor supposed they would separate. He gazed at Jay's face as she dozed. Her jaw was open, her breath dry. He took a lip salve from his pocket and ran it round her mouth, gave her a sip of water. Once, years before, they had parted for no more reason than that they were curious for change, and within days discovered they could not remember each other's appearance. Ashley had sought her out, he later said, merely to remind himself of her face, and soon afterwards they'd begun living together. Now he could summon every detail: the curve of her eyes, the upward turn of her lip, the texture of skin round her mouth. Her features, he realized, had become as familiar to him as his own, more familiar than his parents' and clearer to him now than his brother's.

There were voices in the delivery suite next door. The lights came on and shone into their room through the frosted windows by the ceiling. Jay opened her eyes and gazed blearily at Ashley. The single line of a frown appeared on her forehead. Ella was laughing in the corridor, still smiling as she entered their room and hurried round the bed to the monitor. She examined the printout and made a note on the paper. Then she eased Jay upright for her tablet. 'You're doing very well,' she said. 'I think we'll see this baby before I go home.'

'When's that?' asked Ashley.

'Eight o'clock we change.'

'What's the time now?' Jay asked.

'Ten past ten,' Ashley said, and Jay groaned as she slumped back on her pillows.

'So who's baby going to look like?' Ella asked.

Sitting on the other side of the bed, Ashley guessed Ella was much the same age as Jay, though she wore a wedding ring and lipstick, a perfume which he recognized from the secretaries' office at school. For two hours she divided her attention between Ashley and Jay and the machine. Occasionally she wrote onto the printout, or jotted notes in a file marked *Confidential*, and at intervals they talked. When she told Ashley she had two children, aged three and fifteen months, Jay surprised them by asking, 'What was your first like?'

'We thought you were asleep, Jay.'

'Did you have drugs?'

'Ask me later.' Ella laughed.

But later Jay would have no recollection of this time. From then until midnight she drifted in and out of awareness, unconscious even of the noises from the next room, a woman in the last throes of her labour. 'That's her second too,' Ella whispered, and Ashley walked across to the sink. He poured himself another coffee, drank a little and tipped it away. It tasted faintly of paper, the instructions he'd forgotten to remove from the flask when he filled it. He drummed his fingers on the edge of the drainer. In the other room the midwife was cajoling the woman to push harder, a man's voice quietly encouraging her. There were screams and shouts, a moment's pause, and then the rush of several voices at once. Ella turned towards him and smiled. They heard a baby crying. 'That's a healthy sound,' she said, but when Ashley tried to return her smile he couldn't; he needed to sit down.

'Is there a toilet?' he asked.

Soon afterwards Jay's diamorphine began to wear off. The contractions of the previous hours had built in intensity, dimly registered but painless, and now they emerged with sudden severity. She threw up, a jet of clear water which spattered Ashley's ankle as he tried to jump clear. Ella offered gas from a cylinder attached to the wall, which this time Jay accepted. But the relief was only temporary. With the onset of every contraction there came a brief period of panic as she sought to cover her mouth and nose with the mask. Her hands and whole body were shaking, her teeth chattering. Within half an hour she was writhing on the bed. Ella had to shout to get her attention. Ashley held both her hands and found she wouldn't release them. She rolled away from him, sobbing and frightened. He had to climb on to the mattress. 'I want an epidural,' she cried then. 'Tell them I want an epidural, Ashley. I can't cope with this any more, it's hurting me. Tell them.'

The anaesthetist fixed a tap to the back of Jay's hand. A second midwife secured it with plasters. Ella said, 'I'm just going to take your blood pressure, Jay,' and afterwards left the strap on her arm. A black rubber tube looped up to a gauge on the wall. She made a note in her file and began to set up a drip, a clear plastic tube feeding down to Jay's hand.

'Would you mind if we put a monitor on the baby's head?' a senior midwife said.

Jay replied, 'No, go ahead, anything.'

The anaesthetist made an injection into Jay's spine and Ashley turned his face to the wall. When he looked again the midwives were obscuring his view. He stepped closer. The anaesthetist secured a plastic device to the front of Jay's gown. It contained the anaesthetic. A thin tube curled over her shoulder and down to the small of her back. A blue wire now led from her vagina to the monitoring machine. The anaesthetist dropped his gown and gloves in the bin and waited at the foot of the bed. His hair was dishevelled, as if he'd been sleeping. His shoes were untied. The senior mid-wife eased a tube into Jay's urethra and pressed down on her bladder, filling a bowl. She pushed a plug in the end of the tube and left it inserted for later. Ella dimmed the lights. The anaesthetist and the other midwives departed together. Ashley returned to his seat at the side of the bed. He reached again for Jay's hand but could not hold it; there was a plastic tap in the way.

'I'm pathetic, aren't I?' said Jay.

'You're doing brilliant,' he told her, and thought then he might cry.

The first time they shared a bed was also the last time they'd stayed awake all through the night. The house they were in was newly squatted, a mattress in every room. They'd sat till dawn playing a board game, drinking coffee and tea and smok-ing, eating whatever there was. Perhaps they'd been celebrat-ing; Ashley could no longer remember, only that Jay was strange to him then and he'd clung to her company long after the game became tedious. By morning there were snails stuck to the window, five bicycles coated with dew in the garden. Their friends were already sleeping. In bed he held her tightly and when they finally woke they were still entangled, still wearing their clothes. By then he knew her life story, though she was no less strange than before. Whereas she'd spent her childhood always moving, sometimes unable to distinguish her own mother from the people around her, he had lived his first eighteen years in one house in one town, barely aware of anything beyond it. As he stared at her now Ashley wondered at their coming together at all. Even after five years they had nothing in common except for each other, and yet soon they would become their own family, bound by the baby.

He laid his head on the mattress and pressed his fingertips against hers. Jay's cheeks and neck were flushed red and she was quietly snoring. He allowed his eyes to close too, but in his dream he continued to watch over her. They were in his classroom at school and Jay was sleeping next to the fish tank, Ella sitting by the window. The midwife beckoned Ashley closer and pointed to the children's play area below them, a solitary duck on a spring and a strip of rubberized tarmac. There was nothing else. For a while they watched and waited but the duck was motionless and no one appeared. The tarmac stretched into the distance, smooth and unswerving. Ashley noticed snail tracks on the window and turned to tell Jay but she had already gone. He woke with a start. Ella tapped the printout and smiled. 'You were all sleeping,' she whispered. 'Baby too.'

During the rest of the night many people came and went from the room. Jay's contractions continued unfelt, monitored by the machine and discussed in murmurs by the midwives. Ashley tried not to hear what they were saying, and looked away when he noticed their glances. Occasionally Ella would leave for a break and each time a different midwife would occupy her seat and pick up her clipboard. Ashley was given cups of coffee from a machine down the corridor, and eventually a slice of cold toast. At intervals he descended four flights of stone steps to the nearest men's toilet, shivering in the chill air of the stairwell and reading from his cards as he went. It was a relief to be free of the bedside, and once he took his coffee with him, intending to remain for the length of a tea-break. He locked himself in a cubicle and lowered the seat, listening to the hum of a ventilator, the water in the pipes. When he looked again at his watch he found that barely two minutes had passed. His pulse quickened. He tipped his drink in the bowl and hurried back up the stairs, taking the last flight at a run.

But there was very little for him to do, and nothing to miss. He slept for another half hour, tried to read a book and couldn't concentrate, chose a tape for the machine but didn't play it. There was no anticipation now, and the longer the labour continued, the further the birth seemed to recede. The baby had become an obstruction and he wanted it out so Jay could come home, so she could return to herself. At seven thirty he heard metal buckets in the corridor, polishing machines and loud voices. Stretching her arms, Ella said it would soon be the end of her shift. She pulled on a glove to examine Jay's cervix, and suggested Ashley open the curtains. The fog had cleared. Above the city centre the sky was cloudy and dark but further east there was sunshine, like winter passing to spring. Looking down at the gardens he noticed a play area, a few swings and a slide, and for a moment he felt hopeful, a brief swell of excitement. Then Ella said, 'Would you mind a syntocinon drip, Jay? It'll speed things along. You're still only eight centimetres and the baby's not turning, it's really not coming on.'

'We're going to ask you to do some pushing in a little while, Jay. You'll have to imagine it's like a big jobbie. Really push hard, like you're having a massive big shite. I'll want you to take big deep breaths and really push down on your bum. Two or three pushes with every contraction. You'll feel like your bum is going to explode, but I promise you that won't happen, it won't explode . . .'

The obstetrician was called Marjorie and she wore a red jumpsuit, red lipstick, streaks of pink in her hair. They had not met her before, and neither did they recognize their new midwife, whose name was Angela and who'd arrived to relieve Ella at eight. She was pleased to meet them, she'd said, shaking Ashley's hand, touching Jay's arm. She was new to the team, and surprised they hadn't been told to expect her. She read through Ella's notes and explained that Marjorie would be returning at ten for the birth, assuming the syntocinon didn't work too quickly, didn't force the baby out before they were ready. She laughed, then quietly added, 'I don't think you'll get to cut the cord, Ashley, not this time. It all depends, but probably you won't.'

'It was just an idea,' he'd answered, and felt more relief than disappointment.

Now, as the clock came towards ten, the room became busy with nurses and midwives, cluttered with trolleys and spotlights, equipment for the birth and any complications. Marjorie unclipped her pager and stood at the foot of the bed, Jay's legs splayed before her. Angela placed a hand on Jay's bump to feel for the coming contractions and kept one eye on the printout. A line of pubic hair rose over Jay's belly like the shadow of the crease in a peach, and Ashley concentrated on this as the pushing began, willing the bulge to deflate under Angela's hand, the baby to slip painlessly out. 'That's good,' he said as she heaved, 'you're doing great, Jay.'

Then Marjorie shouted, 'Really big breaths, Jay! Bigger breaths than that!'

And Angela called, 'Harder now, Jay. You're doing very well, but harder now, tuck your chin and push harder, *push harder!*'

But although Jay's face coloured almost to purple and her breath began to gurgle in her throat, she made no progress at all and the strain was too much, she said she couldn't continue. Ashley squeezed her fingers, dampened her face with a sponge. Barely three minutes had passed. Marjorie came to the side of the bed. 'You've got it all wrong, Jay. All the effort is going into your throat. I want you to imagine a big jobbie and push down on this end, concentrate on your bum end.'

'But I can't feel that end,' Jay complained.

Marjorie pushed a couple of fingers inside her. 'Can you feel that? Can you push towards that?'

'Yes.'

'Okay then.'

'I'll wet this,' Ashley said, and edged towards the sink with his sponge.

The pushing continued and the clock approached the half hour. Angela announced the onset of every contraction and loudly coached Jay through her breathing. Ashley found himself straining with Jay, his face contorting like hers. But each time the baby began to descend it slipped back again, Jay became too exhausted to go on, couldn't press any harder, and finally Marjorie said, 'No good, it's getting distressed. The baby's as knackered as you are, Jay. We're going to help it out. We're going to use suction. Is that okay?' Jay nodded, and in moments the bottom section of the bed was removed and her feet raised in the air, strapped into stirrups. Ashley was forced against the side of the mattress by the bustle around him. Jay looked directly into his eyes, and he kissed her forehead, suddenly too frightened to smile and afraid she might notice. She tugged her fingers from his, and squeezed his hand in her own.

Marjorie was sitting on a stool between Jay's legs, a spotlight angled over her shoulder, and when the pushing resumed Ashley watched in several directions at once, but mostly Jay's face. Her hand was pressed to his belly. She was pallid now; the shadows beneath her eyes were like bruises, her lips darkly swollen. When he dared to look at Marjorie he was surprised at the effort involved; she was up on her feet, red-faced and straining, tugging and pulling, like a dentist levering to extract a difficult tooth. He glanced away. Angela shouted. Then the baby came all of a sudden, purple and blue, back rounded towards him. 'It's a blue baby!' he said. 'A little blue baby.' He noticed its hair, and the slime, its creased gummy face. It wasn't real. Angela laid it over Jay's belly, and he looked for its penis, he was sure he would see one; but their child was a girl. 'It's a girl, Jay!' he grinned. 'A blue one.'

'A girl,' she repeated, and sank back to her pillows, still clutching his hand and distantly smiling.

In seconds the umbilical cord was cut and their baby transferred to a table behind Ashley where a doctor and a nurse sucked its lungs clear with a stainless steel tube. Ashley tried to watch but couldn't, his heart was beating too fast and his legs were unsteady. He thought he might fall and looked towards Angela, saw the afterbirth as she expelled it, fat and purple like an internal organ. It slopped on to a dish and Angela peered at it quizzically, noticed he was watching and smiled. 'Very grainy,' she explained, 'it might be overdue.' He nodded, then Marjorie returned to her stool and began stitching Jay where she'd torn. 'I see a clot,' she announced, and poked inside to remove it, a small explosion of blood hitting her shoulder and chin. Ashley sat down. He looked at the clock and calculated their baby was born at 10.44 am, but he could not remember the date. A face appeared round the door and said, 'Congratulations,' and a woman in grey began restocking the shelves. Angela left with the placenta, but promised to return with some tea. Then a nurse tapped Ashley's shoulder and showed him his daughter, now swaddled in hospital green. Jay held open her arms. He went to retrieve his camera from their pile of belongings, padding gingerly through the streaks of red and brown on the floor, and took half a dozen pictures of Jay cradling the child, not sure if he was holding the camera steady, if it was in focus or not. 'She looks like your brother,' Jay told him, and he replied, 'Not so tall.' Then the nurse took the baby away – downstairs, she said, for observation, but not for long, he was welcome to come. And Ashley nodded again, but remained in his seat. For a few minutes then they were left on their own. They looked at each other. Ashley touched the side of Jay's face with his hand. There were scales of dry skin on her lips. He leaned over and kissed her. 'I love you,' he said finally. Then, 'Thank you.'

Jay sighed, and her sigh became a yawn, and she murmured, 'Don't mention it. But I'm not doing that again.'

MAY

*O*F *COURSE you'll be wanting to know whatever became
of the half-done tiling around the fireplace. Well, I finished
it, just – using the very last tile in the box – and then Angela the
midwife came to call, and sat in Jay's rocking-chair, and rocked
forwards, and cracked the most prominent tile of all, the one at the
front in the middle, a calamity which would never have occurred
if we had not been burdened with a baby, and so I've made a note,
that if Maggie doesn't measure up to expectations I shall one day
present her with a list of my grievances, beginning with this
cracked tile, for which she'll be obliged to repay me in sundry tools
and materials from a DIY superstore of my choosing. She's fast
asleep as I type, and apart from the crack in the hearth I have
absolutely nothing against her. She is most agreeable. There
should be some photos enclosed, from which you'll see that she
bears a passing resemblance to me, and a striking resemblance to
you, except that she remains quite minuscule. She seems fairly
satisfied with her parents, so far, and doesn't cry half as much as
expected, not yet. Mostly she sleeps and the critical times grizzle-*

wise are when she wakes for a feed, gets her nappy changed, or when we transfer her from downstairs to upstairs. She is very sensitive to changes of environment or altitude. By instinct Jay is inclined to feed her on demand, comfort her whenever she cries, hold her as much as possible, and sleep with her in our bed. I've done some reading on the subject, of course, and I'm now of the same instinct. Unfortunately our midwives – Angela and the rest of the Green Team – aren't so sure, and neither is Ma Brook, who is on the phone daily. Childcare is a bit of a battleground, I've realized.

Everything is now different of course, but not <u>so</u> different, not yet, and the first surprise of parenthood is that Maggie has taken some getting used to, a bit like a lodger, or one of Jay's freeloading friends – the 'fierce protectiveness' I was so looking forward to didn't arrive instantly but has crept up on me slowly. The books call it 'bonding', and we're getting quite good at it. I've had regular fits of mawkishness since the birth (April 22nd, 10.44 am), including a mannish convulsion of sobbing on the bus home from the hospital, but the second surprise of parenthood (more of a disappointment) is that the anticipated sea-change in my outlook on life and in my relationships with other humans did not occur. My fist-waving attitude to the world-in-general remains, and I experience just as many bursts of everyday irritability as I ever did, though these are now pretty much confined to my working day. At home I'm still floating a little, curiously at ease with bad smells and domestic chaos, quite content to sit and moon over baby in preference to almost any other activity. One notable thing about the newborn, or this particular newborn, is that she's extremely adept at every facial expression this side of misery, with a fetching sideline in mentally subnormal leering and gawping, but she can't seem to express happiness. She does smile, but apparently that's a reflex occasioned by her farts. There are no smiles when Mummy feeds her, or Daddy changes her, or Mummy tells a long inconsequential story, or Daddy buries his nose in her belly. But an explosion of intestinal gas, that's a cause for great infantile joy and hilarity.

Mummy, on the other hand, is struggling to find any great cause for joy or hilarity, maternal or infantile. The birth was fairly horrendous really, the opposite in almost every detail to what we'd expected. I did my Seventies-Man-in-spangly-tee-shirt bit, of course, diligently mopping Jay's brow and mumbling words of encouragement, but generally I hung uselessly about and got in everyone's way. Jay assures me this was more than enough but I'm sure I missed a trick somewhere, she shouldn't have ended up in hospital quite so early, in quite so much pain, on quite so many drugs, with quite so many tubes stuck in her, if only I'd paid more attention in our NCT classes and known when to face down the medics. Or not. We'll never know for sure unless we do it again, but it seems there's more chance I'll have a vasectomy than Jay will ever have another baby. In fact, a vasectomy seems a very likely prospect, just as soon as Jay feels strong enough to perform it. Since the birth she's spent most of her time in bed or sitting on a rubber ring, submitting to one indignity after another, including a return visit to the maternity hospital, baby and all, for an over-night stay and an operation under local anaesthetic to 'scrape' her womb, which was dangerously clotted and painful. After the trauma of the birth this in itself was a bit of a smack in her teeth, and she's still suffering from piles (inside and out), constipation, cracks in her nipples, a viral infection, loose stitches, and baby blues . . . for which she's taking three sets of pills, one medicine, a tube of nipple cream and two varieties of bottom cream, one called Anusol, which tickles me, though not her, except that I have to administer it.

The only real advantage of Jay's condition is that it's given us an excuse to keep intruders at bay, including Ma Brook, although I don't think we can hold out for much longer. I took a few days off work so I'd be on hand to apply the various bottom creams (including one for Maggie; she has a nappy rash already), but finally I crept back in last Friday. I was hoping to keep a low profile but immediately found myself under siege from all the teach-ers I'd previously taken most pains to avoid. The staffroom confederacy of parents has claimed me for its own. They seek me out with bundles of garish girlie toddler-wear, eager to share their birth stories, flourishing colour snapshots of the event, and asking knowingly about 'smelly nappies' – of which we have loads – and 'sleepless nights' – of which we have none. Actually, the scepticism or resentment when I confess to sleeping like a baby, as does the baby herself, is palpable, and has provoked some very acidic replies – 'Ah, yes, yours will be the perfect baby, of course.' But the cast-offs are welcome, satin-pink as they mostly are. The kids are fascinated, and blunt – 'You should get married, Mr B, or she's going to grow up with everyone calling her a bastard.'

Which continues to prey on Father's mind too – he made his second-ever phone call the day after the birth, almost inarticulate with near-excitement (as opposed to merely inarticulate) but still managed to ask if 'wedding bells are on the horizon at all' and if we'd 'given any thought to a surname at all'. In fact, we took Maggie to be registered as a Brook just last Friday, where the man with the fountain pen whispered privately to Jay, 'You do realize that you can at any time in the future apply to have the baby's name changed back to your own, if anything should happen . . .?' So much for getting wedded; it seems we're already prime candidates for separation.

Dad's phone call aside, one other minor miracle occurred with the birth, which is that Jay's Easter cactus flowered for the very first time ever (it was a gift from Daffy Daphne, her mother, about eight years ago). And what's more, your second letter from Thailand arrived just as the cactus was flowering, perhaps even as the baby was emerging. How about that? Our cup overflowethed. The lined paper is a positive boon, by the way, and the printed place names even more so. I read the full seventeen and a half pages to Jay as we lay in bed with Maggie on our first day home together. It was a very happy hour, and for once our pleasure wasn't tinged with green-eyed envy, although I don't know how long this particular effect of parenthood can last. More of the same *would be greatly appreciated, seventeen and a half pages every Tuesday morning if you wouldn't mind, please.*

One less welcome effect, which I'm worried may become permanent, is a creeping nervousness of the wider world, a heightened sensitivity to hazards and other people's unhappiness. I find I'm suddenly quite fearful of crossing the road, and strangely troubled by your smallness in the great vastness of the continents; I worry about you, I imagine a big boot treading on you. After this latest letter I tried to chart your progress in my home atlas and was very disturbed to find my index finger travelling between mountain ranges I'd never previously known the existence of, and more disturbed still to realize that even the finest of fine-tip marker pens would grotesquely exaggerate your size in relation to the enormity of the landscape. 'How tiny he is,' I thought. 'I do hope he's careful.' (I should add too that at least half the places you claim to have visited do not in fact exist on the maps and were very probably narcotically induced.) At school I read extracts from your letter to my first-years, who were surprisingly puzzled by the image of you swimming in the sea with 'dangling abandon', but amused by your bowel problems. With blithe disregard for the National Curriculum we plotted your position on the Peters projection pinned to my wall, then consulted our distribution and density maps and confirmed that you were indeed a dizzying distance from the nearest Large Red Dot, lost in a wilderness of underpopulated green. You'll know a Large Red Dot when you meet one, by the way – it's the thickness of 100,000 people, possibly arranged as an age–sex pyramid, and a pretty precipitous age–sex pyramid too – loads of kids at the bottom, very few over-sixties above, rather like a school, in fact. On which topic – population growth, not schools – I'd be only too happy to expand, but the Maggot and her mother have woken and I'm afraid it's time to get out the bum creams.

There was a baby bath, a potty, a top-and-tail bowl and a

bucket for soiled nappies. There was a bedspread knitted by an elderly aunt and several tiny cardigans knitted by herself. There were dresses and vests and a small pile of romper suits rescued from a neighbour, a rubber cot-sheet saved from Ashley's childhood, and a bundle of sheets and blankets bought from a clearance sale. There was a brand-new push-chair with a detachable rain-hood and holdall, and a safety mattress for the cot he had yet to assemble. There was a wooden chair and a trolley of bricks, a box of old teddies and a threadbare rocking-horse which he recognized from the attic at home. There were books and paints and crayons, some plastic ducks for the bath, a wicker basket for toys. And finally there was Ashley's own christening gown, a bri-nylon frock still in its original wrapper.

As his mother brought each item into the living room, Ashley forced himself to say, 'Thank you,' but sensed he might just as well stay silent. She was too busy to hear him. He glanced repeatedly at Jay, who disguised her annoyance by nuzzling the baby, now lying asleep on her shoulder. She caressed the back of her head. Ashley picked up an old teddy, turned it about and tossed it back to its box. When eventually his mother closed the front door and hung her coat over theirs in the hallway she was flushed with her efforts and seemingly oblivious to Ashley's discomfort. Vigorously rubbing her hands, she came and sat beside Jay on the sofa. 'That should give you a start anyway,' she said, and waited expectantly, her hands now poised in her lap.

Jay paused a long moment, then raised her face from the baby and quietly said, 'Would you like to hold her, Phyllis?'

Ashley's mother made a soft clucking noise as she accepted the baby, gingerly supported her head with one hand, her backside with the other. 'Isn't she light!' she whispered, and looked first to Ashley, then Jay. She was blushing. Ashley smiled. He stepped around the gifts on the floor and went to the window. There was a vase of scented flowers on the sill.

He took a long breath. Outside a small girl in white pumps was standing beside his father's car, wiping her foot on the tyre. A dog turd was stuck to the sole of her shoe.

'Where is Dad?' he said.

His mother cradled the baby as if afraid she might crush her. Without lifting her gaze she replied, 'Gone to fetch a paper.'

Ashley looked at Jay, who stifled a smile, began inspecting her fingernails. 'He's not going to sit in the car again?'

'Think so,' said his mother, and added confidentially to Jay, 'he doesn't want to come in while you're breastfeeding. He says it'll only embarrass you to have another man in the house, especially so soon after the birth, not while you're still a bit poorly.'

Ashley said, 'She doesn't feed Maggie twenty-four hours a day, Mum.' He stared at his mother, who touched the baby's nose with her own, examined her face, her tiny hands. Maggie continued to sleep, her lips parted, and Ashley thought of germs, wanted to snatch his daughter away. He said, 'Mum, you're not serious? You did tell him?'

'Tell him what?'

'That Jay doesn't have her tits hanging out all day!' His mother sat for some seconds quite motionless, apparently absorbed in the baby, then began very quietly to hum, a nursery rhyme or a lullaby. Ashley sighed heavily. 'Her *bosoms*,' he corrected himself, but still she was offended. He turned to the window and waited, saw his father approaching from the other side of the road, a small man with a jutting jaw, rheumy eyes. He walked slowly, without momentum, as if unaccustomed to being out of doors, and when he reached the car he was clutching his newspaper close to his chest. The sun glared momentarily from the windscreen.

Ashley's mother said to Jay, 'I remember when my two were born. Ken worked a full shift, both times. And even then he had to have a sleep before he came to the hospital. A proper sleep, not a nap. I wondered if he'd ever turn up, but he said they'd turned him away – this was when Ashley was born – they'd turned him away for not coming during proper visiting hours. But they didn't have visiting hours, not in the maternity ward, it was come as you please, more or less. And I told him that, but he wouldn't have it, even when I asked the nurse right there in front of him. No, he said, they'd turned him away. And that was that. Not a word of apology, nothing. No interest in the baby either.' She stopped, and swallowed, and then said, 'But this one's lovely, isn't she? A little treasure.'

'I'm taking her out,' Ashley said. 'This is ridiculous.'

As he stepped down to the pavement, leaving the door unlatched behind him, Ashley felt suddenly taller, conscious of the child on his shoulder, his father hunched behind the wheel of his car. Maggie stirred a little, a kittenish cry, and he kissed the side of her head. His father looked up and smiled, and his teeth were a surprise, too regular, too evenly white. He folded his newspaper away. Ashley opened the passenger door. 'New teeth?' he said, ducking down.

'That's it,' said his father, and pushed the plate out on his tongue, swallowed it back. He turned in his seat, and said, 'So this is Maggie, is it?'

Ashley eased the baby from his shoulder and laid her face-up in his arm. His father showed no inclination to take her, and Ashley was glad, he wanted to keep her between them. 'This is Maggie,' he confirmed.

'Not Margaret?'

'Just Maggie.' For a long minute they sat looking at the baby, the only sound her breathing, the slight smack of her lips. 'She's sucking,' Ashley said finally. 'She must be dreaming of milk.'

'All she knows, I suppose,' said his father, and produced

two notes from his wallet. He fumbled to force the money into Ashley's pocket, to have it out of the way.

Ashley took it from him. 'Thank you,' he said.

'You'll not be needing any more baby gear, anyway.'

'Not now.'

'I told her, "Some of that stuff's years old, Phyllis. They won't be wanting all that." But she wouldn't have it. She wouldn't listen.' He shook his head, dismissed his annoyance with a laugh. 'I expect you've got most of it already, haven't you?'

'Some. Not all.'

'You can always pass the rest on. But don't tell her, she'll be wanting it back.' He laid his finger in Maggie's palm, smiled as her hand closed around it. His fingernail was horny, squared-off. The skin of Maggie's knuckles appeared translucent.

'Why don't you come inside?' Ashley said.

There was a pause, and his father said, 'How's Jay keeping now, all right?'

'Yes, fine, still a bit sore, a bit uncomfortable, but fine, she's fine.'

Seconds passed. His father sighed. 'I'll drop by another time,' he said. 'On my own. I don't suppose your mother's told you? She's after a separation?'

'Sorry?'

His father nodded, gazed out at Hazel's caravan. Ashley watched him closely, the watery sacs beneath his eyes, bleary whites, red rims. 'A separation,' he said. 'We were watching the telly the other week and she said, "I'm leaving you. I've had enough." This was before we got your news, before the baby was born.' He shook his head, then suddenly laughed. His dentures clacked. 'I told her, "But you can't go now, Phyllis. There's still that fish in the fridge. It'll only waste if you go now."'

'And?'

'She went straight through and cooked it. She must've been serious.'

Ashley shifted in his seat, held Maggie closer. 'What brought this on?'

'Twenty-seven years married to me. That's what she said. But I don't know what she's got to complain about. I drive her here, there and everywhere. I can't see what she stands to gain by going.' He coughed, and said, 'Anyway, she's got nowhere to go to. No one would have her.' He tapped his hand on the steering wheel. Ashley waited, but his father had said all he wanted to. As the silence lengthened they both gazed down at Maggie. Her eyes were flickering open, her arms and legs jerking. His father dipped his face towards her and said, 'Hello then, young lady. Hello then, young lady,' but the baby started to cry. 'Oh well,' he joked, 'that's another one doesn't like me.'

'She needs changing,' Ashley said. 'Why don't you come inside? I'll make us some tea.'

'Another time,' insisted his father. 'I'll come when you're more settled.' He reached for his newspaper, began to unfold it.

Ashley hesitated. 'Shall I bring you a cup out?'

'Yes, son, okay. You do that.'

'Right.' He opened the door. 'See you in a minute then?' But his father didn't respond and Ashley carried Maggie indoors, feeling smaller now, cramped by the car. In the living room Jay was sitting alone on her pillows on the sofa, staring down at the gifts on the floor. Gently jigging the baby, Ashley sat with her. Jay slumped against him, rested her head on his shoulder. From upstairs there came a scraping sound, an irregular knocking. 'What's happening?' he asked.

'She's sweeping the bedroom, making herself useful.'

Ashley shook his head dismally. The baby was wailing. He got down on his knees and pulled a plastic mat from under a chair, a canvas bag of changing gear. He said, 'She's making herself at home, more like.'

Singapore at last! Well, I can admit to you now, I've been expecting accounts of hideous bowel-wrenching diseases with almost every letter, it's been a great worry that none has yet happened, something very hideous indeed was clearly in the offing, so I'm relieved that your lurgy struck there and not some opium shack in the doctorless wilderness, <u>and</u> was safely delivered into the cool scrubbed hands of Dr Hui Lee. This really is a journey of discovery – mountains I've never heard of, villages that don't exist, and now a fever of genuinely horrible improbableness. Or improbable horribleness. But can Singapore really be so improbably clean, quite so horribly full of shopping malls? Not that you often bothered to visit him, but you may recall our maternal grandfather spending his Tuesday afternoons at the 'Pensioners' Parliament' in Ravensby Conservative Club, where all the important issues of the day were discussed and debated and blamed on the wives and the blacks. Singapore sounds the kind of place that would result if ever the Ravensby Pensioners' Parliament came to power. The penal code, anyway. Fine 'em! Jail 'em! Hang 'em! Though I don't suppose any group of old men so terminally arthritic and splenetic could come up with somewhere quite so full of gleaming emporia, or approve of anywhere quite so perilously far-flung. It amazes me too that you should arrive on practically the other side of the globe, in <u>that</u> place, and come to the conclusion that what's been missing from your life all this time is a <u>hobby</u>, and what's more, an open-air hobby. Presumably we can now anticipate years of weird and wonderful anecdotage interrupted by tedious references to your latest discovery in the undergrowth – 'Did I show you the <u>Galium odoratum</u> cuttings I took last Sunday? Fascinating, fascinating.' Or maybe that wouldn't be such a bad thing. Maybe a hobby is the answer for us all. I'm wondering if perhaps my future mental stability depends on developing a keen interest in <u>Galium odoratum</u>.

No doubt you've been keeping abreast of what's happening in our soon-to-be-tarmacked neck of the woods by reading the various Evening Telegraphs of the globe, but you won't appreciate the full calamitous lunacy of it all until you know that practically every other major road scheme in the country is now 'under review' or 'abandoned forever', whilst ours, trailblazing through an official site of special scientific interest, an official area of outstanding natural beauty, an official civic amenity with picnic tables and guidebook, ours is about to be laid as a matter of urgency, the contractors already appointed, the security guards already recruited, the coils of jaggy fencing already stockpiled. Not only which, but the 'exchange land' being offered in return for said civic amenity is a square of hedgeless farmland on a landfill site over a mile from the Common. Not only which, but this will have to be cordoned off for ten or fifteen years whilst some new trees are grown. Not only which, but an appeal against this idiocy was summarily rejected on the established precedent that a carpark or a piece of the moon could be offered in exchange providing it was of identical square acreage . . . ! I wonder how all this would appear from the pointy end of a Himalayan mountain, or indeed from a lunar crater. And I wonder if a sudden interest in Galium odoratum will be of any use when all the locally available Galium odoratum is about to be buried under three feet of industrial aggregate . . .

Ashley entered by the back door. He heard a soft slap of water in the bathroom, a faint giggling. Three large containers stood in a line in the kitchen. Each was marked with a daub of blue paint and he presumed they were water-butts, though he didn't know whose. He dumped his pile of jotters on the table and laid his coat over them. The bread bin was open and empty. A jam jar stood lidless on top of the fridge, red jelly dripping from a knife to the floor. The sink was clogged with tealeaves. Sugar spilled across the worktop and dissolved in a pool of yellowing milk. 'Jay?' he called, and pushed against a heap of clothes to get into the bathroom.

'It's Mr B.!' cried Hazel.

A young man with a beard was towelling his back, standing up in the bath. He said, 'Ashley? Right?' and brought the towel behind his neck, his arms stretching wide. His penis lolled in a bush of black hair. Damp curls covered his thighs. 'I'm Coz,' he said.

'Don't mind me,' said Ashley. Hazel was reclining with her head at the taps, her small freckled breasts above the water line. As she slipped beneath the surface Ashley said, 'I was looking for Jay.'

'She's outside on the bus, Ash. Mum's here, she brought us.'

'Not Daffy Dee . . .'

Hazel nodded and grinned at him. 'Nice tie,' she said.

'Thanks,' Ashley replied. 'Nice tits.'

'*Mister* Brook!' exclaimed Hazel, and he closed the door on her, tugging the tie from his collar. He trailed it into the living room, where he found a red tricycle and another trolley of bricks. They were second-hand, but the trike had been re-painted in gold and green hoops, a polka-dot flag attached to the handlebar. He switched on a lamp. Jay's mother's coach was parked slightly up on the kerb, very close to the window and stealing the light. He stood and stared at it, his hands in his pockets. He had no desire to go out. When he heard Hazel and Coz in the kitchen he quickly stacked the toys in his arms and carried them upstairs.

Soon after the birth of their baby Ashley had cleared most of Jay's things to the back bedroom. And for once she hadn't resisted, though still she refused to throw anything away. With his own possessions he was ruthless, discarding a shirt if he bought a new one, revising his bookshelves with every addition. There had been few remnants of his childhood in their house; he wouldn't have known what to save. But now he was accumulating things for Maggie, most of it unwanted. He lowered the trike and trolley to the mattress. The last time Jay's mother had visited she'd arrived with a standard lamp, their kitchen table and a spin-drier which didn't work. There were many other things too, mostly discovered in lay-bys and roadside ditches, in the margins of woodlands. Some she bartered or sold on. It was how she made her living, finding and selling, sometimes fruit-picking or labouring, claiming benefits when she could. The spin-drier still sat in a corner of this room, a battered white cylinder just light enough to carry. He took it downstairs. There was no reason why they should keep it.

The smell on board Dee's coach was thick and warm, like meat on the turn, and it lodged at the back of his throat. He had not known her to take baths, and there was no shower on the bus. He presumed she bathed in rivers, if at all, and although she wore scent and burned joss sticks, her own smell always remained, lingering long after she'd gone. Pushing the spin-drier ahead of him, Ashley called, 'It's fucked, Dee. We can't use it,' and noticed Jay's glare of annoyance. She was sitting on a bench with Maggie at her breast. Dee was kneeling on a mat by the burner, heavy grey plaits falling to either side of her face. Quietly he said, 'I just found Hazel in the bath with a hairy man. Is she safe, do you think?'

'She's wise,' Dee replied, and smiled benignly, as though to a child. Ashley nodded, irritated. He stood beside an open half-window, and Dee said, 'Sun's come out today, that's nice. We've had two days of cloud, spirits go down a bit.'

'Yes, Daphne,' he said. She continued to look at him. He crossed his arms on his chest, gazed around at her coach. The walls were panelled and varnished, the floor laid with cork tiles, scattered with rugs. Blue and purple fabric billowed the length of the ceiling, falling as curtains to cover the rear window. The concertina doors which enclosed her bedroom were open, a large pile of blankets and sleeping bags heaped on the mattress. 'It's looking good now,' he said.

'Bodywork's a bit rough.' She sighed. 'Engine's tired. It needs attention.'

'The "hairy man" is mending it,' Jay told him.

'Right,' Ashley said.

Dee rose to her feet and picked up her kettle, began to gather her cups from around the living area. 'Coz,' she said sadly. 'Sometimes I worry. I wonder if I should've done more forcing with Hazel. I try to be a help to her, but she wants to be her own person, which is good, she has her own view, but we're travelling in different directions now.' She shrugged, piled her cups in a bowl, the kettle on top. 'She looks to her friends for guidance now.'

Jay said, 'Dee's worried she's mixing with the wrong sort.'

'Teachers?' Ashley said. 'Bank clerks? Accountants?'

Jay's mother frowned and looked at him quizzically. She said, 'A lot of the new ones are coming straight from the cities, and they're bringing the city with them, all the problems. They're running away, it's understandable, but the vision is missing.'

'I see,' he said.

'It's hard to know, I suppose, all the prophesies, where we're going, what the future holds. But they could find their way. They could develop.'

'Right,' he said.

'And now there's Maggie,' she said.

Ashley looked down at his daughter, her face obscured in the folds of Jay's clothes. Jay's eyes were closed and she was slowly shaking her head. 'Is there a connection?' he said.

Dee sighed wearily. She came towards him, took one of his hands and rubbed it. 'Maggie's beautiful,' she told him.

'Thanks,' he replied. Her gaze was searching, unblinking, and he turned his face to the window, saw Hazel struggling from the house with a water-butt, Coz following behind with two more. His fatigues were oil-smeared, his boots without laces. As they clambered on to the bus Ashley eased his hand from Dee's grip. 'Bathroom's free now,' he said, 'if you'd like one.'

'Not today,' she smiled. 'Maybe tomorrow.'

Jay looked up at her mother. 'How long are you staying?' she said.

JUNE

IT IS LESS than a month since I last wrote and a mere matter of days since I scribbled on my post-it pad that the baby has colic, that Jay is in the doldrums, and that both Jay and the baby cry mostly in the mornings. But this is already untrue. I spend so much time watching for consistencies in Maggie's behaviour, looking for character traits, trying to interpret her every need and fear, that I latch on to just about anything which occurs more than once, so that she seems to pass through one phase after another, and all these phases seem to last weeks when in fact they're usually over in days, if not minutes. She never really had colic, just a few days' bad wind; Jay is far more often cheerful than not, and doesn't cry any more than she used to; whilst the Maggot actually cries around the clock, on and off, and is especially grumpy in the evenings. In fact, she found her voice a little while after I last wrote, spent a couple more days testing the acoustics of each room (the bedroom reverberates best), and now has it pitch-perfect, such that last Sunday I constructed a kitchen storage unit inside-out, back-to-front and upside-down, despite being two doors away from her and wearing a Walkman. A baby's cry is a small miracle of nature and strikes to the very core of your being. It is most distracting.

But perhaps she feels she has plenty to cry about. To add to her colic-that-wasn't, she has also endured her first cold and I have removed the first stringy snot from her nose; she has suffered her second nasty nappy rash, an horrific sight indeed; and she has scared us half to death with her first-ever fever. She gets through about eight nappies a day, sometimes more, and invariably splats the back of your hand with some fresh poo the moment you lay a clean nappy beneath her. She cries when she wets herself, and sometimes just before a fart; she cries when she's bored or lonely and wants attention; she cries the cry of distraction when she's hungry; and she cries inbetweentimes for no reason at all. She is quiet when strapped to a chest; quiet – usually – just after a feed; quiet – sometimes – when laid on her mat for a nappy change; and quiet – mostly – whilst we're asleep.

What she likes . . . she likes very much to be fed.

Maggie the Maggot is a time-consuming fleshy wriggle and her mother's life has changed drastically, such that she can't really do anything without first considering the baby – some days she can't even leave the room without Maggie throwing a tantrum. She has to abandon whatever she's doing before she's finished; never gets a lie-in or a full night's uninterrupted sleep; and often has to put her dinner aside so Maggie can guzzle hers. For a while at first she wasn't even sure she liked Maggie, or actually wanted her, but she didn't tell me this until very recently, not until <u>after</u> she'd decided that she did like her, and did want her. The turning point seems to have been the realization that the baby is portable. She now takes Maggie with her most days to the Road Campaign office, and yesterday breastfed her while being interviewed by the local gumshoe about a forthcoming festival, a summer solstice party-type-thing on the Common. I worry sometimes that she's doing too much,

*she gets awful-tired-looking, but probably I'd worry far more if
she sat at home getting grumpy. Probably. For me the baby is
more of a hobby, evenings and weekends, with none of the physical demands on my body. Perhaps I'll feel different when I
begin my job share (after the summer holidays) and take on
more of the burden, but for the moment there's no greater pleasure in life than wiping the sloppy jobbies from Maggie's backside. Which is sad, isn't it?*

It was the nearest Sunday to the solstice and three days into a
heatwave; the tarmac on the roads was tacky and tugged at
their shoes, the sun glared from the pavements, radiated back
from the cars along the kerbside. With the baby strapped to
his belly, Ashley stayed as close as he could to the hedges and
gardens, crossed the road when he spotted some shade. His
neck was burning, feet sweltering. He looked repeatedly at
Maggie, her pudgy arms and knees smeared in suncream, her
head protected in a lacy bonnet. Any clothes seemed too
many for him, but he worried she wasn't covered enough. On
the other side of the street Jay was avoiding the shadows, her
dress hitched up in a bustle, legs wading through sunshine.
She carried Maggie's changing gear in a satchel on her back.
The estate was unfamiliar to them and they made their way
by following the noise from the Common. A brass band was
playing but the notes became trapped in the gaps between the
houses, echoing from several directions at once. When they
came to the end of a cul-de-sac Ashley sat on a garden wall and
said, '*Shit!*' He waved an arm down the street. 'We should've
got off at my school, Jay! We knew the way from there.'

Jay lifted the sunglasses from her nose and lodged them in
her hair. A film of sweat covered her freckles. 'Well, we
didn't,' she said.

'Or got a lift with Hazel this morning.'

'She was going to sell her caravan. She might not even turn
up.'

'She said she would.'

'Hazel says lots of things.'

Ashley eased his hands between himself and the baby, tried to let in some air. 'It's just so hot,' he complained, and sat around on the wall, inclining his head to the music. The house beside him was large and its many windows were leaded, a heavy curtain of ivy falling from the eaves. He peered into the passage between the house and its garage, and found a stocky toddler in a swimsuit gazing back at him, round-eyed and curious. Ashley attempted a smile, and said, 'Hello,' but the little girl took a step backwards. A pearly string of water spattered the pavement beside her. She cringed, and squealed, and suddenly began running towards him, a heavy-thighed woman chasing behind with a bucket. Ashley rose and waited until the woman noticed him. 'Excuse me,' he said, 'sorry to bother you, but how do we get to the Common from here?'

'We're lost,' added Jay.

The woman laid down her bucket and shielded her eyes, one arm vaguely outstretched to stop the toddler running further. She wore lilac leggings, a baggy white blouse with the collar turned up. For a moment she stared at the sling strapped to Ashley, then turned her attention to Jay. With an air of reluctance she said, 'You can come through here, I suppose.'

'Sorry?'

She lifted the child onto her hip and padded away from them. 'This way,' she said, not looking back. Her garden was long and wide and they passed a group of adults in deck-chairs sitting around a paddling pool. There was a plastic slide on the lawn, a swing, and a giant turtle containing a sand pit. A play-house stood in the shade of some apple trees. 'There's a gate at the bottom. It's through there and up.'

'Right,' nodded Ashley. 'Thank you.'

'Drop the latch when you're out,' instructed the woman; and then warned them, 'I'll be locking it after you.'

'Yes,' said Ashley. 'Will do.'

The gate was heavy and opened outwards just far enough to squeeze through. Beyond it they found a bridle-path indented with hoofprints. There was a ditch and a stand of tall, mossy trees; then the land began to rise steeply, clear blue sky above the horizon, a heath of yellow and green below it. As they edged their way through the browning gorse, sweating and bothered by insects, Jay said, 'Did you hear what they said?'

'Who?'

'Those people.' She imitated an upper-class accent. *'They weren't too smelly were they, dear? Oh no, quite well scrubbed actually.'*

Ashley sighed. 'I think you imagine things, Jay.' He held a prickly branch out of her way. 'Paranoid.'

'Ashley, you were too busy doffing your cap to notice.'

At the crest of the hill there was a footpath and a row of benches facing the Common, all of them occupied. Ashley wanted to sit down but everywhere he looked there were people. As they walked amongst the groups on the grassy slope they passed families with picnics laid out on blankets, couples with pushchairs and babies, a knot of elderly women holding placards. Unable to see his feet for the sling, Ashley kicked over a bottle of cider and quickly apologized to a man in black denims who half-rose to challenge him. A few yards further on a young woman leapt out in front of them. Her hair was pink and green and she began laughing when Jay failed to recognize her. Then she and Jay started talking. Ashley hesitated, but carried on walking.

In the milky haze of the distance there was farmland and a railway, a honey-coloured viaduct where the track crossed a river. Gazing down at the isolated oaks of the Common he saw traders and performers, stalls and platforms, a bouncy castle and a solitary white teepee. There was a rank of portable toilets, and a cluster of uniformed musicians outside a beer tent. The band had stopped playing, but there came a constant beating of drums, shrilling whistles, and a noise of children as loud as any school playground. He noticed Jay's banners where the oak pasture met the denser green of the woods. They formed the backdrop to a stage, from where a woman with a microphone was addressing a small audience. Her voice was thickly distorted. Ashley tried to signal to Jay that he was heading that way, and she nodded, but he couldn't be sure if the nod was for him or the friend she was talking to. In the hot soupy air he felt a sudden blaze of irritation and descended without her.

Closer to the banners the crowd began to tighten and he stopped when he could squeeze no further forward. There was a patter of applause, and an elderly man in a flimsy green waterproof accepted the microphone. The man pushed at the bridge of his spectacles and cleared his throat, felt inside each of his pockets. He looked questioningly behind him, and waited for a film crew to signal their readiness. Then he delayed a few seconds longer. He was the chairman of the oldest of the campaigns and formerly a teacher at the school where Ashley now worked. When finally he spoke his voice was assured and his speech well-rehearsed. The amplifiers crackled, suddenly became much clearer and louder.

'I'd like to thank you all for coming to Hogslea Common today,' he began, 'to reaffirm your opposition to the Department of Transport in its determination to bulldoze this beautiful wood, one of the most ancient and beautiful in England, in whose place we shall soon be given a road, a new motorway by stealth. It is a motorway which every one of us here knows to be unnecessary and which can only create more problems than its solves, create more traffic than it diverts, encourage yet more business out of the city, cause yet more pollution and accidents, and destroy yet more natural habitats. It is unwanted, and for sixteen years we have campaigned to show it is unwanted. For sixteen years we have lobbied and protested. And we have been polite, we have been reasonable, we have opposed this idiocy at every turn with polite and reasonable argument. We have gone through all the right channels and followed all the correct procedures. We have written letters and got up petitions, we have submitted our arguments to countless meetings and briefings – and to three Public Inquiries – and at the end of all of this, at the end of sixteen years of being reasonable and polite, the system has failed us. The faceless wonders of the civil service have failed us. Our elected representatives in Parliament have failed us. The British Government and the bureaucrats of Brussels and the high and mighty of the British judiciary have all failed us. They've all failed us. And so the time has come to be impolite. The time has come to be unreasonable . . .' He paused for breath and there were cheers and whistles, a few shouted remarks. Maggie's arms began to flail. Ashley hoisted her up to look at her face, bobbed his head until her eyes found him. For a moment he thought she might smile, but instead she produced a dribble of vomit. 'The time has come to break the law if we have to, to chain ourselves to the bulldozers, to occupy these woods, this common, to make a physical nuisance of ourselves at every turn . . .'

Beneath her bonnet Maggie was sweating. Ashley began to back out, untying her hat as he went. The sunlight pierced his eyes. Surveying the slope from below he recognized a few children from school, but couldn't locate Jay or her friend. Soon the baby would need feeding and her nappy changing. He cast around for somewhere more obvious to stand, but there was only the crowded hill or the stage and so he drifted towards the shade of an oak tree, searching the faces around him for anyone he knew and using Maggie's hat to wipe the sick from her chin, the dampness from her hair. He wasn't aware of the ring of spectators around the tree until he reached it, and didn't notice Hazel until she prodded his arm. 'Seen Jay?' he said.

She pointed in the direction he'd come. 'Behind you.'

Ashley turned sharply, but Jay was some distance away, talking to Owen from the Inquiry. Her thumbs were tucked into the straps of her satchel and her legs were planted firmly apart, a posture which emphasized the fullness of her breasts, the roundness of her belly. Several inches taller than her, Owen stooped to listen but his gaze was fixed on the trestle table between them. Ashley wiped the sweat from his forehead, and stuffed Maggie's hat in his pocket. He pointed to the tree, and asked Hazel, 'So what's this all about?'

'It's brilliant,' she told him, 'just unruly. There's so much energy here, Ash, everyone coming together like this, it's amazing, so connected . . .'

Ashley narrowed his eyes and smiled from the side of his mouth. Hazel sighed and stopped speaking. They both looked at the tree. Seven or eight young men were straddling the branches, one playing a tin whistle, the others clapping their hands or beating on drums whilst beneath them some girls in pointy hats were skipping and twirling as they circled the trunk. An older woman was beating on the bark with a couple of sticks, and all of them were hollering and whooping. Amongst the spectators Ashley noticed a couple of his own first-year boys, gazing disbelievingly from their bicycles. With more impatience than he intended, he said, 'Did you finally get rid of that caravan, Hazel?'

'That obstruction, do you mean? That fucking eyesore, that heap of old rust . . .'

'That's it,' he smiled, but Hazel looked at him sternly.

'Yes, I did,' she said. 'Only you shouldn't be so sarcastic all the time, Ash. You're really negative, you know, really cynical these days.'

'Sorry,' said Ashley. 'I'm just a bit tired. A bit hot and bothered and tired.'

'Yes, well . . .' Hazel shrugged.

She removed half a roll-up from behind her ear, pinched out the plug of burnt tobacco. As she tried to get her lighter to ignite, Ashley noticed the nicotine stains on her fingers, the grime beneath her nails. She smelled of woodsmoke and patchouli and he thought momentarily to tease her, but instead he asked, 'Would you like to hold Maggie?'

Hazel looked at him sceptically, and then nodded, quickly discarding the cigarette. Ashley unbuckled the sling and gratefully eased the baby into her arms, dropping the sling to the grass. He tugged his shirt-tail from his belt and flapped the front to let in some air. A photographer was standing in front of him, taking pictures of the dancers. Ashley stepped to one side, and three men slipped between him and Hazel, one brandishing a didgeridoo, another a heavy brass bell. All three were stripped to the waist, their ribs and stomach muscles as sharply pronounced as those of the dog that raced after them. Hazel rocked Maggie from side to side, pulling faces, making noises. Some of the dancers and spectators were chanting, and Ashley made out the words 'Strong is the spirit, great is the strength of the trees . . .' Then the bell clanged too close to Maggie and she started to cry. On the main stage a local pub band was about to start playing. There was a screech of feedback and Maggie's cry became a gulping wail.

'I'd better fetch Jay,' Ashley said finally, but when he looked round he saw first the microphone that was angled above her, then a reporter from the local TV station. The same woman had covered the Inquiry and the making of the banners, and was reputedly related to someone in government, though she claimed to support the campaign, occasionally phoned Jay at home to ask how things were going. As Jay spoke, a football scudded across the stall behind her and the interview was halted whilst two boys and a dog fought to retrieve it. When they resumed filming Ashley said to Hazel, 'Here, I'll take her.' He gathered Maggie to his chest. Her nappy was damp and she continued to whimper as he threaded his way through the onlookers towards Jay. He stood next to Owen a few feet behind the soundman.

Hazel nudged between them. 'Wait up,' she whispered. 'You left the sling.' Then to Owen, 'How's the beetles?'

Owen grinned but didn't reply, and they strained to listen to Jay. 'The idea of the tree adoptions,' she said, 'is not that the trees belong to the people who buy them, but that we belong to the trees. We have a duty towards them, to protect them from the road builders. And I think you'll find a lot of people are prepared to take that duty further. We've already had over a hundred pledges of support for non-violent direct action, and many people are quite prepared to go to jail over this.'

The reporter nodded, and said, 'And are *you* prepared to go to jail over this?'

'Yes,' said Jay distractedly. 'Whatever it takes to prevent this road.'

'So you still believe the road *can* be prevented?'

'Sorry,' said Jay, 'but can we stop there? Look . . .' and she showed the reporter the milk stains darkening her dress at her nipples, indicating Maggie with a smile of apology.

Annoyed or uncomprehending, the reporter frowned in Ashley's direction, and raised a hand as if to ask him to come forward or move further away. Then she sighed and said, 'Fine,' and dropped her arm heavily. 'Okay, thanks, Jay,' she said. 'We should get something out of that.' She turned to talk to her cameraman and Jay slipped the satchel from her shoulders, loosened the buttons of her dress. She sat in one of the chairs behind the trestle and accepted the baby with barely a glance at Ashley. He watched as she guided her nipple into Maggie's mouth, stroking the baby's cheek with a finger.

He said, 'I thought she might need changing first, Jay.'

'Did you.'

'She's quite wet.'

'You shouldn't have fucked off with her then.'

Maggie sucked greedily, her eyes anxiously searching for Jay's as her hand plucked at her breast. A few yards away two jugglers were exchanging skittles in the air. Behind him he heard a man saying, 'If they build through here, they'll be disturbing a lot of ancient energies. I think you'll see a definite magical aspect coming into effect. It'll be dangerous for them, it really will.'

Ashley glanced round and saw the reporter earnestly nodding. He said, 'How long are you planning on staying, Jay?'

'Don't know,' she shrugged. 'Till this evening probably.'

'What about Maggie?'

'What about her?'

'I don't think she should be out in the sun so long.'

'Oh, Ashley,' she said, finally meeting his eye, 'would you please stop *fretting* all the time. For Christ's *sake*!'

Ashley took a deep breath. He stood very still. Near the teepee in the distance two women in long flimsy skirts were slowly describing shapes in the air with their hands, their elbows wide and legs bent at the knees, their heads poised, barely moving. A small troupe of drummers filed past them and into the trees, pursued by a photographer and a couple of dogs, and one of the women flopped to the ground, apparently laughing. Ashley heard the man behind him telling the reporter, 'It's, like, you wouldn't build a road through a cathedral, so why build one through here?'

'And do you think of it *as* a cathedral?' the reporter asked him.

Ashley said, 'That was such a load of shite, Jay, what you told her. All that crap about going to jail.'

Jay lifted her face from the baby, looked at him directly. Her eyes were cold and bright, her mouth taut, and she said very quietly and carefully. 'Why don't you just fuck off home, Ashley?'

I ought to thank you for the hill-tribe titfer you sent so many moons ago, which is a joy to us all, if still a little large for the littlest of us. I should guess the Maggot will take another couple of months to expand into it, but really there's no telling because she is growing by the feed and is already – says our health visitor – above-average in height and weight, though thankfully 'all in proportion'. I'm actually more worried about her intelligence and suspect we may be nurturing a mentally retarded giantess. She ought to be smiling by now, proper 'social smiles', not fart smiles, but no matter how many hours I spend looming over her, grinning gamely, saying, 'Hi-yah, hell-o, hi-yah,' she refuses to remove her eyes from the corner by the bookshelves, just where the potted plants cast a shadow of leaves onto the wallpaper. In fact, I don't think she can see me. Her vision is extremely selective. She likes this corner, and the hideously grotesquely red fireplace, of course, and the folds in the grey bedroom curtains, and she always knows where her mother is, but somehow I just don't figure. Not that I mind, she's only young, and my own vision is equally selective.

More galling by far is the instant attachment she forms to anyone smelling of incense and cannabis, in particular Daffy Daphne, who smells a lot worse than that, and who came to stay for a little while last month, although when I say 'came' and 'stay' I don't mean she actually came into our house very often, or stayed for more than the few seconds it took to evacuate her bowels. She has a morbid fear of catching something horrible from our electrical appliances. In fact, she has a paranoid aversion to electricity of any kind (and water) and prefers to hole up in her Bedford Panoramic, which she appears to run on the energy generated by three dozen guttering candles. Her arrival, of course, was unannounced – 'spontaneous', as she would say – but not something for which I was entirely unprepared. Since the birth of the Maggot I've been diligently meditating, ten minutes every morning, on the virtues of Old Age Hippies; diligently smiling, ten minutes every afternoon, whilst picturing Daffy's face; and diligently chastizing myself, ten minutes every evening, for the canker in my soul, my negativity and cynicism. And I was almost there; I was almost looking forward to seeing her again, but then there she actually was . . . Hippies give me heartburn.

(Hippies and heatwaves. You might like to know – it's finally a number 06 outside, which is to say 'widespread dust in suspension in the air, etc,' and not only has this provoked some extreme electrical disturbance between my frontal lobes, it has also brought about an explosion of street life in Telegraph Lane – a chart hit from every window, a gaggle of drunks in every doorway, a cacophany of children till well after their bedtime. It is doing my nut in – Maggie's likewise – and I think if ever I manage to travel beyond the new northern bypass, it'll have to be on the cold-climate tour – Iceland, Greenland, Alaska, etc – which is a shame because it means I'll never get to confirm the existence of Keli Mutu, which is – ahem – 'one of the truly authentic sightseeing experiences available on this planet'.)

However – Daffy Daphne, mad grannies in general . . . – we had hoped that becoming a grandparent would entice Daffy back down to earth, but instead she seems to have spiralled even further into orbit, her perceptions becoming ever more strangely distorted, such that she now seems to believe that she and Jay have always had a very close and meaningful mother-daughter relationship, and that such relationships are inevitable (and that fathers are entirely irrelevant to the sum of human happiness. Ha!). Which is almost as much garbage as our own mother claiming she's always loved babies, or that she truly enjoyed being a mother to us two, which is what she *actually said when she last visited. Since when she's been regularly on the telephone (every Monday and Thursday, exactly*

*five minutes after cheap rate begins – no spontaneity there) to
share with us the fruits of her experience, inasmuch as she
carps about our sleeping with Maggie ('You'll roll on top of
her'), Jay's feeding her on demand ('She'll never get into a
routine'), our picking her up whenever she cries ('You'll spoil
her'), our preferring a sling to a pram ('What about when she's
older?') and Jay's refusal to contemplate ever having another
one ('An only child is a lonely child'). Soon, no doubt, she will
extend her repertoire of rubbish to include homilies on how to
keep our relationship a happy and lasting one.*

*If only she or Dee knew something about fish. I'm afraid the
last surviving (and most prolific) mother of my fry, suffering a
strange kink in her torso and clearly exhausted from the trauma of
constant childbirth, finally expired last week. I was able to dispose
of her body with dignity, wrapped neatly in one of Jay's handbills
and laid gently to rest in the litter bin. Her spouse, however, had
an altogether less happy end. He developed the familiar flossy
growth on his belly, for which I prescribed thirty minutes' immersion in an anti-fungal solution, from which he emerged strangely
blue-looking. I left him to recover over the solstice weekend, but
when I returned he was no more. Gone. Eaten. Presumably cannibalized by the other males, who will no doubt also now develop
flossy growths, and die, and be eaten . . . My fish monitors, Stacey
and Clare, seem to have lost heart and can no longer be bothered
to feed the sorry specimens that remain. I did warn them, but I
don't think they really appreciated what they were getting into.
Breeding causes many unforeseen stresses and strains, many
strange symptoms.*

JULY

BELOW IN the carpark Clare Morrison was pursuing a sheet of paper as it skittered and rolled over the tarmac. She was laughing, but couldn't catch it, and when finally it flattened to the railings she grabbed it triumphantly and held it flapping over her head. Across the road the leaves of the poplars reversed in the breeze, showing their silvery undersides. Her friends began cheering. As Clare raced back to join them, Ashley lowered his window. He had picked two teams of four and sent them down with trundle-wheels and chalk, clipboards and sheets of squared paper. In the central aisle of the carpark, visible to the rest of the class, they had drawn rectangles as large as double-decker buses. They had estimated the number of car-shapes that would fit inside the buses; and now they were drawing these too, boys competing against girls. It was an exercise suggested in one of Jay's leaflets. He had promised to try it, but the pupils in the classroom were getting restless, bored with looking on. Some boys at the back were dropping threads of spittle on to the roof of a waiting delivery van. He warned them not to lean so far out of their window.

'Right,' he said then, tearing open a fresh ream of paper, 'return to your seats, all of you.' He laid two sheets and a pair of scissors on each of the desks. 'A bus measures eight and a half by two and a half metres. I want you to cut a rectangle of the same dimensions, in *centimetres*. That's your bus, okay? Eight and a half by two and a half. It holds seventy people. Now. A car usually carries two people, so you need thirty-five cars for every bus. The cars measure three and a half by one and a half. Three point five by one point five. Lay the cars next to the bus on your desk. Then . . . hold on.' He picked up Jay's leaflet. 'Then, *imagine the effect on congestion, pollution and accident rates if more journeys were made by bus.* Actually, we'll discuss that later, when the others get back. Everyone happy? All understand what you're doing?'

But they would rather ask their friends than have him explain a second time. He quickly wrote the dimensions on the board, then paused and nodded, and returned to stand by the window. He gazed across at the science block. The circular shadow beneath the cherry tree was pink with rotting blossom, the newly mown bank speckled with daisy heads. Jay's bicycle stood chained to a drainpipe nearby, oddly luminous in the sunlight. For the past week he had used it instead of the bus, wondering whether to buy one of his own. Jay had already bolted a bucket-seat over the rear wheel, for Maggie when she was older, and every morning as he set off he carried the thought of the baby from the house like a breakable, a small precious thing too easily lost in the crush of traffic at junctions, the four-lane rush on the roads. Now motionless against the far wall, the bike appeared out of place, something familiar mislaid. He saw himself approaching the bike in bright sunshine, crouching to unlock the chain, leaving unseen for home in mid-afternoon. It was ten past two. There was a glint of light at the edge of his vision. The doors of the main entrance swung open, and his head of department strode out to the carpark.

'Shit,' he said quietly. The girls nearest turned to see what was happening. 'Concentrate on your work,' he told them. He slipped Jay's leaflet into his drawer and dragged a pile of marking from the edge of his desk to the centre. He found his red pen and sat down.

'She's giving them a row,' said a voice at the back.

'Get on with your work,' said Ashley.

He made a few ticks in a margin, flipped over the page and made a few more. But he could not concentrate. With his head in one hand, he scratched on the desk with his pen until eventually the classroom door opened. The eight children ducked in beneath Mrs Gumley's outstretched arm, hurriedly laid their equipment by the blackboard and returned to their seats. She was wheezing from the stairs. The droop of her chin shook when she spoke. '*Your* pupils I believe, Mr Brook. Doing heaven knows what in the carpark. The *carpark*, Mr Brook, which I think you'll find is out of bounds.' She fixed him with a momentary glare, then looked around for the school regulations, pinned by the door with the fire drill. She prodded the sheet and turned to leave, proclaiming loudly into the corridor, 'Against the rules, Mr Brook!'

The door clicked quietly shut and the class remained silent, expectant, as if she might suddenly return. Ashley brought his hands together as though in prayer, resting his chin on his thumbs. He pressed his nose and lips to his forefingers. A soft wind blew through the open windows, a few flakes of white paper drifted to the floor. At last he took a deep breath, and nodded to the girl nearest the regulations. 'Roshni, what does it say?'

The girl stood and placed a finger where Mrs Gumley had poked at the notice. She read aloud, '*There must be no*

*snowballing in or around the playground or the vicinity of the
school because of the danger of eye injuries to pupils and
pedestrians.'*

There was laughter. Ashley waited, and said, 'Roshni?'

'But that's the one she pointed at! You can look if you like,
Mr B. The one about the carpark is down here.'

'And?'

'The car-parking area is out of bounds to pupils at all times.'

'Ah,' said Ashley. He folded his arms and tilted back in his
seat. 'I see,' he said. Outside the delivery van was leaving,
circling the carpark. He stood and gazed after it, and when it
had gone he stared at the chalked marks on the tarmac. The
boys had ignored his instructions, lining their cars bumper to
bumper next to their bus, whilst the girls appeared to have
cheated, their car-shapes overlapping inside their bus-shape.
He shook his head and smiled. If he described the outcome to
Jay she would blame him for not teaching the exercise properly. But if he pretended it had been a success, she would
expect to be told every detail. He opened his drawer and took
out her leaflet. Underneath it were several postcards and letters from Douglas, and he selected the most recent of these,
an aerogram from Indonesia. At back of the class by the fish
tank a boy was straining to keep his arm upright. Ashley
realized he'd been waiting for some time. 'Sorry, Craig,' he
said. 'What is it?'

'Mr Brook, will you get the sack now?'

Ashley expected laughter but none came, and only a few of
the boys bothered to smile. 'I very much doubt it,' he said,
and passed his litter bin to the nearest desk. 'No, I don't think
so. Collect the bits of paper, would you, Laura?'

'But it's true you're leaving?' Clare Morrison asked him.
'Everyone says you are.'

'They do?'

'You're going to live in a tree,' she said.

'I *am?*' Now there was laughter, a joke shared by his pupils.

In the weeks since the festival, the Common had been regularly in the local newspaper and on the TV. Several of the oaks had been occupied by the protesters, treehouses constructed and squatters' rights declared. The earth-movers were less than a hundred yards away, and a banner had been strung from one of the trees saying 'Action to Save Hogslea,' the initials A S H picked out in green. The acronym was Jay's, and she'd known it would annoy him. He shook his head, and said, 'No, Clare. Actually, I'm going to work half the week only, so I can spend more time with my daughter.'

'Aaah,' said some of the girls. Ashley grinned and tossed a small cardboard box to the next nearest desk. The boy sitting there rose reluctantly to gather the scissors.

'We saw you up the Common with your baby,' Craig told him.

'Did you now?'

'Your girlfriend's a hippy. Your wife, I mean.'

'My *partner*, you mean. Who isn't my girlfriend *or* my wife. And I think that was her sister you saw.'

'Right,' said Craig. 'She was nice-looking, though.'

'I'll tell her.' Ashley looked at his watch. The bell was due shortly. He held up Jay's leaflet in one hand, the aerogram in the other. 'Right, listen, a few minutes to go. Two choices. We can discuss congestion and pollution on the roads, or else I can read one of my brother's letters. Which is it to be? No, don't bother . . .' He opened Douglas's letter and sat upright in his seat. '*Another day, another world-famous volcano,*' he began, but the bell was already ringing. His class erupted for the exit, not waiting to be dismissed, and he dropped the letter to his desk. He locked his hands behind his head and stared at the ceiling, murmuring, 'Thanks,' when his litter bin was replaced, his box of scissors laid beside him. Before his next class arrived he would have to visit the departmental base for some textbooks. The small, cluttered room doubled as Mrs Gumley's office, and she would expect him to explain why his pupils had been left unsupervised; why they were engaged in an exercise not on the syllabus; why he had allowed them to breach school regulations. The only alternative was to improvise his next lesson too, forgoing the textbooks and avoiding the office. He didn't see that it mattered. There was less than a week till the end of the term. It might even be possible to evade her until after the summer break. He rose from his chair and stood again at his window. A cloud passed overhead and he watched the dimming colours in the car-park, Jay's bike retreating into shade. He was still standing when the last of his fourth-years arrived from PE, hurling their sports bags to the back of the room. 'Right,' Ashley said then, clapping his hands but unable to prevent himself yawning, 'have I read you the letter from Indonesia, the one about the volcanoes?'

Dogs, Douglas – the Begley bitches, for instance, or Beaver's mean-minded mutts – they do resemble their owners, it's famously true, but so do cars – for example, the Gumley Motor, my head of department's conveyance, which is small and bulbous, old and probably obsolete, bulging in all the wrong places, its engine as bronchial as her lungs, coughing and spluttering, bellowing exhaust as it goes, leaving a trail of grey every evening from the school gates to the next junction, a foul little cart which hates me every bit as much as she hates me, possibly even more. This evening, impatient with some traffic lights on my way home, and wishing to speed ahead to see my baby, I mounted a kerb on my temporary bicycle and managed to advance fifty yards up the next street before rejoining the road, whereupon the Gumley Motor swerved into the kerb, horn honking, exhaust fuming, and forced me so far off-balance I very nearly copped it from the following bus. I dismounted. Car and Gumley sped into the distance, cursing my lucky escape. My morale is dented, though happily not my cranium or Jay's bicycle. But for how much longer can I continue to work for a woman bent on my assassination? Luckily, the end of term occurs very shortly, which will keep me out of her road for six weeks at least, though I fear instead for the safety of my fishes, as the woman is a workaholic and will no doubt spend her holidays alone in the school, allowing ample opportunity for sabotage.

Not that spiking the tank would really make very much difference. My fry are mostly eaten now, my mollies losing their bloom, the danios all dead, black widows bereaved, neons dimmed, guppies grim, catfish sulking. Happily, however, the anticipated epidemic of floss-like fungal growths did not occur. You will recall I had a single sick fish, which I immersed for thirty minutes in a medicinal solution, and which then disappeared, presumably cannibalized, and thus presumably infecting all the other fishes. I now have grounds to believe that he was not eaten, but simply disintegrated, turned to liquid and evaporated. The thirty minutes' immersion ought to have been thirty seconds. *I suppose it's the equivalent of administering an acid bath for a mild case of athlete's foot. Fearful of fishy retribution, I have since avoided any water not safely contained in a teacup. And in view of the precariousness of life in the tank, I've adopted two dozen papier mâché models from the art department, average length eighteen inches, which I intend to hang next term from the slats in my collapsed ceiling, directly above the aquarium. They look tatty and ridiculous and will draw nothing but abuse, I'm sure, but I like them enormously, not least because they require no maintenance and shall not die on me. Always assuming they're not pulped by Mrs Gumley in the meantime.*

As for my other helpless dependent, the Grub seemed to get wind of my anxieties about her almost as soon as I posted that last letter, and immediately began smiling like a maniac. She's cooled off a little since then – now she only really smiles when she thinks I'm not looking. You might even call it a smirk. But her most usual expression is still rather solemn. There is no question of defective intelligence. Left to her own devices, and *given that she's neither hungry nor soaking, she becomes fierce-somely introspective, clearly wrestling with the great questions of being. Literally wrestling. Never in the history of philosophy or prodigies can there have been a more <u>physical</u> thinker, a more <u>pugilistic</u> philosopher. Arms, legs, fists and every last facial muscle are brought to bear on the issue at hand. Also her sphinc-ter. She shits and farts like nobody's business. And since you're bound to ask, her motions are still rather liquid; they're a sort of Colman's English mustard colour; but they're not smelly, at least not from a normal nappy-changing distance. And yes, the first ones were kind of greeny-black, rather like pondslime, but smellier. Her wee is perfectly clear and tends to bubble up straight after she's been scrubbed and re-creamed. She is mostly very endearing. There should be a photo enclosed of when she became rather rotund, a right tub, but since then she's length-ened somewhat and redistributed the blubber. In fact, she's length-ened a lot, and produced a lot more blubber to redistribute. Her appetite is gargantuan, gluttonous, gannet-like, and we've had to introduce her to solids early – although, properly speaking, solids ought to be in 'quotes' (thus: 'solids') because what we're shovelling into her is still pretty oozy. She doesn't yet have the knack of swallowing anything not squirted directly to the back of her throat, so most of these solids seep out again, if they aren't actually spat out in disgust. What does go down is then expelled explosively from her nether end – and is giving her the start of another nappy rash.*

However, such is her rapid growth she is already sporting her hill-hat, not to mention the rest of her three-to-six-months gear, which is a joy because we're now into some seriously bright garmentry. On the other hand, apart from sometimes grinning like a lunatic, she is also quite capable of bawling like one and occasionally devotes an entire day to it, from morning till well past our bedtime, constant grizzling. These days are very trying, very tiring, and worse because there's usually no explana-tion for them. She's too busy bawling to explain, so all we can do is grit our teeth and take regular turns at hiding in the bed-room. These days occur once, sometimes twice a week, which is just about tolerable. Two in a row is enough to bring an almost grown man almost to tears. And almost has, several times.

The bedroom smelled of soiled nappies and paraffin. Jay was feeding the baby and didn't look up. Ashley smiled, and continued to smile as he navigated the wardrobe, the table and chair and the clothes-horse. He slumped down on the bed and waited a moment. He felt as if he were still moving. He wanted to take off his boots, but when finally he lifted his foot it slipped from the edge of the mattress. He sighed and flopped forwards and tugged at one of his laces, but the knot became tighter. It was funny. He collapsed backwards and snorted. Beside him Jay was sitting with her knees slightly raised, the baby lying on a pillow in her lap. Ashley turned to face her and said, 'Sorry.' The only light came from an oil-lamp on the floor at her side. It cast a webbed shadow on the ceiling and wall, and everything appeared to flicker. 'All right?' he asked.

'Tired,' she said.

'A bit scratchy?'

'Yes.'

He moved a little closer. The baby was drowsy, sucking forgetfully. Ashley narrowed his eyes and focused on the top of her head, the soft steady pulse of her fontanelle. He tentatively touched her, his fingers still stiff from gripping the bicycle's handles. Outside in the street there were people sitting on doorsteps, standing in groups at the entries to the flats. He had passed some boys playing football in the centre of the road. Music was blaring from open windows. It was midnight and still very warm.

Jay looked at him and said, 'What are you grinning for, Ashley?'

He kissed the baby and hauled himself upright and immediately the room started to spin. He flared his eyes and took a long breath. His breath became a yawn. He hung out an arm and wagged his hand at the window until finally he could say, 'I saw these two women up the street there. They were serenading some guys in one of the flats – it looked like they'd been to a wedding or something, and they were absolutely *huge* women, enormous. The oldest was about fifty and she kept lifting her blouse to show off her bra. She had this massive black brassiere, and this huge wobbly belly. She thought it was hilarious . . .' Jay watched his mouth as he spoke, but didn't appear to be hearing him. She gave no response. His throat tickled, and when he coughed he tasted the cigarette he had smoked a couple of hours earlier. He swallowed sourly. He had been drinking since four o'clock, first in the school staffroom, then at the sports club where the teachers had gone to play bowls. It was the last day of term. He didn't know why he had stayed out for so long. 'That's all,' he said, shrugging.

Jay slid her little finger into the side of Maggie's mouth and eased her off the nipple. There was a tiny mattress in the middle of their bed, their pillows parted to accommodate it. As she laid the baby to sleep, Ashley gently supported the soft weight of Jay's breast in his hand. Her nipple was dark and gluey. He tried to kiss the side of her face, but she pulled away and tucked herself into the cup of her bra. 'Don't paw me, Ashley,' she snapped. 'I've had her at me all day. I don't need it.'

'Sorry,' he said. Jay flipped back her fringe and looked at him coolly. He offered a smile. 'Rough day?' he said.

'Yes,' she said, and set about rearranging her pillows. Ashley placed his feet on the floor, his elbows at rest on his knees. As he prepared to stand up, Jay said, 'There's a nappy for you take down.'

He nodded. 'In a minute.'

'And you're not sleeping with us, not like that.'

'No,' he said. He crossed to the open window and knelt on

the floorboards, inhaled several times deeply. With his chin on the window-ledge he said, 'I don't know why I bother, Jay. It's always the same – I talked at cross purposes with every-one. No one got my jokes, and I didn't get theirs, and every time I got up, whoever I was talking to went and sat some-where else, they fucked off.' He grinned and looked round, 'I'm a fish out of water, Jay – one of the English teachers told me.'

Jay was lying on her side facing Maggie. She touched the baby's neck with the back of her fingers, arranged the sheets away from her face. 'You drink like one too,' she said.

Ashley quietly belched. He carefully stood, and pressed his forehead to the cool of the glass. 'Thanks,' he murmured. 'Actually, I ended up in a corner by the fruit machines with the school librarian and he told me *all* about his new auto-mated catalogue, and *all* about his new automated issuing system, and *all* about his new PC at home – he's the world's most boring bastard, Jay, totally obsessed with gadgets and computers and his fucking tedious *systems*.'

Across the street some women were sitting on stools and deckchairs, cans of lager and lemonade by their feet. Ashley knew which flats they lived in, recognized their voices, their children. Music drifted from an open doorway behind them. An adolescent boy was dancing with his mother on the pave-ment. She held a can in one hand, a cigarette in the other, and as they drew closer, miming the words of the song, the boy suddenly pushed his tongue in his mother's mouth. She forced him away and spat at the road. 'I'll fucking get you for that!' she shouted. 'You fucking slimeball!' The boy began cackling. The other women were laughing.

Ashley turned from the window, and said, 'I suppose my mum phoned, Jay?' But Jay's eyes were closed. She appeared to be sleeping. He neared the bed and stood over her. 'Jay?'

'Mn.'

'Did she?'

'Tomorrow,' she said.

There was a long silence between them, more laughter outside. Ashley knelt on the bed and looked closely at Maggie, the milk blister on her top lip, her mouth still shaped for the nipple. 'Jay?' he whispered.

'Ashley, you know she phoned, she always phones. She twittered on for nearly an hour – I couldn't get her off. She thinks I'm wonderful.'

'Sorry?'

Jay sighed and rolled on to her back. She opened one eye, then the other. 'She said I was great because I was breastfeeding Maggie – she's been hungry all day, she was feeding when the phone went. Your mum said the reason *she* didn't breastfeed was because your dad wouldn't let her, because it wasn't the done thing and he was embarrassed, or jealous, or *something*. She just wanted to gripe about your dad, that's all.'

'Any more about leaving him?'

'No, she started raving on about trees. She thinks it's wonderful what I'm doing to save the trees. Basically, she just thinks I'm wonderful, full stop. Suddenly everything about me is wonderful.'

'What's she on about? She doesn't give a shit about trees. Or you.'

'Sssh,' Jay whispered. Then, 'She's got a bee in her bonnet about a tree in your back garden, Ashley. About your dad cutting it back. She got herself totally irate just talking about it.'

'But that's *her*, Jay. He cuts it back every year because *she* tells him to.'

'Whatever.' Jay yawned. '*That*'s what she talked about, for almost an hour, and now I am really tired.' She rolled away from him, reached down to extinguish the lamp.

Ashley sat on his pillows. He felt he was sinking, falling backwards, and as he began to accelerate he touched the wall with one hand, the bed with the other, and steadied himself.

Outside in the street the boy and his mother were shouting at each other. Ashley felt for Maggie's hand in the dark. He pictured his parents' tiny back garden. Its solitary feature was the beech in one corner, heavily truncated, like an arthritic fist raised to the sky. There was nothing else: the enclosing fence, the washing line, a neat rectangle of grass. He whispered hotly to Jay, 'It's because she didn't want any leaves on her lawn, Jay, that's why he had to cut it back. She wouldn't even let us have a birdtable in case it got covered in birdshit.' Once she had even objected to the noise the birds made; she'd flung open the kitchen window to scare them, later played the radio at full volume, then sat sobbing on the settee. It was the summer holidays. Ashley had offered to fetch the shopping from the arcade, and when his mother didn't respond he'd left anyway, taking Douglas with him. They'd bought the usual things, everything they could remember, and then they'd called at an aunt's house. He and Douglas had eaten that day with their cousins and walked home when their father came to collect them. 'She didn't want *any*thing in her garden, Jay, nothing. We were never allowed out there. If we wanted to play in the field at the back, we had to go out the front door and all round the houses.' Jay was silent. Ashley expelled a heavy breath, leaning backwards. His head bumped on the wall. He swallowed to stop himself belching, tasted vomit, the bile in his throat. His forehead was damp and cold. If he moved, he would be sick. The dark shapes around him drifted and blurred, he felt himself drifting with them. In his head he heard voices, the clamour of the sports club, his mother urgently whispering. He tried to stand but found himself sitting again. He dived forwards and supported himself with a hand on the wardrobe. Outside the music had ceased. There was a hiss in his ears. Ashley aimed himself at the door and kicked the nappy as he neared it. 'Sorry,' he blurted.

'Night,' said Jay.

AUGUST

O *H BOY, the phone rings, I dive downstairs to catch it, but*
it's for Jay, the phone is always for Jay, only Jay is out, she's
on another circuit of the back-to-backs, she's trying to calm the
baby, walking her round and round, so I say ring again in twenty
minutes, and grab another can from the fridge ('seriously smooth')
and bomb back up the stairs and sit again at my tupewroter and
crack open the can and watch as 250 ml of beer spumes all over
the curtains . . . my head hurts, seriously smooth this isn't, sober me
neither, it's the fourth can of the afternoon and I'm already well
into tomorrow's hangover, but I've been on baby-duty all morning
and this is the holidays, my holidays, so why should I not get
slaughtered if I want to, if I need to?

Because I have grown-up responsibilities.

There is no stress, I've decided, like the stress of trying to
mollify a bawling bairn. Even as I wrote my last letter Jay was
developing a kidney infection which depressed her milk produc-
tion and spirits just as the Grub was entering her Three Month
Growth Spurt and demanding seconds and thirds at every feed

— she decided she wouldn't accept anything but the breast and embarked on a ten-day tantrum that was just about the worst experience of our life pre- or post-parenthood. As Jay's kidneys revived, so did her milkflow, and the baby began to calm down, but she remains very difficult to please, and especially difficult to feed. She has now embarked on another marathon moan, another five-day fret, which is by far the least endearing of her many accomplishments, and which appears to be entirely unrelated to the motions of her bowels, or the state of her appetite, or the hours she's slept, or the amount of stimulation she's enjoyed, or the average room temperature, or anything at all. She doesn't cry but emits a constant, unrelenting stream of half-moans. The pitch doesn't vary and the rhythm is constant — it is a sound 'wholly or predominantly characterized by the emission of a succession of repetitive beats', causing 'serious distress to the inhabitants of the locality', and is thus outlawed under Clause 58 of the very sensible Criminal Justice and Public Order Act. Not that she cares. Eah. Eah. Eah. Eah. Eah. Eah. It's a difficult noise to spell, and a very difficult noise to live with. No matter where you are, cloaked in no matter how much other noise, it penetrates right to the bone. Every task is twice as hard to accomplish and twice as exhausting. Threads are lost. Tempers frayed. And it's worse because when she's this unhappy her only consolation is the breast, which she wants every ten minutes, literally, liberally, day or night, which is irritating for Dad but soul-destroying for Mum. Things become very tense, very dark. It's like I said when we were expecting — we invented our perfect child, but the closer we came to the actual day the more misgivings we began to have and slowly the perfect child spawned its own demonic alter ego. Both are true, except that the angel child sometimes still refuses bottled milk and the demon child is still eminently kissable. I didn't know I had so many kisses in me, I'm a kissing machine, they just keep popping out. Pop pop pop . . . In fact, in case you suppose there's little more to fatherhood than tears and tantrums, here are Five Fantabulous Facts about Maggie.

1. She is now able to roll from her back to her belly, a notable gymnastic advance, but only ever rolls onto her left side, which is where she usually finds Jay when she wants a night-feed. She never rolls onto her right side, ever. One day in the far future, not long after she has left home, some hairy oaf will pass her a joint and say, 'What's your favourite side for sleeping on then, Mags? Got one?' 'Oh, I dunno,' she'll reply, 'my left side, I suppose.' 'Me too!' the hirsute one will exclaim. 'I wonder why that is.' 'No idea,' the Grub will yawn, 'but I'll bet my dad the ex-teacher has a theory about it.'

2. Her favourite TV programme is the ITV Chart Show and she is quite the Baby Groover, she has even invented her own dance craze, known as The Twitch. As I can never remember the lyrics to any pop songs, or even the words to any nursery rhymes, the tune I most often sing to her is the Pearl & Dean theme music that heralds the ads at the cinema. This is accompanied by the most technicolour smile in my repertoire, eyebrows almost shooting off the top of my head, and the Grub loves it. No doubt when she's older she'll develop an insatiable craving for hotdogs, ice-creams, popcorn, Gordon's gin, Martini, Kia-Ora, Coca-Cola, Hamlet cigars, and Sunkist orange pop – highly puzzling to her, but eminently explicable to her father the ex-teacher.

3. Her little bod is a marvel to behold. Her ankles and wrists are no more than creases in her skin, but despite the amplitude of flesh she is remarkably compact. There's a dimple on the knuckle of each finger, and the tiniest of dimples to the left of her nose which only appears when she grins. Jay's favourite view is the back of her neck, which is surprisingly slim and perfectly formed. I'm more fond of her paunch.

4. She is incredibly sweet-smelling; even her breath smells sweet – it's probably the sweetest thing you ever smelled – somewhere between a raspberry-ripple ice-cream and a Milky Bar, but it doesn't do to spend too long trying to decide which, she doesn't yet know the difference between a nipple and a nose. Sucks either. She is at her very most fragrant first thing in the morning, not merely sweet-scented but sweet-tempered. Her cheeks are rosy, she smiles at everything, the merest word produces a squeal of delight. Then she does her nut for a feed.

5. *What does Maggie dream of? She dreams of breasts (or noses). Her* REM *is really* RLM − *Rapid Lip Movement. Sook, sook, sook, she goes.*

Sook, sook, sook . . . You can't tell from where you are, of course, but between the first and last of these sooks exactly three days have elapsed, seventy-two more hours of RLM *and complaining, and now the Grub is once again at her fragrant loveliest. Today, in fact, is the notable 8th of August, a sunny, squally sort of a day on which your latest postcard has arrived and during which Maggie has made her national television debut. Of course, the admirable nape of her neck did fleetingly appear on the local* TV *news a couple of months ago, but she was feeding at the time and only the most dedicated of fans (a dewy-eyed dad, for example) would have recognized her. This afternoon, however − on the notable 8th of August − the world-renowned and respected* BBC Lunchtime News With Andrew Harvey *broadcast exclusive semi-live footage of the Maggot as charming New Age cherub bravely (blithely) defending the venerable Old Age oaks of Hogslea Common from the bullies and bulldozers of the Rabid Roads & Construction Co. The cameraman was evidently much taken with her, and why not, has she not fragrance? And now, even as I type, the child-star's mother is busily coaching her for the next big break − a promised exclusive in the local advertising freesheet − and if all goes well we may soon be able to sell her on to an agency as an established media package.*

The road, incidentally, has been delayed by a colony of beetles and a cacophony of barristers. The beetles − Selatosomas cruciatus (linnaeus) − are somewhat rare, a 'relic population' no less, and haven't been seen in the British Isles since these ancient oaks were merely middle-aged. In the entomologically small world of bugs and grubs this is a momentous discovery, sufficient even to trouble the conscience of Her Majesty's Minister for Roads and Ructions. The fact that the Minister's conscience remained untroubled for months and months until beetle-mania suddenly broke out in the national media is neither here nor there. The earth-movers have been halted whilst a plan is devised for transplanting the bugs from the irretrievably doomed oaks to others not in the immediate path of the road. This is, by all accounts except the Minister's, a risky if not totally risible scheme. One option is to fell the currently occupied oaks and dump the trunks at the feet of some more distant trees, from where it is hoped Selatosomas cruciatus will complete the rest of the journey himself. The new trees will require to be not only oaks, however, but 'oaks of identical age and microclimate'. A second option is to coax a few biddable adults from their cracks and knotholes in the doomed oaks and introduce them to the cracks and knotholes of the favoured oaks and hope they don't die of homesickness, or indeed air pollution, before they can multiply. A third option, and the best hope it seems, is to discover an existing colony in one of the more far-flung trees, and simply add a few healthy incomers to swell the numbers. Teams of crack government scientists are already on the case, magnifying glasses in hand, but they are rapidly running out of accessible trees to explore – too many of the oaks have already been colonized by humans . . .

Hence the barristers, who are busily debating in the High Court whether a judge was correct to conclude that the trees are now legal dwellings because the occupants have received letters (of support or abuse, I don't know) through the Royal Mail. Not that this will count for much in the long run either way. If the sheriff's officer and his bailiffs and their army of privatized strong-arms do not evict the tree-dwellers as squatters in the short term, the trees will be compulsorily purchased – or somesuch, I don't know – in the long term, with the same outcome. Hence the presence of national television, for which this is all wonderfully odd and amusing, a perfect heartwarming nonsense *of no real consequence or seriousness with which to end other-wise routinely gloom-laden newscasts. No doubt it will limp up the order of newsworthiness once the first bones are broken, but in the meantime Jay is becoming pretty worn out by it all (not that she'll admit it) because she has been doing far too much of the donkey-work (not that she'll admit that either) and now seems to believe she would benefit from a week or two in a tree-house, which is one good reason at least for the Grub to keep guzzling because the longer it takes to wean the baby off the breast, the less chance there is that Jay will abandon us for a life of arboreal anti-establishmentarianism.*

Big word!

Speaking of which and whom (weaning and Maggie, I mean), there has been some progress towards bottle-feeding. I don't know if I've mentioned before, but . . .

Fantabulous Fact Number 6

. . . the Grub has abandoned her philosophical conjectures and has accepted the existence of the wider world, which is to say her toys, my nose, trailing ivy, empty beer cans and sharp imple-ments, all of which she explores with her mouth. Thus she can now be conned into mistaking the whole bottle-feeding business for a sophisticated form of oral stimulation entirely unrelated to sustenance. And I've found she swallows more milk the more complex the diversion. For instance, if I simply sit and pour she gets bored, gets fractious, has a fit of fury, soils her nappy, attempts to gouge out my eyes with her talons, but if I walk around the house in complicated circles, singing, 'Oops, there goes another one!' and pulling funny faces, hopping, skipping, jumping and pirouetting, then she is more inclined to comply. I've also developed a technique for holding both bottle and baby, and singing and grinning, walking and jigging, whilst simultane-ously squeezing the base of the teat between my second and third fingers − that is, since the Grub won't suck, I squirt. And she doesn't mind − why should she? − it's summertime, the living is easy, and no matter how much effort I put in, 'success'

is still measured in millilitres, and Jay still has to make up the difference.

The Grub is in many respects quite like her father. Having given up entirely on thinking, she now grins gormlessly at just about anything, gawps at the television for hours on end, lounges uselessly about, drinks and farts and complains, but above all . . .

(Fab Fact 7)

. . . is adding pounds to her midriff and thighs almost as fast as she is shedding her hair. It was my intention to remove some of these discarded hairs from the carry-cot sheet on which she sleeps, using a length of forensic sellotape, and to insert that piece of sellotape here:

But Jay washed the sheet. The hair loss is actually quite alarming (although apparently quite normal) and looks very like that disease I can't spell but which is pronounced 'alla-peesha' – all tufts and baldy bits. It's not especially fetching, and the effect is worsened by her constant drooling, because . . .

(Fab Fact 8)

. . . she produces an unbelievable amount of slobber – on account of her teething, I understand. It's a messy, wet business and every cuddle results in a shirt-change. I imagine the effect is much the same as taking a midday stroll through steaming Bangkok, or a sweaty afternoon's hike in the Australian outback. Though, of course, I know nothing – absolutely nothing – about the Australian outback. Certainly nothing from your postcard, Douglas. You ought to appreciate that we do get worried – in an admittedly vague and distracted kind of way – by your

long silences, wondering if you've finally fallen off the edge of the world, but it seems this time you made it through to Chuck's Diner in San Francisco, and thanks very much for the card, which is picturesque, but is that all you have to say about your five weeks on the continent of Australasia, that it was there? What is the purpose of your journey if not to keep us informed of the sights, tastes, sounds and smells of everywhere, as I keep you informed of the sights, tastes, sounds and smells of parenthood? And besides, I need you to confirm that there still is a world beyond my baby and me.

Because I do sometimes wonder.

Well, of course there is a world beyond my baby and me. In fact, since I hit the dot on the previous line – four days ago – the big wide world has been shouting through our letterbox, hammering on our front door, skulking in our back yard. You couldn't tell, of course, being so far away, but even as I paused to consider the philosophic possibility of a world-out-there I was overcome by a pressing need to swallow lots of beer. Which was a problem because I'd resolved never to use our local off-licence again, or at least not for a couple of weeks, as my face was becoming far too well known in there: they begin stacking my cans on the counter even before I appear; they ask after my health, my wife, my beautiful daughter; they call me son, dear, lovey, even Ashley. Besides which, there's a bellicose tribe of floppy-haired hoodlums camped permanently outside the shop, demanding money with menaces (26p, curiously; they always want 26p, the price of an evening paper).

So, to save my blushes, and my 26p, I slipped out the back way and went half a mile in the opposite direction to the CENTRA STORES FOODMARKET *(TIGHTS* 39p! *CHAPPIE DOG FOOD* 31p!) *where they sell alcohol from a hole in the wall at the rear of the shop, from behind a wire grille, protected by a bank of surveillance cameras and machine-gun emplacements. It was Saturday evening, just before dark, and it was* uncomfortably, stickily warm, but I got my beers, and some chocolate for Jay, and all was mellow with the world, I may even have whistled as I ambled along, I may even have hummed the Pearl & Dean theme tune, but as I turned happily into the alley behind our terrace I saw *The Silhouette Of A Man* slipping into our yard, which of course I'd left unbolted in my haste to get to my beers, and what's worse, I knew him, he was one of the floppy-haired hoodlums from the off-licence, and I didn't have 26p. Actually, he's always around and seems to live permanently outdoors, always seems to be talking to policemen, or waving at police cars, or ducking out of their way, and one night last February I saw him getting beaten senseless by a gang of similarly scrawny delinquents. I should've turned round and come in by the front door and called 999, but instead I crept up on him in the near-dark, armed with a four-pack of beer and a giant-sized bar of Bournville.

He heard me, he was waiting. 'Sorry, mate,' he said, with a matey hand on my arm. 'I just came in to get away from this guy.' I edged past him, and he said, 'Is there anyone out there? Did you see anyone?' 'No one,' I said. 'Right, mate,' he said. I held the gate open. He said, 'So what's the time now then, mate?' 'Nine-ish,' I said. 'Right, mate,' he said. This went on for several minutes until finally he backed into the alley, but even then he didn't leave, and didn't look round for whoever he was supposed to be hiding from, he just stood and waited for me to close the gate on him, all the while smirking. I could see why someone would want to beat him senseless, or bundle him into a police car – his face is set in a permanent smirk and it is very provoking. And quite unnerving. I spent the next half an hour upstairs in the dark, peeking from behind the curtains, a ridiculous and shaming carry-on because he is six inches shorter than me, not much older than Jay's sister, and weighs slightly less than a shadow at dusk. And of course he was long gone.

However, he returned the next evening, hammering on our

*front door at bedtime. I squinted through our spy-hole and saw
him squinting back at me, still smirking, and I actually ducked,
I got down on my cowardly haunches and tried to hide from
him. 'Are you going to open up, mate?' he shouted. 'I want to
talk to you a minute.' His speech was slurred. I stayed crouching, not sure what to do. He began talking through the letterbox.
'Are you coming out or what, mate? Open the door, I want to
talk to you a minute.' I said, 'What do you want?' He said,
'Open the door a minute, I just want a word.' I felt stupid, so I
opened the door, about four inches. 'What do you want?' I said.
'Listen, mate,' he smirked, 'how long you lived round here
now?' 'What do you want?' I said. He stood on our doorstep,
swayed backwards, came up again and spoke into my face. 'I
want to know what you're dealing in,' he said. 'Nothing,' I
said, 'I'm not dealing in anything.' 'Listen, mate,' he said, 'can
you lend us a fag?' 'I don't smoke,' I said. 'Are you being
cheeky?' he said. 'No, I'm not being cheeky,' I said. He offered
his hand. I hesitated, then shook it. He moved in closer. 'Going
to give us the lend of two quid till tomorrow?' he said. 'I
haven't got two quid,' I said. 'How long have you lived here
now?' he said. 'On your way,' I said. 'On my way?' he said.
'It's late,' I said. 'Do you think I'm a junkie?' he said, 'because
I'm not a junkie, no way.' 'I wouldn't know,' I said. 'Can you
lend us a fag?' he said. 'I don't smoke,' I said. 'You're being
cheeky,' he said, 'aren't you? You're being cheeky to me.' 'I'm
not being cheeky,' I said. 'Do you live here alone?' he said. 'No,
I don't live alone,' I said. 'Nearly three years,' he said then,
'that's how long you've lived here.' 'Really?' I said. 'Your
woman rides a bike,' he said, 'here, shake my hand. Come on,
shake.' I took his hand and he gripped mine tightly and whispered, 'She rides a bike and she's called Jay and you're called
Ashley and your kid's called Maggie . . .' At which point I managed to free myself and shut the door and retreat up the stairs
to lie quaking on the bed beside Jay.*

She was awake and also quaking. So we lay and listened to

him chattering through our letterbox, though we couldn't make out a word, and even after he'd given up and slunk off we remained all of a tremor, because in his absence every incomprehensible word was a crystal-clear threat to our personal safety. The front door suddenly seemed far too thin, the big wide world pressing against it too firmly. Nothing was quite so solidly ours any more – the floorboards, the nice new wallpaper, the typewriter – we didn't belong where we were and the people in the street suddenly seemed that much poorer and paler, uglier and sicklier, every one of them slyly determined to burgle or rob us or kidnap our child. We both slept very badly and all the next day our minds were elsewhere, we kept dropping things, bumping into the furniture, losing our place. Every sound was someone breaking into our house and I spent half the day scurrying from window to spy-hole to window and back again. Since when he hasn't been seen, although he continues to stalk my dreams, whispering threats, demanding 26p, revealing my deepest dark secrets and fears. But did I always used to be this jumpy, this easily unnerved, this scared? Did I only become so easily jittered when Maggie was born? Am I suddenly so vulnerable because she is? Am I frightened on her behalf because she is too mindless to be frightened? Ought I not to have acquired some fierce protectiveness by now? Should I not be more of an adult than I was, less of the cowering child? Would you rather I told you about the weather?

I believe I've neglected to give the Met Office a mention in recent correspondence, and doubtless you're as anxious to know the state of the skies in England as I am anxious to know the names of the beauty spots in Queensland. Well, it is currently a number 91, which is to say, 'slight rain at time of observation', and bully for that. The sun disappeared behind a blanket of cloud almost as soon as the school holidays began, but the temperature has remained uncomfortably high. The heat is clammy and constant and I feel as if I'm crawling with insects, little beetles, a small colony of Selatosomas cruciatus. We are in want of a downpour,

a thoroughgoing 63, 'rain, continuous, heavy', and not this pass-
ing drizzle. But, since the drizzle is there and all that we have, I
shall pull on my galoshes and kagoul and get out and make the
most of it. I need some more beers, and the waterproofs will serve
as my disguise. Although, before I leave you, perhaps I should
mention – also at time of observation – some crop-haired hooligan
is standing on the bonnet of a windowless car across the road and
pissing all over the front seats. This is the first vehicle to be trashed
this summer although there were six or seven of them last year.
You'd think they'd find something better to do with themselves,
wouldn't you? Didn't we use to go around collecting car registra-
tion numbers and jotting them down in homemade notepads? And
wasn't there widespread dust in suspension in the air as we did
so? Perhaps you were too young to remember. You were always too
young, as far as I can remember, never old enough for anything.
However, Unfortunate Effect of Fatherhood No. 17: all the world's
children are mine, even this crop-haired hooligan is somebody's
son, he could be my son, he ought to know not to piss on wrecked
cars, somebody ought to tell him . . . I shall go and fetch Jay.

SEPTEMBER

ASHLEY PUT down the telephone and rubbed his ear. The floor was strewn with leaflets and toys, the remains of their dinner and tea. There were snapshots of friends on the Common, bits of underwear and magazines. It was the usual mess, and Jay lay in its midst with her chin in her hands, pulling faces at Maggie. Ashley said, 'That was my mum.'

'I gathered,' said Jay.

'She wanted me to explain what the hippies are up to.'

'I heard.'

'So how did I do?'

'Sounded like you knew your stuff, very impressive.'

'I've been doing my homework,' he said. He picked up a leaflet and stretched himself out on the sofa. 'Listen to this one. I'm going to send it to her. *In the groves and glades of the coppice, in the dingles and ditches, gullies and ponds, you will discover an endlessly various and unpredictable tangle of trees, shrubs and wild flowers. Here are bluebells and oxlips, primroses, violets, and drifts of sweet woodruff; here are dormice, shrews, badgers and bats; here are chiffchaffs, woodpeckers, tits, pipits and nightingales.*' He rolled on to his side. 'Sounds nice, doesn't it?'

'Very.'

'Trouble is,' he said, 'I could recite that blindfold, but if I ever saw an actual chiffchaff or pipit, I wouldn't know what it was. Badgers and bluebells is about my limit.'

'Same here,' said Jay. 'So what?'

'I feel deprived. I've only ever seen the countryside from car windows. I was thinking, when we were kids we used to drive past this bit of wood just outside Ravensby. There was a sign on one of the trees which said *Private. No trespassing* and I thought that meant the whole of the countryside. I thought that's why we never went there.'

'Sad,' she said.

'And now I'm the world's greatest expert on Hogslea Common.'

'Hardly.'

'So how big is it?'

Jay spread her arms wide. 'This big,' she said.

'It's 125 acres,' he told her. 'The coppice is ninety-four acres and the wood-pasture is thirty-one.'

'Very good.' Jay yawned. She reached across the floor and drew a leaflet towards her. 'So tell me about the coppice.'

'The coppice is a relic of the primeval forest that followed the Ice Age. It contains most of the native trees of England, and coppicing means the harvesting of poles from the stumps of trees like hazel, hornbeam and lime. Are you listening? The stumps are called stools, and some of the stools are eighteen feet wide. They're nearly 800 years old . . .'

The baby squealed, her arms and legs flailing, and Jay tickled her nose with a bunny. 'And?' she said.

'And it's survived this long because the Church and the medieval gentry couldn't agree who owned which bits. They squabbled about it but they never cut it down – or not all of it. Then when they tried to enclose it the commoners revolted. *Then* in the last century someone found iron ore near where my school now is, and for a while they coppiced the trees to make charcoal – to fuel the foundry. They needed the trees more than they needed new fields for farming. Then eventually the Corporation bought it on behalf of the people. So it belongs to us now, it's a public amenity.'

'And the pasture?'

'That includes the pasture.'

'No,' she said. 'What's there?'

'Pollards and grass,' he said. 'The grass used to be grazed by the peasantry, or their animals at least, and the branches of the trees were used for firewood. Commoners' rights. Now it's a picnic site and the pollards are populated by rare beetles and social undesirables, and soon it'll all be a road. The road will plough through the pasture, and then it'll plough through the coppice, and then you'll have to find something else to print leaflets about.'

Jay sat up. She lifted Maggie on to her lap and began to undress her.

'Ask me another,' Ashley said.

'What did your mum say?'

'My mum said she'd seen the social undesirables on the box and she didn't think they were serious-minded and she was sure they weren't local. They're doing themselves no favours.' He made a face at the baby. 'By the way, the pollards are oak, pedunculates not sessiles, and they're about 500 years old.'

Jay looked at him. 'So why didn't you tell your mum I was going to join them? I'm local, and I'm serious-minded.'

'Because you're not going to join them, Jay. You're not going to live in a hammock.'

'Oh,' she said into Maggie's ear. 'Daddy's putting his foot down.'

'Daddy's going to tidy up this mess,' he said.

'No,' she replied, 'Daddy's going to bathe baby. It's Daddy's turn. *Then* he can tidy up the mess.'

A curious thing about Jay, but the less energy she's supposed to have, the more she seems to find (or perhaps this is all relative, a question of perspective, because I very rarely seem to be anything but knackered). The ladies in the office at school ask after her often, and express their admiration, but clearly disapprove. A Good Mother, as we know, stays at home and does the ironing and eats chocolate and bawls at baby and washes nappies and gets depressed and puts on make-up for Daddy and eventually joins a coffee-morning circle with lots of other Good Mothers and one day goes back to work as a school secretary and regrets the waste of her life. But Jay is not a Good Mother. Apart from being a smelly hippy roads protester, she has also made arrangements to return to her work (I mean her proper job, the Community Arts Project) a month early (Fridays only to begin with), a move made feasible by Maggie's sudden and inexplicable craving for formula babymilk (although only if administered by Daddy). The Grub can now suck a rubber teat and swallow six ounces of WySoy at one sitting with a minimum of assistance or distraction. Unfortunately, the more she consumes, the more her appetite seems to increase rather than diminish, the more energy she has to burn, and the less inclined she is to sleep during the day or through the night, during which she wakes regularly and frequently, not only to slurp at Jay's melons but also, horrors, to play. Baby time is not like regular time, her cycles are very much shorter and have begun to dictate ours. She feeds, she sleeps, she cries, she plays, she shits (although in truth she hasn't produced a jobby for almost a week; she's busy gestating her first grown-up stool, which I hope to capture on camera for you), but never to any particular pattern. The days are full of incident, and they are very unrelaxing. Not that I ever complain. Not publicly anyway. The other thing the ladies in the office admire-but-not-really is my job-sharing, which seems to evoke for them pitiful images of the Lonely Father sitting at home watching game shows, aimlessly wandering the park with his pram, bashfully accepting a seat on the bus as the real men pile on in their overalls, forever ignored by the Good Mothers, never invited to coffee mornings . . .

All of which is true enough, though still marginally preferable to work. The first day back was a Wednesday, my half-day, an in-service, non-teaching day, and happily the end of my week. I strolled in at nine thirty, lounged around, left three hours later, spoke to practically no one in the meantime, but still came home as tense and tired as on any other working day. So it isn't the day-long human interaction that exhausts me. It's my own company. It's being there. It's not being elsewhere. I'm a soul in turmoil, evidently, and this can be rather enervating. Do you ever have those dreams where you're trying to smash someone's skull through a wall but no matter how hard you strain, you can't do it because your limbs are like bread dough? All you want is the satisfaction of cracking some bone and seeing some splatter, and all you get is madder and madder and weaker and weaker . . . My work is actually nothing like as bad as this, and I don't know why I pretend to despise it so much . . . Soul in turmoil, you see? But what to do? Stick it out, I suppose: what other employment would provide half so much grist to my mill, give me quite so many excuses to feel undervalued and unappreciated? (Or offer quite such long holidays (relatively speaking, Douglas, relatively speaking).) And then there's the horror of applying for new jobs, shaking strange hands, suffering fresh awkwardnesses . . . Crumbs. (Apparently they've lined up six candidates for the vacant half of me, but aren't prepared to tell me anything about them, and don't seem to know when the interviews will take place.) So I'm actively scanning the vacancies columns, even going so far as to red-pen the likeliest openings, but then quite comfortably talking myself out of asking for further particulars. Turmoil, utter turmoil.

Added to which, the continuing carnage in my aquarium . . .

Clare, the Principal Feeder, returned from her summer break a year older and a year more sensitive to the agonies of other creatures and found the sight of such death and putrefaction quite traumatic. She announced in class the next day that she'd had a nightmare in which Mr B. appeared as a puffa-fish floating around the school corridors, growing 'huger and huger', turning 'all red and purple', until suddenly I – he – burst apart like a balloon and splurged 'this gooey white fishstuff' all over the desks and windows. She was obviously baffled by this. Her friends, unfortunately, weren't. However, we have now arrived at a very adult agreement not to have any more fish (in fact, she and Stacey have already flushed the survivors down the girls' toilet) but we will still maintain the tank for the sake of its aqueous glow, the bubbling aerator, the gentle hum of the motor. To this end, Clare and Stacey and Clare's mum, Mrs Morrison, took me in the Morrison motor to the High Glades Garden Centre and Tropical Fish Franchise last Monday lunchtime, where we bought bogwood, fresh gravel, several submarine plants (live ones), several life-like Plantastics (fake ones), a ceramic castle, a sunken galleon, some plastic seashells, and an algae-magnet on a stick to keep the glass clean. And, since we were there, I also satisfied all my indoor gardening requirements because I'm afraid my pot-plants are dry and top-heavy and dropping like dry, top-heavy pot-plants from window ledges in every direction, except for the ones which have rotted. We passed a very pleasant last-Tuesday-lunchtime overhauling the aquarium, which now looks a picture, good enough to swim in, and I intend to pass a very pleasant next-Monday-lunchtime re-potting and re-propping my copious greenery. I may even introduce a Selatosomas cruciatus or two because, I'm sorry to report, the famous Hogslea beetles are temporarily homeless. You may not be aware, but the whole of the Common is now owned by the County Council, and within the County Council there has been much conflict between Commercial Planning (who want to napalm the lot and build megastores) and the Conservation

*Unit (who want to napalm Commercial Planning and lay
nature trails). But it seems they've concocted a compromise between themselves to create a mini nature reserve to the north of
the bypass (or 'development corridor', as it's now known). And
this, realistically speaking, is the beetles' only hope of survival.
Of course, there's an equal amount of in-fighting amongst the
protesters and campaigners, but yesterday the brave defenders of
the beetle-trees finally agreed to step down and allow the woody
hulks to be felled and transported to the reservation. It's a gesture. The bugs will still probably die, and the brave defenders
have already hitched their hammocks in some neighbouring trees,
from whence they're determined never to descend, whatever the inducement. But perhaps you'll have gathered all this
from the foreign-news page of the Oaxaca Argus? And perhaps
from a Mexican – or even mescaline – perspective it all seems
rather trivial? I'd be interested to know. You have my
address . . .*

The approach to Hogslea from his school brought Ashley
alongside the perimeter of the construction site, a half-mile
stretch of cleared farmland. The fence was twice as tall as
himself and crowned with coils of razor wire. Through the
mesh, as he walked, he glimpsed pyramids of plastic piping
and concrete tubes laid out in lines. The afternoon sun
flared from the scoop of a stationary bulldozer. He counted
four towering cranes, and passed a small village of two-
storey prefabs where there were boards advertising the
names of the contractors, the engineering consultants, the
security firm. A few yards beyond this he clambered up a
steep rise from where he could see the whole area. He held
on to the base of a tree. The course of the road was marked
by parallel lines of wooden crosses, the red-brown earth
levelled and rippling with tyre tracks. Diggers stood idle in
every direction, the broken mud heaped in piles around
them. Immediately below his position there was a white

kiosk marked *Site-A-Loo*. Ashley watched as the door opened and a man ducked out, replacing his hard-hat, re-fastening his belt. He tramped over the mud to join a mass of other men. They wore reflective vests emblazoned SECURITY and they were linking arms around a large rusting digger. The wide scoop to its rear was lowered, the clawed bucket in front raised up on hydraulic supports. With a belch of brown smoke it began to roll forwards and the guards set off beside it. Every part of the vehicle rumbled and clattered, the wheels squeaking inside the tread of the caterpillars. Ashley slid down to the fence and continued along the perimeter, watching the digger and its escort through the wires until they reached the main gates at the start of the Common. Then a voice said, 'Where you going, boss?'

Two men barred his way, their arms folded, legs apart. They wore black jumpsuits and elaborate helmets with visors and neck-shields, but no identifying numbers or logos. A few yards beyond them sat a grey-bearded man in a Landrover, a small white Camcorder strapped to his hand. He closed one eye and fixed the camera on Ashley, the lens slowly extending.

'I need to get across there,' Ashley said, and gestured to the crowds on the Common. He loosened his tie. 'I've come to collect my daughter.'

'We can't allow access, sir, I'm afraid.'

'Sorry?'

'Out of bounds, boss.'

The men remained quite rigid, watching him warily. A chain-saw snarled in the distance. The main gates rattled open, and as the digger rolled out the air suddenly swelled with shouts and ululations, drumbeats and whistles. Ashley raised his voice to make himself heard. 'Look, my daughter is some-where in that lot and she ought to be at home. She's five months old. I've come straight from work to collect her.

I'm a teacher. I'm hardly likely to start climbing trees, am I?'

'And your wife's across there too, sir?'

Ashley hesitated on the word, but said, 'Yes. My wife's expecting me.'

The man nodded gravely. 'Well, I suggest you take the wife home as well, sir. Kiddies need their mums. Be a shame if Mum spent the night in a police cell.'

Before Ashley could reply the men stepped slightly apart, inviting him to squeeze by them. The bearded man lowered his camera. He rubbed his eyes and yawned and Ashley set off along the edge of the Common, avoiding for now the crowds and the digger. The earth was soft underfoot and he passed a group of workmen lounging in the grass, drinking from bottles of cola and smoking. They wore red bibs and red hard-hats, earphones looped round their necks. A blue butterfly flitted amongst them. The ground was littered with wood shavings and there was a sappy smell of sawn timber, bonfires burning out in the haze. A couple of drummers, bare-chested and bearded, hammered with sticks on a pair of plastic barrels, and three young women tumbled out from some bushes, laughing as they parted around him. Then Ashley saw Hazel's boyfriend, sitting alone on a tree stump. He wore a thin, baggy anorak and his hands were in the pockets, bunched together at his knees. 'How's it been?' Ashley asked him.

Coz eyed him dimly, nodded when he recognized him. 'Predictable,' he said.

'Seems fairly good-humoured.'

'Nah, they're dying to lay into us, they just need an excuse.'

'Right,' murmured Ashley.

A helicopter clattered overhead, black against the pearly sky, and Ashley gazed around at the Common. The oaks were widely dispersed, and although no two were alike, each one suggested in its folds and contortions a face or a torso.

These were the dark, twisted shapes of fairytales. In the whorls of the trunks there were knuckles and knees, furrowed brows and bent backs. There were eyes and gaping mouths in the rents left by fallen branches. He said, 'Seen Jay at all?'

Coz shrugged in apology. 'Over that way, Ashley. She's somewhere about.'

'I suppose I'd better find her.'

Coz answered with a nod, and then said, 'You could try the site office. They're bound to be keeping tabs, yeah? They'll think you're one of theirs, you look like a sheriff's man.'

As he walked away, Ashley slipped out of his jacket and pulled off his tie. He saw a girl looking out from one of the trees. She leant her elbows on the rim of a cavity, her face in her hands, and glumly watched the struggle in the distance. In the boughs above her there was a rudimentary tree-house, a platform of planks with a roof of tarpaulin. Other shelters had walls of striped canvas or pieces of plywood, and a few were enclosed in screens of interlinked twigs, hurdles of wattle and daub. The foliage of the oaks was sparse and bristly, but most had also been decorated with tinsel, wing-mirrors and hubcaps, bent nails and pieces of gnarled tin. As Ashley drew closer the girl ducked into her tree, and when he looked again she was walking behind him, wearing a sombrero. He passed under the banner with his name, its ties coming loose, the fabric drooping.

An electrified voice crackled above the noise of the protesters. *'All reasonable steps have been taken to ensure your safety but you are placing yourselves in a position of danger. I repeat, you are placing yourselves in a position of danger and your safety cannot be guaranteed'*. There was a buzzing pause, an answering cacophony of jeering. *'If you do not come down from the tree, then all reasonable force may be used to remove you. You are liable to a criminal charge of obstructing the sheriff'*. The man speaking held a clipboard, the megaphone strapped under his arm. He was being filmed by a camera crew, watched over by a knot of men in white hard-hats. The men were young and burly and beneath their yellow bibs they wore rugby tops or tee-shirts, the sleeves rolled high on their arms. Ashley didn't go any closer. He tugged his shirt loose from his waistband.

A cordon of police three and four deep encircled one of the oak trees, each man gripping the arm to his left. There were women officers behind them, bailiffs and tree-surgeons, and a yellow lorry from which a platform rose slowly, shakily extending into the crown of the tree. The men in the cage rasped through the outer branches with chainsaws, began to pull apart the ramshackle dwelling as the squatters clambered over the boughs to escape them. The wood creaked and fell crashing, lengths of blue rope trailing behind it. A woman with dreadlocks became trapped a few feet from the cage. The chainsaws whined around her, then choked and fell silent. One of the workmen was wearing a harness, tubigrips on both arms. He grabbed the woman by her hair, and there were yells and howls from below as she was hauled by her vest into the cage, screaming, 'Get off me! Fucking get off me!' Clods of earth flew over the heads of the police. The protesters on the ground jostled with the cordon and there was a shouted 'Piss off!' Then, 'Grab him! Grab the fucker!' A beer can spun through the air and struck the side of the cage, and immediately a scrummage of bailiffs fell on the man who had thrown it. In the rush of bodies a cameraman tumbled over, filming the sky, and Ashley fell backwards, tripping on a didgeridoo. 'You fucking prick!' a woman yelled at him. She could have been Jay. He got to his feet and retreated, then paused for a moment, and turned and walked on.

He might have continued walking. He had not wanted to come; he had not wanted Jay to come either. Sounding much like his own parents, he had pestered her for days, arguing long after her mind was decided, never expecting to convince her. He hadn't convinced himself, and didn't know why he persisted except that decisions now should be mutual,

Maggie was also his child. They had responsibilities, he'd said. And he was being responsible. 'Yeah, yeah,' she'd replied. He pulled on his jacket. In the area beyond this tree there were others, already felled and dismembered. Only the stumps remained, waiting for a digger to uproot them. The heavy machine from the site stood twenty yards out from the gates, still surrounded by guards, temporarily stalled by protesters. They were mostly women. A line of private police and bailiffs attempted to keep them away, but more than a dozen were already sitting or lying in the path of the digger. Men in yellow hard-hats carried them off like sacks of cement, dumped them near a group of police. Ashley came to a picnic table and sat down. Jay had called him predictable and boring, and said their responsibilities were wider now. They couldn't hide Maggie away from the world; they had a duty to change it, make it better for everyone. 'Oh, sure,' he'd replied. Nothing she'd said was surprising; and he'd answered as they both knew he would.

There was a scuffle amongst the watching crowd, and then he saw her, standing with Hazel and Owen. He got to his feet. Owen was holding the baby, Jay's satchel slung from one shoulder. Ashley guessed why, and hesitated a moment before deciding to run. He set off at a sprint, but his jacket blew open and he felt foolish, conspicuous, already doubting his urgency, what he hoped to achieve. He walked the final few yards, and Hazel and Jay broke through the line before he could reach them. They raced over the ground in short jolting strides, almost falling into position, sitting with their backs to the digger. The onlookers were cheering. Ashley pushed through to Owen and took Maggie from him without speaking. She was warm and heavy, and he held the back of her head, buried his nose in her hair. 'Do you want the bag?' Owen said mildly, and Ashley accepted that too.

'Thanks,' he said.

A workman approached Jay from behind. He bent and

tucked his arms under hers, cradling her breasts. There was a roll-up clamped in his mouth, black rubber gloves stuffed in his pocket. When he dragged her away she went limp, her belly exposed, and his arms rode up to her throat. Ashley winced as he watched. He momentarily lost sight of her, and tried to edge sideways. A female security guard pushed him back, but there were people behind him, pressing forwards. He hitched Maggie on to his hip, the satchel dangling from the crook of his arm. He felt the pressure of the woman's hand on his shoulder, and dimly registered a warning. 'Back off,' she was saying. He shrugged her away, all the time watching Jay, but again she shoved him, more forcefully now, and Owen's arm came swiftly between them. 'Would you cool off? The guy's holding a baby, for Christ's sake!'

There was a moment's stillness. Jay passed from view, and Ashley glimpsed Hazel, one man holding her legs, another her arms. He thought to leave then, to try to find where they were going, but the black-clad form of a bailiff moved across him, nudging in front of the woman. He wasn't wearing a hard-hat. He had his hands on his hips, and shuffled from side to side as he inched closer to Owen. There was no room to move. He pressed his forehead to Owen's, forcing him to arch backwards. 'Come on,' said Ashley, 'this is stupid,' and the bailiff relaxed, casually glanced over his shoulder. His eyes briefly met Ashley's, and then he tautened and swivelled, driving his head into Owen's. 'Fuck off!' he yelled, his fists now clenched at his sides. 'That's a *lady* you're pushing!'

'There's no need!' someone was shouting, 'There's no need!'

Owen collapsed to a crouch, holding his face, and Ashley yanked him away by his shirt. There was blood dropping from his nose. He held his head back, mouth gaping, and allowed Ashley to guide him to the picnic table. An elderly woman hurried after them. 'It won't do,' she was saying. 'It's criminal. Absolutely criminal.' She wanted to staunch the blood with her cardigan; she was fumbling with the buttons, her hands shaking.

Ashley said, 'Here,' and gave her the baby. He dumped the satchel on the table and found a fat roll of toilet paper. He reeled off a length and passed it to Owen, then helped him on to the bench. The old lady sat too, and Maggie craned her head to see Ashley. She squealed, showing her gums, and he held out his hands to take her. It was the first time she'd recognized him. His heart was racing and he was breathless, as if he'd been fighting.

A flock of birds banked overhead. Then the digger lurched forwards, the area now cleared of protesters. Two lines of policemen marched alongside it. Ashley said, 'How's it feel?' and Owen opened his eyes and closed them.

'Not broken,' he said. A trickle of blood rolled to his ear. The old lady dabbed it with her sleeve. She was weeping, shaking her head, and Ashley gave her some tissue.

He walked a few yards away. In the nearest tree there was a pockmarked sign saying 'No Construction Traffic Beyond This Point'. There were crusts of lichen on the trunk, ruffs of crinkly white fungus. He saw ferns sprouting from the sleeves of moss on the branches, a small bird darting from the abandoned treehouse. 'Look at the bird,' he said to Maggie, and squeezed the fat on her knee. Behind him the claw of the digger descended on the tree-stump, crashing into the wood, and when he looked again he saw Hazel and Jay, trudging out of the distance towards him. Jay lifted an arm, and Ashley smiled and waved back. He pointed for Maggie. 'Here's Mummy,' he said. He was angry, and wished he wasn't smiling.

OCTOBER

OUTSIDE THE rain fell vertically, a steady hush in the yard. There were splats on the window ledge and in the empty flowerpots by the doorstep. Ashley drummed his fingertips on the worktop. 'Right,' he said, 'milk.' The kettle was bubbling. He fished for a bottle in the sterilizing tub, caught the kettle on the whistle and poured it. He counted eight scoops of powder, flicking the excess away with his finger, tipping them in. Maggie stood bandy-legged on Hazel's knees. She was gurgling and flapping her arms, her chest enclosed in Hazel's hands. Ashley screwed the teat to the bottle and shook it. A spray of milk hit the clock and he saw it was five past twelve. He ran the cold tap and stood the bottle in a saucepan, then left it to cool in the flow. 'What time did she go off?' he asked. The tea-towel was soaking. He dried his hands on his jumper.

'Eleven.' Hazel yawned.

11 am sleep, he wrote on a pad. *11.50 awake (cheery)*; *12.05 change*; *12.15 milk*.

'So, nappy,' he said, and pushed the breakfast things to the edge of the table, making room for the mat, the water, the sponge, the cream and a nappy. He would need a towel too. He went to the bathroom.

'I'm really amazed you're using disposables,' Hazel called after him.

'Sorry?' he said, draping the towel round his neck. He lifted Maggie on to her back and unclipped the poppers on her sleepsuit and vest, tugged her legs free and stripped off the nappy. It smelled of ammonia, warm and hard where the wet had absorbed. He tossed it to the floor by the bin.

'I can't believe you're using disposables.'

'Me neither.' He sighed. The sticky tab on the new nappy wouldn't open. It ripped when he forced it. 'They cost 14.1p each, and they keep fucking breaking.' He threw it aside and went to fetch another, stopped and gave Hazel the towel. 'Would you wash her?' he asked.

'I mean, it's such a waste,' Hazel said.

'I know, I know,' he replied.

In the living room he took a deep breath. The floor was strewn with Hazel's belongings. He heaped them impatiently near the door and dumped her rucksack on top. A car sped by the window, bumping over the ruts in the road. He stood and looked out. Across the street a woman was sitting in the entrance to the flats, wearing her slippers and holding a can and a cigarette. She yelled into the lobby and dragged herself to her feet. A small girl with red hair appeared beside her. 'You mind that lager,' shouted the woman, and as she stumbled indoors the girl sat down in her place, nursing the can in her lap. She gazed up at the rain, then directly at Ashley. Like the other children in Telegraph Lane, she often spoke to him when he was carrying the baby. He thought to wave but drew the curtain instead. There was a bag of nappies under the sofa.

In the kitchen Hazel smeared a finger of cream around Maggie's creases, and Ashley turned off the tap. He opened the new nappy and cautiously tested the tabs. 'Ready?' he said.

'Nearly,' said Hazel. A glass pendant hung from her neck, a necklace of beads and a pouch for her lighter. They dangled over the baby, just out of reach of her hands. Maggie kicked her legs in frustration, and gazed wide-eyed into space when Hazel stepped back. 'There,' she said, wiping her hands in the towel, 'all done.' She sat cross-legged in a chair and watched as Ashley gripped the baby's ankles in one hand and slid the nappy beneath her. 'It's just so typical really,' she persisted. 'If you think of all the babies in the world, and all the nappies they use up. No one ever considers where the nappies come from . . .'

'Boot's,' said Ashley.

'Trees, *actually*, Mr B.'

'Trees are a crop,' he shrugged. He tucked Maggie into her suit. 'Just like the cotton in terries. And you don't use water to clean these. Or detergents, or electricity.' He eased the baby into Hazel's arms. 'Besides which, what's so special about trees?'

'Ashley!'

He handed the bottle to Hazel and waited to see if Maggie would take it. Then, smiling, he said, 'I don't know why you get so worked up about conifers, Haze. They're ten a penny, and it's not like they're being wiped out, is it?'

Hazel tilted her head sideways and stared at him. Her mouth was tucked at the corners, pressed to a pout. It was a gesture he recognized from school, something girls did to him often, defensive but scolding. He supposed it meant he was missing the point, and deliberately so, as if he ought to know better. He leant back on the worktop and folded his arms. Hazel spoke as if to the baby. 'But it's, like, if you live on the land and you're aware of the elements and seasons and things

– if you live and work next to nature, instead of working against it – then you get to see that every living thing has a character, like people. We're related, *Mr B.*, we have a relationship with the environment. But the people in houses can't see that. They think everything's disposable and they put nothing back.'

'We do our bit,' he said.

'I just think it's really weird, you and Jay living like this. Jay, anyway. You're just such a *family*.'

'Jay's different from you, Hazel. Older for one thing.'

'She's not that different. She didn't use to be. I don't know how she can handle being stuck in the same place every day, with a mortgage and practically a husband and everything. We had a really natural childhood. We were brought up by loads of different people, which is the way it should be, that tribal energy, living with people who are working towards something really brilliant. I'd die if I thought I was going to be stuck here for the next fifteen years or whatever.'

'So would I,' said Ashley. He heard the flip of the letterbox, something landing in the hall.

'And stuck with the same person – who never goes out anywhere. Always eating dinner at just the same time, always trying to be the perfect parents, just like all the neighbours. You're so protective of Maggie as well, no one's allowed to touch her. I really worry about her, what she's going to grow up with.'

'Thanks for worrying,' he said. 'But you're touching her now . . .'

'And you're watching me . . .'

'And besides, Jay isn't stuck. She happens to be out right now, and our neighbours really aren't much of an example to follow. You should take a look.' He went to collect the mail.

'So why do you live here?' she said when he returned.

'Because there's a flush on the toilet, Hazel. And the bin-men come every Tuesday, and the postman always knows where to find us.' He flapped his brother's letter on his palm. 'Plus, we don't have to talk to our neighbours if we don't want to, which I'd say was a definite advantage over living on sites with argumentative types like you.'

'People on sites are really passionate about life, Ash. They care about things.'

'Conifers, for instance.'

'Yeah.'

'You're turning into your mother, Hazel.'

'Fuck off, Ashley.'

He looked for a knife and sliced open the envelope. The postmark was Belize. There were ten pages, the place names written in capitals. 'I'll leave you with Maggie then. Half an hour all right?'

'Take as long as you like. She won't miss you.'

'What time are you going?'

Hazel didn't reply. Ashley cleared the discarded nappies to the bin. 'I'll be in the bedroom,' he said.

A few questions, Douglas:

1. When you sleep what do you dream of? Is it all dirt roads and jungles, machine-guns and mountains, or do find yourself in England again, a boy-nuisance again? Because your child- hood self is a frequent presence in my dreams, haring about like a mad thing, causing no end of grief and commotion. Not that I mind, of course – at least in my dreams I don't get blamed for your mishaps.

2. Do you ever wake and not know where you are – what day, month or season it is? And do you ever sink a little dis- tance when you realize? Are you ever troubled by not knowing what is to come, menaced by thoughts of what you'll have to return to?

3. In other words, do you get homesick for England, ever? Do you get homesick, or nostalgic, for aspects of England – the apple-blossom snows of May, say? The shirtsleeved start to the football season? And do you get homesick, nostalgic, for things that made you sick when you were at home, the creeping clouds of October, say; the drear, damp drizzle of December; the gloom and doom of Ma Brook on the telephone . . . ?

4. Do you ever experience moments of panic, realizing how far from home you are? Or do you more often experience moments of elation? Does the world seem bigger or smaller to you now? More or less crowded? More or less cluttered with children? And how does it feel to be always surrounded by a foreign language? Is <u>this</u> the stuff of your dreams?

5. Do you find yourself drawn into conversations with your fellow travellers, and are you grateful or resentful of the opportunity? How easy is it to ignore another Westerner? And how close have you come to fighting one? Does it help if they share your rank, sweaty odour?

6. Do you feel yourself to be on holiday still? Or are you on the great motorway link-road of life, voyaging to understanding, wisdom, disinterested oneness in beingness? I mean, will you ever be the same again; will your thoughts run on straight lines again; and will you ever wash again?

7. And what does a poste restante <u>look</u> like?

It was eight o'clock and Maggie's bedtime. They were using her buggy now, the pushchair Ashley's mother had brought. It resembled a small stripy deckchair on wheels. Ashley strapped her in and gave her something to hold, a rattle which she gripped to the mound of her belly. He arranged the buggy to face him and sat on the sofa. There was a rubber foot-rest between the front wheels. He pushed on this with his heel, drew it back with his toes, and pushed gently again. In twenty or thirty minutes the motion might lull her to sleep, but beyond that she'd become restless, then fractious, and Jay would have to take her upstairs, breastfeed her in bed until she started to drowse. It was anyway rare for Jay to stay up beyond ten o'clock. Her sleep was always disturbed. Three and four times every night Maggie would demand extra feeds, and whilst Ashley continued to dream, Jay would lie on her side in the dark, in the half-light of dawn, listening to the clock, to Ashley's breathing, waiting for the baby to settle. Maggie wouldn't accept nightfeeds from a bottle. Even when she wanted to play and Ashley was woken to take her downstairs, she would complain if he took her to the kitchen, wail if he attempted to feed her.

Jay got to her feet now and turned off the overhead light. She switched on a table-lamp and took a book from the mantelpiece. The gas fire burned on three bars. She lowered the heat and undid the top buttons of her shirt, tucking her hair behind either ear. Ashley emptied his beer to a glass. The newspaper lay beside him and he pulled it closer, flipped it on to its front. He scanned the TV page, the radio listings and the weather report, then sighed and gazed over at Jay. She bit her lower lip as she read. Her skirt was tented by her knees, her elbows on the armrests of the rocking chair. Conscious of him watching, she screened one side of her face with her hand. Ashley closed his eyes. He thought it might encourage the baby, but when he next looked, a blurry glimpse through one eye, she was staring intently at the bulb of her rattle. He said quietly, 'Can I read you something, Jay?'

'Is it long?'

'No.' He reached beneath the sofa for his book. 'Quite short.' He had marked the page with his brother's letter. 'Listen. *More and more he was becoming convinced that it was only through children that one could connect with anything any more, that in this life it was only through children that one came home, became a home, that one was no longer a visitor.*' He scanned quickly to the end of the page and looked up.

Jay was fiddling with the neck of her shirt. She refastened one of the buttons. 'Is that it?'

'Yes,' he said.

'You're very mushy, Ashley.'

'Thanks,' he said, and waited a moment. 'Is that a bad thing?'

'I suppose not,' she shrugged, and bowed her head to her book. Ashley drank from his glass. He wanted her to say more but Maggie had twisted in the buggy, curling as if to sleep, her eyes almost closing. He concentrated on pushing. There was a blare of music next door, then shouting. He heard 'Bitch!' and 'You dirty fuck!', a long pause, doors slamming and silence. Jay was listening too. She laid the book in her lap and stared at the ceiling, rocking back in the chair. Finally she said, 'It doesn't really apply, though, does it? You haven't *become* a home. You always were a home.' She smiled and faced him. 'That's why I like you.'

The baby was sleeping. Ashley leaned forwards, carefully unfastened her straps. 'You should tell that to Hazel,' he grinned.

'Why?'

'She thinks I'm boring because I never go anywhere.'

'That's true, you don't.' She rose from the chair. 'And you are. A bit.'

'Is *that* bad?'

'I'll take her up,' said Jay, crouching next to the buggy. She gathered Maggie into her arms and lifted her gently, pausing before she straightened, watching to see if she'd stir.

'But is it?' Ashley whispered.

'Maybe,' she sighed, and opened the door with her foot. 'I haven't really thought about it.'

The door swung closed, and as Jay mounted the stairs Ashley looked around the room for his diary. He wondered if he should telephone someone, but he could think of no one he wanted to talk to. There had been many calls in the weeks following Maggie's birth, brief exchanges of cards and letters and photographs, arrangements made to meet friends, vague promises quickly forgotten. And when he had moved himself to go out – to pubs, to other people's houses – he soon sensed that the baby was of interest to no one but himself. Other parents listened to his stories, just as he listened to theirs: politely and patiently, waiting for the opportunity to talk about their own children. The only letters he wrote now were to Douglas; the only phone calls he received were from his mother, regularly on Mondays and Thursdays, and always just after six. And yet, when the phone had rung two Thursdays ago, he had prevented Jay from answering it. 'It might be important,' she'd said.

'It might not,' he'd replied, and they'd stood and waited until the ringing had stopped. Later, when Jay was out of the room, he had slipped the phone off the hook. His mother would call again on Monday, he supposed; sooner than that if it mattered. But for the next two weeks there was silence. He tried to remember the last time they had talked, and whether he'd said anything to offend her, whether she'd suggested a visit to Ravensby with Maggie and Jay. It was something she often mentioned, and he usually ignored. Perhaps she was expecting a date, or confirmation, some excuse at the least. He heard Jay's footsteps descending the stairs, and looked at the clock. Reluctantly he rose from the sofa and carried his glass to the telephone. He finished the last of his beer and placed his hand on the receiver, hesitated a moment, then punched the number from memory.

No doubt you'll have a few questions of your own, Douglas, and no doubt the answer to your first will be '91', which is to say, 'slight rain at time of observation'. In England it's raining, always raining; spitting when it's not teeming. In addition to which, also at time of observation and since we're looking, I've just seen a couple of teenyboppers in rainhats pushing a pram down the street, both scoffing an ice-lolly (in this weather!) and both smoking a king-size cigarette (at their age!). And as they ambled along they took a bite of lollypop, a drag of fag, a bite of lolly, a drag of fag . . . The pram wasn't theirs. I think the infant inside belongs to

*Caroline, our next-door-neighbour-but-one, who has children to
spare and the biggest deepest voice of any woman known to man
and the biggest deepest bosom. She wears a tee-shirt (in this
weather! at her age!) which says* FUCK THE GOVERNMENT
across her chest and LET'S RIOT! *in the shadow beneath. She
is a phenomeness and Jay thoroughly approves of her but I just
wish she'd stop shouting – if you pause and cup an ear to the
nearest poste restante you might even catch an echo of Caroline giving her kids a hard time. She's yelling at them now and
the walls of this terrace are trembling. I'm not joking. The
plant-pots beside our skirting board are rattling in their saucers.
(I say plant-pots – what we have is a collection of wonky
cylinders which Jay made at night school last year, when she
last decided to improve herself. This year she was trying to
cultivate her own weed, but she's made just as big a hash of
that and the seeds aren't sprouting – every last jugful of water
floods out the bottom and over the saucer and leaves a nasty
brown ring of rot on the floorboards. Besides which, she's on the
wagon from all forms of intoxication. (It used to be that I worried about rings of rot on the floorboards. A positive effect of
parenthood is that now I couldn't give a toss. A negative effect
is that I'm now too worried about other things, particularly
other people's children. I want to dash out and lecture those
schoolgirls on the hazards of smoking, I want to stop Caroline
from belting her kids, I want to teach the world to sing in
perfect harmony, grow up on trees and honey bees and snow-
white turtle doves . . . But enough. (Close brackets.)))*

*And as for your inevitable second question, the state of our
parents' marriage, the answer is variously '03 – clouds generally forming or developing', '13 – lightning visible, no thunder
heard' and '18 – squalls'. Trouble looming, in other words.
Ma Brook's soul is a seething tempest of umbrage and loathing.
She has a good mind, she says, to talk to a solicitor now. A
good mind! I think not. Her perceptions are so thoroughly
skewed, so consistently off-beam, I don't think she has the slightest*

inkling how nutty she is. But then, how could anyone live for twenty-seven years with Pa Brook and not lose their grip on what's real? Everything comes filtered through the murk of his incomprehension. Lately, it seems, she's been trying to explain to him what grieves her. She told him, for instance, that he never listens to a word she says; to which he replied that it wasn't his fault, his ears are blocked from so many years in the Works, but if it'll make her happy, he'll see about having them syringed. Is this facetious, or is he genuinely that dim? Mum is convinced he's mentally defective. But she also believes him capable of extreme cunning and wickedness – for instance, he recently chipped the glass on their unusual coffee table, then spilt hot tea on the heir-loom sideboard, then mended the dodgy handle on their walnut wardrobe with an oversized black bolt which apparently looks ridiculous and is fastened too tight for her to remove. But wasn't he always this dyspraxic – or 'hamfisted', as we educationists say? Mum thinks not; she suspects a determined campaign to ruin all their best furniture. But why on earth why? Because, she says, she won't then be able to flog it off to raise funds to leave him, and won't want to furnish her new home with it either. This is the measure of the man's deviousness, and she is furious because the strategy is proving so effective. Every time he damages something she deducts the amount from her expected capital after leaving him, and adds the cost of a replacement to her likely expenses. Dad thinks she's barmy, though not because she credits him with such roguery, but because he can't imagine any sane person wanting to leave such a happy home in the first place.

Meanwhile, in answer to your third question-to-be, yes, there have been some highly exciting developments at the Grub's nether end: authentic jobbies, real turds, genuinely poo-shaped poos! Proud parents we are. And thrilled. We actually witnessed the emergence of an eight-inch-long, three-quarter-inch-wide, steaming sausage of processed carrot and potato just last week. The Grub was lying naked on her changing mat at the time. I was in the kitchen, losing my temper, I can't recall why.

'Ashley! Ashley!' trilled Jay, 'Quick! Quick! Get some tinfoil. You can put it in a time capsule!' And such was the excitement that Jay enjoyed an immediate bowel movement of her own. Still no photos, however – no film, I'm afraid – but when you get back you'll have to ask me to get the package from the fridge and we can unwrap the tinfoil for a quick peek. Presuming it survives that long. Presuming neither one of us deliberately damages it before then, a pawn in our own non-marital breakdown . . .

Ashley sat fully clothed on the edge of the bath. The walls were peppered with mould. Gauzy cobwebs clung to the corners. On every surface there were smears and crusts of dried soap, and the skirting was shadowed with grime, but despite the baby neither of them could find much enthusiasm for cleaning, the house seemed to resist all their efforts to improve it. 'We ought to lay some more tiles,' he sighed.

'They'd fall off,' Jay told him.

'Might hide the damp, though.'

'Doubt it,' she said, and lay back in the water, resting a heel on the rim of the tub. Sweat glistened above her top lip, on the bridge of her nose and over her forehead. Ashley traced a finger along the line of her shin.

'You've got a varicose vein,' he said.

'Thanks.' She dropped her leg in the water. 'I've had a baby,' she said.

Ashley nodded and smiled. Her abdomen was softer now, paunchier than before, her breasts still swollen with milk. Fine grooves showed like scars where the skin had been stretched. 'You wouldn't know.' he said.

'Would you stop gawping at me?'

'Sorry.' He looked around for a sponge. 'Shall I do your back?'

'No.'

Ashley trailed his hand in the water, and knew that he ought to get up. Jay's baths, as she frequently told him, were the only time she had to herself, though once she would have taken them with Ashley. He remembered long conversations carried over into bed, their voices muffled in the darkness, in their closeness, the talk drifting as often to sleep as to sex. But now their bed was divided, too crowded, and sex had become something planned in advance, hemmed in by tiredness, the discomfort of the living-room floor, worries that Maggie would wake.

Jay soaped her face and sluiced it with water. Ashley reached for a towel. 'Here,' he said, and as she dried her eyes he perched himself on the toilet seat. He leaned forwards with his chin in his hands. 'Did you mean what you said earlier, Jay? About me. Do you think it's a problem?'

'What did I say?' she asked, not looking at him. She splashed beneath her arms, over her breasts and her shoulders. He didn't reply. 'No, of course not,' she said then. 'It's nice, I told you, that's why I like you. Don't worry about it.'

'Yeah, well,' he yawned. 'I do.' He rubbed his eyes with his fists, blinked around at the room. 'I was wondering,' he said then, 'maybe we ought to live somewhere different.'

'Move house?'

Ashley shrugged, and Jay sat up in the bath. She brought her knees to her chin, wrapped her arms round her legs.

'Why?' she said cautiously.

'Change of scene? You know, if we're getting into a rut . . .'

Jay rested her face on one knee and spoke to him softly. 'We'll still be us, though, Ashley. Wherever we go. We can't just leave ourselves behind, even if we are in a rut.'

'Suppose not,' he said. He tore a strip from the toilet roll, crumpled it into his hand. He dropped it to the bin and stretched out his arms. 'What about a holiday then?'

'Like where?' She laughed. 'It's nearly November. Butlin's won't be open.' She looked at him narrowly. 'Unless you mean Belize?'

'Guatemala now,' he said. 'But no. He'll be home soon enough.'

Jay slipped under the water, ducked her head and came up. 'Good,' she said.

'Is that "good" he'll be home, or "good" we won't go?'

'That's both,' she said, and reached over her shoulder. The shampoo bottle was empty, hissed when she squeezed it. 'There's some more in the cabinet,' she told him. Then, smiling, 'We could always join the camp in the woods. For a week or so.'

He faced her reflection in the mirror. 'Or we could visit my parents,' he said, and tugged at the latch of the cabinet. Jay's cap and a tube of spermicide fell out, a bag of condoms tumbling after it, spilling into the toilet bowl and next to the bin. He gathered them up. 'Mum wants to see us,' he said.

'So send her a photo.'

'I did.' He found a sachet of shampoo and knelt at the side of the bath, tearing it open. He emptied the lotion into his palms and smoothed it over her head. As he massaged her scalp Jay closed her eyes and he looked at her breasts, their plumpness, the wet sheen on her skin. He began to get an erection. 'I suppose sex is out of the question?' he murmured.

Jay smiled, and quietly replied, 'Fuck off, Ashley.'

He raised himself over the rim and dipped his hands in the water. 'Hazel said that as well,' he told her, and kissed one of her nipples.

'You didn't ask her for sex?'

'I'm a family man,' he said, and stood to open the door. 'Far too boring.'

NOVEMBER

T HE CUBICLE was fusty, a smell like worn trousers, stubbed cigarettes. Ashley closed the seat lid before he sat down. He started to yawn and took off his watch, dropped it into his pocket. He raked a hand through his hair and slackened his tie. It was a Tuesday afternoon and his only free period, but there was still an hour to the bell, then a meeting to follow, an extra hour of in-service training. He had meant to look at the programme over the weekend, but the document now lay at his feet, fresh from its envelope. He tucked his arms to his belly and leaned forwards to read it.

Effective teaching, it told him, *is constituted by a range of attitudes and strategies defined by researchers as follows. The effective teacher is approachable and bears the qualities of patience, tolerance and understanding. S/he has a good rapport with pupils and shows real interest in what pupils say and do. S/he makes him- or herself available for pupils with learning difficulties . . .*

The door to the Gents swung open. Ashley heard two pairs

of feet and quickly fastened the lock on his cubicle. *The effective teacher is well prepared and organized prior to lessons with a clearly established lesson plan. S/he ensures that the lesson plan is enacted in an orderly manner, and defines appropriate expectations of behaviour and performance both for the pupils and for him- or herself. Such standards are set early and remain consistent and realistic throughout . . .*

He gave up; he was too tired. Beyond his door a voice said, 'The trouble is, the lad isn't interested in chess or computers, whatever his mum says. All this fuss and when it comes to the crunch it's a load of fucking hee-haw. He'd rather take his chance in the playground.' It was the head of PE. He coughed and spat at the sink, turned on the taps.

'Special needs, though,' said another voice. 'It's always the same – it's the mother needs the attention, not the boy. She sissies him.'

'And every other cunt. They all do it, Gillian especially. I feel for the lad.'

'Yes, I heard that about you.'

There was a noise like a scuffle, trainers squeaking on the tiles. Ashley waited until they had gone and picked up his document. He went out to the sink and straightened his tie, splashed his face with cold water. The towel dispenser was jammed, as it had been the previous week. He wiped himself dry on his sleeve and crossed to the urinal. There was a penny coin in the runnel, edged with verdigris and staining the porcelain. He remembered seeing that last Tuesday as well. He fixed his gaze on the wall.

When finally he went through to the staffroom he found a couple of teachers from Science standing by the mail trays. Ashley hesitated but couldn't avoid them. He met their smiles with a yawn. They were sharing the last of a cigarette, both wearing their lab coats. 'It's that young Mr Brook!' said the first. 'Remember, Gillian? The one who used to teach geography.'

Ashley sagged his shoulders and grimaced. 'Rough night?' Gillian asked him. She pinched her eyes against the smoke and passed the stub to the man, who ground it into a plant-pot.

'Three hours,' said Ashley. He reached for his mail slot. 'Then I missed my bus again. I nipped in by the side door and the first person I met on the stairs was the boss. Same thing happened yesterday.'

'Little one teething?' asked Gillian. She slipped her foot out of her shoe and scratched at the back of her leg. Ashley glimpsed the dark nylon over her toes. Gillian was much discussed amongst the male staff for wearing stockings, not tights, and for not being married, even for playing netball at weekends. Her name was inked on two of the desks in his classroom, and behind the door of the Gents' cubicle.

Already edging away, Ashley leafed through his memos and said, 'It's just a cold. She wakes because she can't breathe, then she's high as a kite and won't go back down again.'

'What time does she wake?' demanded the man. He started to follow. Gillian eased her foot into her shoe and came with them.

'Two-ish,' said Ashley, faintly smiling.

'And what's her bedtime?'

'Eight. Usually.'

'Well, you know the answer.'

'I do?'

'Obvious,' said the man, and reached for the doorknob. 'You go to bed when she does. Half nine at the latest.'

Ashley shook his head. There was a yellow slip amongst the papers; he was supposed to be covering for someone. 'But if I did that,' he said, 'I'd have no life at all.'

'Well,' the man said, guiding Gillian through the door. 'Either you have no life in the evening or you have no life at school the next day. Simple choice. Which is more important?'

Ashley paused to examine the slip. He read it twice. The room number was Mrs Gumley's. He remembered she had a conference at another school, and that she'd warned him well in advance. Sighing, he said, 'I don't think I'd call my job here a life.'

Gillian scolded him softly. 'Your job is what you make of it, Ashley.'

'Thanks for the advice,' he said, and turned for the stair-well. 'I'll sleep on it, shall I?'

Ashley climbed the stairs two at a time and hurried down the corridor. He no longer taught any sixth-formers. When his group had begun their exam year Mrs Gumley had taken sole responsibility for teaching them. She said she wasn't suffi-ciently impressed with their performance so far, or confident that he could improve it. But almost immediately their num-bers had dwindled from seven to four, and with each loss she had become more unhappy with Ashley. Clearly they were unused to hard work or rigorous marking; they were too accus-tomed to leniency. And so she had set extra assignments for those who remained, and often left them unsupervised, retreat-ing to the departmental base and her paperwork, returning later to gather their essays.

Arriving now, twenty minutes after the start of the period, Ashley found her classroom deserted. He stopped in the door-way and rested his head on the jamb, wanting only to sleep. He would need to find an excuse, but knew there was none. Whilst the other teachers were collecting their memos that morning, he was still travelling to school on his bus. And during the morning interval, when he ought to have been in the staffroom, he had remained instead at his desk, staring out at the frost, the last leaves showering from the trees over the road.

He wandered up to Mrs Gumley's desk and lowered him-self to her chair. The clutter of books and papers before him was much the same as his own, and the room identical save for the ceiling, here collapsing directly over the blackboard. A pair of thick woollen socks lay flat on a radiator. The windows were damp with condensation. Listening for footsteps, any noise in the corridor, he carefully pulled open a drawer. A small ceramic figure rolled from a box of tissues, a gnome on a plinth inscribed THE WORLD'S GREATEST TEACHER. He lifted the flap of a packet of photographs and recognized a group of children in rainhats and anoraks, posing before a tumble of stones, a scree slope somewhere in Wales. There were pens and staples and confiscated cigarettes, a tangle of rubber bands, empty notepads, but no clue to her mind, nothing he wanted to find. He pushed the drawer closed and tried the next one, which was empty, and the last, which was locked. Whatever she thought of him, he supposed he would hear it tomorrow. He gathered his mail and got to his feet, leaving the room as Robin Crawley arrived at the top of the stairs.

'Hello, Mr Brook! Only me!' Robin showed his hands palms outwards. 'I was just coming to find you.' Ashley leant on the wall. Robin's hair had been shaved at the sides and slicked back on top. He wore a black-and-yellow striped tie and two-tone brogues in beige and brown. The heels of his shoes clacked on the tiles. 'Listen,' he said, 'We're having a Chinese take-away tomorrow lunchtime, in the staffroom. Shall I put your name down?' He mimed the writing.

'Not me,' said Ashley.

'Well, just come along for the company. You don't have to eat.'

'No thanks.'

Robin continued to smile, and hitched up his trousers, holding the creases. 'It's a special occasion, we're celebrating my new shoes. Like them?'

Ashley noticed the bulge of Robin's groin. 'Have you thought about new underpants?'

'Boxer shorts.' Robin grinned. He looked quickly over each shoulder, and whispered, 'Silk ones.'

Ashley smiled wearily. 'I'd better be getting on,' he said.

'But there's more.' Robin laughed. He produced a book of tickets from his pocket and stripped out the top two. 'Prefects' Christmas Dance,' he said. 'Take a couple and pay me later, yeah? You could bring the girlfriend along.'

'Maybe,' said Ashley.

Robin touched him on the elbow. 'It'd be good to meet her again. I saw her on the box the other week, with the baby? She's doing a great job out there.' Ashley was silent. Robin twitched his eyebrows, his mouth. 'Still very pretty,' he confided.

'Robin,' sighed Ashley. 'Do you ever let up?'

'Nope,' said Robin, and scratched at his chin. 'I don't believe I do.' He grinned broadly and lifted his hands. 'Right, message received, I'll go and irritate someone else. But you'll think about the dance, won't you? And the Chinese tomorrow?'

'I'll think about it,' said Ashley, and watched as Robin departed, his shoes clicking down the corridor. The price on the tickets was £13. Ashley crumpled them into his fist and tossed them aside. He walked to his classroom and for several minutes he stood just inside the door. He gazed around at his plant-pots, the empty desks and the fish tank, the maps pinned to the walls. In one corner lay his pile of papier mâché fish, their colours dulled by the damp, a grey coating of dust. There was another fish on the shelf at his side, a blue-and-green-streaked ornament he'd been given last term by his first-years. He thought of the gnome in Mrs Gumley's drawer, and remembered how little the presentation had meant to him. He carried the fish to his desk. Very shortly the bell would be ringing and the meeting about to begin. Chairs scraped in the next room along, a teacher bellowed instructions about homework. Ashley dropped the fish in his bag and gathered his coat from the back of his chair, decided to leave now by the side door. He would phone in sick in the morning. Perhaps he would talk to Jay that evening.

Novembrrrrrrr.

I'm ill, Doug. The chill blanket of winter is tucking in around us, there's a hint of Vicks in the air, fistfuls of tissue on the carpet-that-isn't, bronchial splutter on every surface. It's a cold but that's not the whole of it. There's an itch at the back of my left knee, a rash beneath my arms, a pain which shoots from my left testicle to the region of my pancreas, a permanent low-level sore throat, and a really unnatural propensity to tiredness, or drowsiness, a mad desire for sleep at all hours. The cold was my reward for taking a sicky from school, and like the tiredness it's a gift from my daughter. I can't say I'm grateful. In fact, I could possibly furnish you with a list of Five Less Than Fantabulous Facts About The Grub. Despite our best intentions and conscientious reading, for instance, it seems we were quite wrong to assume that smiling attention and copious bodily contact would produce a self-contained, confident and contented child. Maggie has her own agenda this month; she belongs to the Nature, Not Nurture camp and just can't help being miserable, a bedroom tyrant, sleeping for no more than two hours at a time. During one particularly bad week Jay aged sixty years, forgot the name of the Prime Minister, and began calling me 'Eh? Speak up'. It's got so bad we will shortly be shifting the Grub to her cot by way of retribution and rewarding her nighttime awakenings with no more than boiled water. I fear deep psychological traumas ahead, for all of us. Although on balance – of course! – I'd still say I was pop-poppingly enamoured.

And so, a few more Fantabulous Facts.

1. On her good days she is much tickled by her own reflection. Held in front of herself in the mirror, she grins and yelps and paws the glass with slobbery fingers. But she also grins and yelps and paws the glass when I hold her up to the living-room window. Presumably she believes the flats opposite are a true reflection of herself also. More psychological traumas ahead, no doubt.

2. The pecking order amongst her toys has taken a sudden reversal. The most neglected was a plastic trumpet, which neither rattles nor bounces and can't be cuddled in bed. But one afternoon she performed a sudden evolutionary leap – discovered how to blow into the narrow end to produce a screech at the wide end. This was accomplished lying on her belly on her changing mat, which is her favourite posture for evolutionary leaping.

3. For two days after learning to play the trumpet she was extremely agitated and grumpy, and spent frighteningly long periods asleep during the day. Then suddenly her mood cleared, she woke up, and – a miracle! – she actually sat upright, unaided, unsupported, perfectly poised and at ease with the world. I handed her a pen and a notebook. 'What's the formula for gravity?' I said. She's thinking about it.

4. Meanwhile, her motor is revving and after several weeks of grinding herself into the floor, she has started to crawl. First gear eludes her, but she has found reverse and edges backwards almost imperceptibly until she gets within grasping distance of Jay's champion begonia. She has it in for the begonia and uses the leaves to polish her first bit of tooth, which is emerging at backward crawling pace from the middle of her lower gum.

5. She has been practising her consonants and has already mastered 'm' for 'mmaammaa' – though sadly not 'd' for 'ddaaddaa' – and has also typed her first message at this very typewriter, here reproduced in its entirety:

gh

It's quite hard for a grown-up like me to recite this authentically, but repeated by Maggie it comes out as a sort of gurgling shriek and a burble. It seems to mean something to her anyway. Possibly it's the formula for infantile gravity.

The Grub's mother, meanwhile, has become the temporary toast of the Telegraph Lane Wifies, though not for her evident loveliness, media friendliness, selfless sleeplessness, or any other of her recognized accomplishments, but for her handiness with a bike spanner. Last Saturday one of the local street kids trapped his foot between the wheel and wheel-arm of his bicycle. He was screeching like an absolute trumpet, and whilst his mates were attempting to wrench his leg off at the hip, and his mother was pacing up and down in the road, and his Auntie Caroline was bellowing bustily, and a dog, possibly his own, was howling like an absolute hound, Jay not only freed him but realigned his gears, oiled his chain, and tightened his brake blocks. Since when she's been unable to leave the house for offers of coffee and biscuits and second-hand babywear. And so, all of a sudden, after three years of being ignored by our neighbours, apparently invisible to all but the tribe of thieves by the beer shop, we do actually exist, we do actually live here. And we're not altogether glad about this – we're not sure we want to live here – but to mark the occasion, and to make the house saleable, and since the toolbox was already out, we spent the rest of the weekend finally revamping our kitchen. Or I did, ailments and all. Jay was too busy basking. And I'm a very proud handiman. Not least because there isn't a single true plane or right angle in this entire house and the kitchen is possibly the most undulating room of all; floor, walls and ceiling all bend and slant at hopelessly oblique angles, but not so that you – a casual observer – would notice, which is a nuisance because how are you then supposed to appreciate the scale of my achievement? You will have to remind me whenever, if ever, you visit to get the plumb-line out and I'll demonstrate. You will also have to take a peek under the sink because I think you might like to admire my first and last venture into the realms of flexible tap-tails and reducer compression fittings, my first and last attempt

at home plumbing, a new plateau in my ascent to manly com-
petence. Assuming we haven't already absconded, assuming you
do actually come home.

A fine drizzle was falling and the street lamps were hazy.
Ashley widened the front door and looked to the top of the
road. He saw a large battered car cruising towards him, and
beside it a dog, trotting to keep up. The driver steered with
one hand and his window was open, his elbow protruding.
The dog's lead was wrapped round his fist. From the off-
licence corner some boys were shouting, 'Walk, you fat bastard!' And although it was too far to see their faces, Ashley
knew who they were; he recognized their voices, the shapes
they made in the dark. Two days before they had followed
him home, asking for cigarettes and money, one of his cans.
A boy called Groucho had clipped his heel, tried to trip him
up. The others had laughed. Ashley had fastened the chain
on the latch when he got in; and he fastened it now. He would
go in the other direction, to Centra Stores in the precinct, and
he whispered to Jay as he left, 'I'm taking the back way.' She
was rocking the baby to sleep in the living room and mouthed
him to be quiet.

He took a deep breath as he opened the door. He had been
drinking since teatime and was tipsy and cheerful, happy to
be out in the air. The yard was lit by the glow of their neighbour's back bedroom, and when Ashley looked up he saw a
face pulling away, the blinds suddenly closing. He smiled to
himself and drew the bolts on the gate, heard a chink of coins
in the alleyway. For a moment there was only the darkness;
and then the forms of bin-bags and boxes, the sheen of the
rain, and finally something moving, a head lifting to see him.
He realized it was the boy who had hammered on their door
in the summer. He was hunched down with the rubbish. 'Bit
wet tonight,' Ashley said, and dragged the gate shut.

'I'm waiting for a friend,' said the boy. His hair was flat to his skull, dripping into his face. There was a pile of loose change at his feet.

'Fine,' Ashley said as he passed him. He thought he saw blood on the boy's knuckles, and stalled a few yards further on, patting his pockets. 'Forgotten something,' he murmured, and turned back to the house. In the kitchen he switched on the light and looked for his keys. There was a smell of fresh paint and fabric conditioner. The washing machine started to whirr. Ashley picked up a vegetable knife and wiped it clean on a tea-towel, but immediately replaced it. He wouldn't have known how to use it. He opened the curtains to let out the light, and locked the door as he left.

'Safe and sound now?' said the boy. 'No worries?'

'No worries,' said Ashley. He closed the gate and pulled up his hood. 'Back in a minute,' he said.

'Right, mate,' said the boy.

The streets were deserted and the rain coming heavier, slanting against him. From the back-to-backs Ashley crossed to a newer estate, and took a route through a wide stretch of green. The pathway across it was marked by a line of skeletal trees, each enclosed in a tube of wire netting. Jay had told him about them that evening. Like the saplings in the local park, their branches had been broken, snapped off at the trunk. As he passed by them he noticed a dog chasing a scent through the grass. It cocked its leg to a bench and raced on, its coat sleek with the wet. Ashley realized he was walking almost as fast as the dog. He checked his stride and turned through a complex of houses, avoiding the short way, a road which led straight to the precinct. He didn't want to return too soon. He pictured the boy crouching down by the bin-bags, his stack of coins on the pavement. He remembered hiding from him last August, and the sound of his voice through the letterbox, the grip of his hand, his smirk. But perhaps he would knock on their door now, whilst Ashley was out. He started to hurry again, then also remembered last winter, watching from his window as the boy was beaten to the ground, taking the blows without moving, curled up like a baby. Ashley reached into his pocket and folded his hand around his wallet. There would be no confrontation. He passed a row of empty properties, already graffitied and boarded, and crossed to the shops. All but the supermarket were closed, steel shutters covering the windows. Ashley took out his money. He wanted three cans. When he reached the grille at the end of the aisle he said, 'Four.'

'Oh, *Ashley*,' Jay said. 'You didn't!'

He wanted to laugh. He flopped down on the sofa and stretched out his legs, snapped open a can. 'Yes,' he said. 'I did'. He shrugged, and spilled some beer on his chin. 'It was only two quid. Why not?'

Jay glared at him angrily. 'But *why* though, Ashley?'

'Because he said he didn't drink beer, he gave me it back.' Ashley pinched his features and imitated the boy's voice. '*I like a bit of hash, mate. I don't want it.*'

'Hash,' breathed Jay. She shook her head. 'He's a *junkie*, Ashley. He'll be round every night, every time he sees you he'll be wanting a handout. Who do you think leaves all those fucking syringes?'

They had found one in the yard, dark with blood, and another two in the alley. Ashley said, 'We haven't seen him in weeks, Jay, and you don't know they were his. They're everywhere, they could be anyone's.' He grinned, and thought he might giggle. 'And he *won't* be round again. We shook on it – he gave me his word.' The boy had offered his left hand, the cuts on the other were bleeding. He said he'd been scratched by his girlfriend.

'And you were drunk enough, and *stupid* enough, to believe him.'

'I do believe him,' Ashley said quietly. The boy had not looked up when he came down the alleyway, and he appeared nervous when Ashley stood over him. His surprise had been genuine, Ashley felt sure. *'I appreciate it,'* he'd said, returning the can. *'But, like I say . . .'* He had showed Ashley his money, and said he was two pounds short of fifteen. 'He was grateful, Jay. I mean really. He wanted to give something back.'

'And did he?'

Ashley rolled the can between hands, wasn't sure if he should tell her. Tentatively he said, 'Sort of.' Jay was looking at him. 'He mentioned that crowd by the off-licence. He said, *I rule that team, mate. They do what I say.* I'm supposed to tell him if they hassle me again, he reckons he'll put a stop to it.'

'He offered you protection, in other words. You're such an *idiot*, Ash.' Jay drew her thumbs over her eyes. She gave a sigh and stood up, began to tidy around him. 'In other words, it's blackmail. The next time he wants something he'll bring the boys round.'

'I'm not an idiot,' Ashley protested. 'He doesn't rule anyone. It's a pile of shite, what he said, and he knows it, but he hadn't got anything else to give me. I felt sorry for him. He's hardly any older than Hazel and his life is just rubbish. I thought you'd approve.' He swallowed some beer, saluted himself with the can. 'I was making the world a kinder place, Jay.'

'So why didn't you offer him a bed for the night?'

'I did, but he said he didn't like beds. *I like a bit of rain, mate, sleeping under the stars and that.*' He waited to see her expression. He wanted to see her smile. 'Joke,' he offered.

Jay gathered a pile of exercise books from the floor, Ashley's marking for the evening. Her face was flushed red and she took a long breath, tipped the books on to his belly. She stared at him until he began to feel foolish. His hands had been shaking when he came in; he'd been light-headed, triumphant. In the kitchen he had spun the knife on the worktop, laughed as he stacked his beers in the fridge. Now the boy's words ran through his mind as a threat, a warning. He should have stayed in the house, in the living room with Maggie and

Jay. He picked up one of the jotters, and limply allowed it to fall.

'I think you'd better sober up,' Jay said very quietly. 'You're drinking too much, Ashley. You should give it a rest.'

He nodded. It was nearly nine thirty. 'Maybe we should just go to bed?' he said.

DECEMBER

THE COACH pulled into Ravensby early. Ashley
stayed seated and watched as the other passengers filed
past him. Maggie was snoring by his side, her arms and legs
thrown out as if she'd been dropped there. He switched off
the overhead light and wiped a cuff on the window. The
depot was sodium-lit from high rafters. A few coloured bulbs
glowed from the staff canteen. When the driver came down
the aisle, collecting magazines and papers, tapping the seat
backs, Ashley pulled himself to his feet. He began to gather
his things. There was a carrier bag under his chair and another in the rack. His rucksack was wedged to the roof and
his coat was bunched up beside it. There was the buggy with
its rainhood, Maggie's changing gear in a satchel, a loose
bottle, and then there was Maggie. The driver didn't offer to
help but said, 'Happy Christmas,' and followed him down
to the steps. Ashley didn't reply, and took his time getting
off.

His parents had said they would meet him. He passed a

man in galoshes hosing the rear of a double-decker, and went to stand just inside the door of the shed. The cold pinched his face when he looked out. His breath came as vapour. Across the uncovered tarmac there was a rank of local buses, angled into lettered bays and most of them empty. An engine began thrumming, a mini-bus beeped as it reversed. Swarms of starlings were shrilling from the dark of the company buildings. Ashley wrapped the flaps of his coat around Maggie and hugged her closer against him, the weight of the rucksack tugging his shoulders. He looked at the clock and wondered if he should phone, or wait somewhere else, but then another coach pulled into the shed and he saw his mother hurrying past him. She searched along the windows of the coach, straining her neck to see over the people crowding out. Her face showed no anticipation, any sense of excitement, but anxiety and anger, as if already convinced he hadn't bothered to come. Ashley jerked open the buggy and trundled it towards her.

'Mum,' he said in her ear. 'Wrong coach.'

Her eyes were frosty but she managed to smile when he showed her the baby. 'Bless her,' she said. 'Worn out, I expect.' Then, 'Come on, we'd better not keep him waiting.'

'Just a minute.' Ashley dropped the satchel from his arm and found Maggie's coat, fumbled to get her inside it. His fingers were numb, and she started to cry. He strapped her into the buggy. 'Could you push her?' he said, and looped the plastic bags over the handles.

'If that'll be quicker,' said his mother. 'He's parked on a double-yellow. I told him not to, the buses are always late.'

'It was early,' said Ashley.

'Especially this time of day. He thinks if we park next to the station, we'll get home quicker. Never mind the traffic's just the same, we've still got to get out of town.' They passed a man and woman arguing in a phone booth, wrestling over the receiver. The man's hand was flat to the number pad. 'All he's worried about is missing his dinner. Chips and burgers all right?'

'Mum!'

A bus had swung into the station. His mother dragged the buggy back from the kerb and glared at the driver. 'Well, that's just ridiculous,' she snapped. 'He'll be another one, can't wait to get home. Where's the station manager's office, can you see it?'

'We haven't got time,' Ashley reminded her. 'Where's the car?'

'It's on a double-yellow,' she said again. 'Up by the Co-op.'

'So how are you?' he asked then, but she was in too much of a hurry to answer.

Christmas is looming, and every morning there's a mini Mount Nilgiri of mail on our doormat, most of it for Jay of course, but also including – at last! – a fat despatch and photo from the Dug in Guatemala. I woke to find it on the pillow beside me, and Jay holding two cups of tea. Oh happy day. We enjoyed this letter immensely, despite the onion-skin paper and your minuscule scrawl, and I think if you were to offer me any four weeks of your tour as a present, I would take a month of Guatemala please, ravenous fleas, gun-toting soldiers and all. I even decided to re-name our kitchen Little Guatemala in its honour, given that neither can lay claim to a single flat surface in all their breadth and depth, etc., and to abandon any further plans for home-improving (such was my scheme for the day) but to assume a Dug-in-limbo posture instead – ie, 'feet up, mind a blank, complete vacancy of being'. Only it's harder than you let on. My own habitual mental limbo was too troubled by this photograph, Douglas . . . Are you aware (Question Eight) of just how weedy you're getting, or of how ragged you look, or quite how bizarre is your facial hair? Your goatee is more of a sheepee, and I recommend you find yourself a razor, or a biddable shearer, just as soon as you can. And a change of clothes, not to say a few squarish meals. We were taken aback, really quite shaken, by your decline into shagginess, Dug; though the view beyond you is happily twice as unfeasible as your appearance – such is your proper role in our life, to beggar belief with mind-bending views, not to stand beggar-like before them. Please note.

In the car in the dark they spoke very little. The radio was tuned to a local station, the volume set no higher than the drone of the engine and the hum from the heater. The presenter's voice murmured just behind Ashley's ear, his words barely distinguishable, interrupted by a muffle of jingles, commercials, records from ten years before. It was a programme of oldies, from when he still lived in the town. He held Maggie closer and pressed his face to the window.

Ashley's memories of Ravensby were mostly of summer. It had been a good place to be a young boy. He remembered wide roads and playing fields, grassy triangles and swing parks, shrubberies to hide in, neat houses with gardens. People paid rent to the Council and did not often move. Every street seemed to connect with someone he knew: there were aunts and uncles and cousins, friends in other estates, and the steelworks had been visible from most of the hills. As they passed the steel site now he saw a sign advertising *Starter Homes and Prestige Apartments*. In the surrounding area there were front-porch extensions, replacement windows and satellite dishes, gravel drives where once there'd been gardens. Christmas decorations were everywhere. But still the estates seemed shabbier, distances shorter and everything smaller. An old cinema was boarded at street level, half-demolished above. He recognized a terrace of prefabs, now completely abandoned, and a carpet warehouse which had once been a primary school. Squiggles of graffiti marked every postbox, phone booth and shopfront. At the next lights his father looked in the rearview mirror and said, 'Same old place, eh?'

'A few changes.'

'Plenty up the town anyway. No end there. Do you remember Queen's Parade, where the market was? That's all shops now, shops and offices. All empty.' He indicated right and pulled out. 'They've put the market on the balcony. And they've moved the big shops out past the works. Free parking. No one bothers with the town any more. Even the little shops, they've had it, they're all closing down.'

'Anyone moving in?'

'Let's just say they're a few shades off black, son. As soon as anywhere goes empty, the pakis move in. There's a lot of them in Ravensby now. I'm not colour-prejudiced, but they know how to charge. And the new factories, it's all jobs for women, ninety per cent female labour.'

'Just as well,' said his mother. 'They're the only people wanting to work. Women and boys.'

Ashley's father didn't reply and they drove on in silence. Like many of the men, he had not worked since the steelworks had closed. He said he was too old, and his skills weren't the right ones, trades in general weren't needed. His redundancy had gone on their mortgage; and whilst Ashley's mother continued to work part-time in a dry-cleaner's, light jobs eluded him. But it was doubtful he could manage even those. When they arrived at the house he carried Ashley's rucksack in from the car, and the effort coloured his face. His mother unlocked the door. 'Take your shoes off,' she said. 'The carpet's been washed.'

Ashley crouched down with Maggie. His father propped the rucksack beside him and rested on the stairs. His breathing was wheezy, and it was some moments before he bent to untie his laces. Ashley said to his mother, 'The house looks very smart. You'd hardly know anyone lived here.'

She tightened her mouth to stop herself smiling; the velcro flap of her anorak rasped as she opened it. 'I like everything in its place,' she nodded. 'If he had his way, it'd be all higgledy-piggledy.' As she leaned across to the coat hooks, Ashley's father gave him a wink. 'Dinner in half an hour,' she said, and toed her feet into her slippers. 'The pushchair can go in the cupboard.'

Ashley carried Maggie and her satchel into the living room. On every surface there were ornaments – pieces of china, glass vases, miniaturized objects in brass. It seemed they had always been there, as old as his parents' marriage, but whenever he visited he would find something new. It was how his mother marked holidays and daytrips, and how they all marked her birthdays. She preferred 'old-fashioned things', she said – china gramophones three inches tall, ceramic figures in period costume, vintage cars that were actually bottles or ashtrays – but she had no time for antiques, anything she thought second-hand, 'other people's leavings'. She didn't forget where each of her ornaments had come from, or how much they'd cost, or who had bought them, but few held any other associations. The most prominent object on the mantelpiece, a clock in the guise of a basket of fruit, had been brought back from Butlin's. Ashley remembered a miserable week of arguments and rain, and he had stopped asking why she kept it.

He looked around for somewhere to sit Maggie. She was already kicking her legs and twisting to be free of him. Her warmth rose like a breath when he took off her coat, soured by her nappy. He pressed his nose to her backside and laid her down on the carpet, then began to unpack the satchel. She started to crawl to the fireplace. There was a group of porcelain swans on the hearth.

His father sat in his armchair and watched her. 'She'll be into everything,' he said.

Ashley picked her up and carried her back to the changing mat. 'That's what I said on the phone.'

'She could do with a harness.'

'She's not a dog, Dad.'

'She'd soon learn.'

Ashley sat cross-legged on the floor and dumped Maggie over his knee, tugged down her trousers, unclipped her vest. 'Couldn't some of this stuff be moved out of her way?' he said. 'Just while we're here?'

But his father was frowning. Quietly he said, with a glance to the kitchen, 'Hadn't you better do that in the bathroom, Ashley? Your mum won't want that smell down here, will she?'

Actually, I can't believe we're so close to the end, only one more letter to go and then I'll have to say it all in the flesh, assuming there's any flesh left on you, assuming I have anything left to tell. Not that I'm altogether sure I want to say it all in person – no offence – as we've grown quite used to this version of you, always somewhere we aren't, unfettered, in transit, forever ignorant of developments in our national decline, and now that your year and a half is about to expire it doesn't seem quite such a long span after all, and I'm worried at the prospect of your returning to this miserable country, more worried than I ever was when you were a mere dot in the South-East Asian mountains; it will diminish us all when you discover your last improbable volcano, cross your final frontier, and rejoin the bus queue in Ladbroke Grove. As I've no doubt said before, I depend upon these airmailed reminders of the world beyond our threesome, our street, my work, and this city (the former car-crime capital of Britain; now cardiac capital of Europe – did you know that?). But perhaps you'll invest the last of your fortune in a Ford Transit and tour the postes restantes of England? We have contacts, you know, and Jay could easily fix you up with an old coach, or caravan, or reconstituted delivery truck . . .

No one spoke at the table. Ashley ate with one hand, forking the food into his mouth over Maggie's shoulder. She sat on his thigh, rocking backwards and forwards, cheerfully burbling. A thread of dribble fell from her chin to the table-cloth. Then his father said, 'You're very patient with her anyway.' A piece of meat was stuck to the side of his mouth. Ashley looked at him quizzically.

'The child's not doing anything wrong,' said his mother. 'What's there to be patient about?'

'Nothing,' said his father. 'No, you're a good little girl.' He smiled for Maggie, bearing his dentures. 'I don't think I've heard you cry once, have I? Your daddy cried non-stop for two years, he never stopped crying.' He looked at Ashley. 'Your mum was never the same after she had you.'

'I thought that was Douglas,' said Ashley before his mother could speak.

'No, not Douglas, he was good up till about three and a half, then he got a bit more of a personality, he got more of a lip on him.' He gestured vaguely to the window with his knife. 'That one, he hated things not going his way. I remem-ber one tantrum in the town centre, Saturday afternoon. He was rolling about on the pavement and screeching like a bloody maniac, you'd think he was dying. *I want my mummy, I want my mummy.* But your mum was in the Fine Fare. I nearly ripped the sleeve off him, trying to get him up again.'

Ashley smiled thinly. 'That *was* me,' he said. He had col-lapsed to the ground so his father couldn't spank him. But he was spanked anyway, lying on his back, turning a slow circle to get away from the blows. He remembered the shoppers parting around them, a swirl of faces and coats, and another small boy gazing on, open-mouthed.

'Oh, that was you, was it?' said his father. He nodded and picked up his tea. 'Bad as each other then.'

Ashley put down his fork. He stroked Maggie's arm and looked at his father, the waxy back of his hand, the jut of his jaw as he drank. Like Douglas, Ashley had been hit regularly, routinely, and once so hard he had fallen against the cooker, striking his head on the grill-pan. He was old enough then not to cry, and remained where he lay, refusing to get up. His father had left him. The door had closed quietly. He remembered bright sunshine, visitors in the living room, some relatives from London. He'd sat cradling his knees on the floor, and when finally his mother had come through to the kitchen it was to make cups of coffee. She had busied around him, minutes had passed, and then she'd examined the mark on his forehead and tutted. 'You'll have to stop answering back,' she'd said.

He got to his feet now, and said, 'I'll get Maggie's supper.' A tin of babyfood was warming in a pan by the sink.

'There's dessert yet,' said his mother.

'Not for me, thanks,' he called.

'Off the puddings as well,' said his father when he returned.

Ashley sat slightly away from the table and eased a bib over Maggie's head. 'As well as what?' he asked, but his father was chewing and didn't appear to have heard him. Ashley touched Maggie's lips with the spoon and she jerked her face to one side. The purée smeared her cheek. He waited for her mouth to open again and tucked the food in, scraped it back from her chin as it began to ooze out.

His mother said, 'Is she eating properly now?' She meant nightfeeds and refusing the bottle.

'Not bad,' he replied, though really there had been no improvement.

'I expect Jay will be glad of the break.'

'Yes,' he said.

'What's she got planned? Anything?'

'She's joined the camp for a couple of days. I told you that.'

'Oh, did you?'

'Yes,' he said, 'on the phone.' He kept his eyes on the babyfood, the spoon. Unlike his father, whose own forgetfulness and deafness had become ingrained, more than merely a habit, his mother forgot very little and her blankness now, as they both knew, was deliberate. She was waiting to hear him explain; she had things she wanted to say. 'Her sister's out there,' he said carefully. 'They're sharing a tent.'

'That'll be her half-sister?'

'Yes, that'll be her half-sister.'

'And what are they hoping to achieve, in this tent, in the middle of winter?'

'You know why they're doing it,' he sighed. He let Maggie play with the spoon and wiped his hand on her bib.

'No,' said his mother, lifting her chin. 'I'm afraid I don't know why they're doing it, not any more. And I'm no fool, Ashley. That road is going to be built whatever anyone says. Isn't that right?' Ashley nodded. 'So all they're doing is making a nuisance.'

'If you like.'

'It's badness, in other words. It's wasting everyone's time and money and asking for trouble.'

'Yes,' he said wearily. 'So the sooner Jay gets a bloody good thrashing, the better.'

'I didn't say that.'

'No. You didn't say that.'

'That's not what I meant.'

Ashley stood the babyfood on the table. He hoisted Maggie around in his lap and took off her bib. His hands were trembling and his finger caught her ear. As her face slowly creased he whispered, 'Sorry, sweetheart,' but she was already crying. He hugged her to his shoulder and patted her back. Finally he got up to make her some milk. His mother sat very still, gripping her knife and fork over her meal. As he passed her chair she pushed the remains of her dinner aside and clattered the cutlery on to her plate.

'What's up?' said his father. 'Lost your appetite?'

'And you needn't think I'm criticizing Jay,' she warned Ashley. 'You needn't go telling her that. Jay's a sincere girl. I'm sure she's acting according to her beliefs. But I happen to think she's got mixed up with a very bad lot.' Ashley watched the electric kettle. 'Do you hear me?' she said.

'I hear you.'

'And there's a child to consider,' said his mother, suddenly clearing the table. 'She has other responsibilities now, besides all that.'

'She's a responsible girl,' said Ashley.

'Let us hope so,' said his mother.

And now a thin postscript from Colombia too! But thankfully no photo. This sounds a very awful place indeed, and if you wanted to impose upon me any two weeks of your tour as an act of malice and malevolence, I don't think you could do much worse than a fortnight travelling here, with the possible exception of a weekend in Ravensby. The letter coincided, in the freakish way of these things, with a Saturday-supplement feature entitled 'How to have a great holiday and not get mugged or murdered or shot at', which I would've chanced immediately to the Christmas mail except, of course, you'll be in Ecuador already, or on the return flight to Guatemala, or shambling off in some other direction. Or at least I hope so. Perhaps the murderous, gun-slinging muggers got to you first, in which case you won't be reading this, and won't feel up to reading the clipping. But it was generous of you to reply to my questions at last, albeit briefly, though a shame you couldn't respond in logical sequence and forgot to answer my Question One, to wit, when you sleep what do you dream of? Strangely, your younger self has now disappeared entirely from my dreams; or, rather, my dreams have disappeared entirely from me, and you with them. Complete vacancy of being, in fact. Which is worrying. I wonder whatever became of us?

Time in his parents' house passed slowly. Ashley stretched himself out on the floor between Maggie and the fireplace. He tickled her nose with a teddy and she clutched at it with both hands, closing her mouth round its ear. It used to be his, and the fur had coarsened to bristles. 'Dirty,' he said, but she started to whine and he let her hold on to it. The carpet was soft and thick and the day-long air in the room was making him drowsy. He yawned and said, 'Soon be your bedtime,' but Maggie showed no signs of tiredness.

'I'll find you those blankets,' said his mother.

'No, really,' he said. 'We'll be fine. It's a warm house anyway. We're more used to the cold.'

'You'll need them,' she insisted. 'You'll see. The central heating goes off at ten.'

'Snow's forecast,' added his father. He gazed balefully at the television. It was the first time he'd spoken since dinner. Ashley propped himself on one elbow and listened as his mother padded upstairs. He glanced at his father, and supposed he should say something.

'How are you then, Dad?' he asked.

'Me? I'm fine, don't worry about me. That's the key to the story.' His eyes followed the movements on the screen. There was laughter from the studio, but his face showed no response. Ashley remembered when they were children, watching their father's favourite programmes without comprehension, laughing when he did. Sometimes he would ruffle their hair, laugh louder when they fought to mess up his own. He used to comb his back in a wedge, held stiffly with spray. He used to shave twice a day.

'Are you growing a beard now?' Ashley smiled.

His father scratched at his stubble. 'No,' he said, still watching the set. 'I'll go up in a minute, when your mother's sorted.'

Ashley nodded. He sat upright and poked Maggie's paunch with a finger. She giggled, and he pulled her to his belly, blew a raspberry into her neck. His father looked down at them. The commercials were on. 'Can you see much of a change in her?' Ashley asked then. 'She was very little the last time you saw her.'

His father considered. He said drily, 'I can't see much of you in her anyway. There's plenty of Jay, she's like her mum all right.' Then, 'I expect she'll be missing her mum.'

Ashley frowned, made himself smile. 'Does it look like she's missing her mum?'

'In the week, I mean. When you're doing the nannying.'

'We get along fine,' Ashley told him. He bounced the teddy on his knee and made it jump up at Maggie. 'It's what she's used to.'

They heard the toilet flushing upstairs. His mother went into the front bedroom. 'And what about your job now?' his father persisted. 'Have you thought any more about that? You'd be wiser going back to that full-time, wouldn't you?'

Ashley shrugged. 'Perhaps,' he said.

His father watched him steadily. 'Well,' he said grimly, 'you want to be careful you don't end up like this other one. I don't know what he thinks he's going to come home to. He's burnt his bridges, that one.'

'His bridges were burnt for him, Dad. He was made redundant.'

'He had a nice girl there. She was a very nice girl, from what I saw of her. Homely. He could've made something of that.'

'Dad.' Ashley shook his head. 'That was years ago. He's been out with at least three other girls since then, and the last one chucked *him*. There was nothing to keep him here. He did the right thing. It was the right time to go.'

Ashley's father was silent. He worked his jaw as if chewing. 'He's too much like your mother is the problem,' he said then. 'Never satisfied with what he's got.'

Ashley sighed. 'Maybe,' he said.

'She's a very dissatisfied woman,' his father said. 'A very dissatisfied woman.'

Jay meanwhile is dreaming of wide-open spaces, or twiggy en-

closed ones . . . I spent my last half-week of term discussing rural push and urban pull with my fourth-years – why folk leave the countryside, why they come to the cities, and what they do when they get there. And do you realize (Question Nine) that the balance of the earth has tilted, that the weight of the people in cities is now greater than the weight of the people in villages? I expect you do. Jay certainly knows, and her sleeping self finds the tilt quite giddying. She dreams of redressing the balance; she sits with the Grub in a tree and discusses rural pull and urban push. It's an odd sort of dream. There's a camp in the woods . . . There's self-employment in small family enterprises, minimal tools, cheap or recycled materials, intensive-labour input, irregular hours, no guaranteed income, a life outside the law, ignored or oppressed by the state. And I think she'd like me to join her, or at least show my face in her dream. But how could I travel? How could I cope with meeting so many new people? And how could I manage to survive so far from an off-licence? I'm sure it's not in my nature to live so close to Nature, and I'm sure it's not in my make-up to wander, or at least not in my upbringing. But then it ought not to be in yours either.

When his father went up to shave, Ashley's mother filled the kitchen sink to bathe Maggie. She rolled her sleeves tightly and dipped an elbow in the water. Her movements were exact, self-conscious, and everything she might need was laid out beside her. 'You won't remember me doing you like this, will you?' she said.

'I've seen the photos,' Ashley replied. He handed her the baby and waited. 'I used to help you with Douglas,' he said. 'I stood next to you on a chair.'

'That's right.' She smiled.

Her arm brushed against his and Ashley stepped out of the way. He turned restlessly about the kitchen, drumming his fingers on the worktop, the cooker. He crossed to the window and parted the curtains. Outside the snow was settling on the stump of the beech tree. Behind him Maggie squealed and thrashed her feet in the sink. 'Maybe I'll take our things up,' he said.

'Yes,' said his mother, frothing some soap in her hands, 'you do that.'

His parents had begun to sleep separately long before Ashley left home. He remembered the needlepoint plaque which had hung from the wall above their headboard. It was a wedding present from his grandmother. EAST OR WEST, HOME IS BEST, it said, and when they'd bought single beds it had remained there, hanging over the space between them. Now his father slept across the landing in Ashley's old room, and the plaque had been moved to his brother's. It was propped up on the dressing table. Ashley shook his head and smiled. He turned it face-down and stretched himself out on the mattress. The furniture here hadn't altered, nor the wallpaper, but there were no traces of Douglas. The previous Christmas Ashley had sent his parents a framed photograph of Jay and himself, and this now covered a ventilation grille on the wall. He stared at Jay's face and smiled; and closing his eyes he wished he had gone with her.

The front door thumped shut, and Ashley jolted awake. He heard the car starting and went to the window, watched as his father drove off. The tyres printed neat tracks in the snow, drew a smooth arc from the junction. Caps of white had formed on the lamp-posts and telegraph poles. Globs of melting ice hung from the wires. Ashley quickly searched in his rucksack for a sleepsuit and took it downstairs. His mother was cleaning the wheels of the buggy, and Maggie lay naked on the carpet, surrounded by Ashley's old toys. Her hair made wet licks on her forehead. There was a bottle of milk warming on the hearth. 'Sorry,' he said, stretching his arms. 'I dozed off. Where's Dad away to?'

'He's dropping a card at your gran's.'

'I thought we were seeing her tomorrow. He didn't tell her we'd visit tonight?'

His mother handed him the buggy and accepted the sleep-suit. 'She wouldn't remember if he did,' she said. 'She's worse than he is.' She took off her slippers and knelt down with the baby. 'Pot of tea if you want some. Coasters are in the drawer.' Ashley brought his cup to the sofa and watched whilst his mother dressed Maggie. She clipped her into the buggy, gave her the milk and tucked a teddy beside her. 'I'll let you push.' She smiled. 'I've done everything else.'

'Thanks,' he said. But the wheels wouldn't run straight in the weave of the carpet. With every few pushes the buggy turned a quarter-circle, backing into the coffee table.

His mother sat down with her tea and said, 'You've got yourself into a bind, haven't you? Doing that every night.'

Ashley leaned forwards and righted the buggy. 'I might just take her straight up,' he said. 'I'll give it a few more minutes.' He continued to push, and tentatively asked, 'So what's happening with you and Dad now?'

'What do you mean?'

He shrugged. 'Just what I said.'

'I'm leaving him,' she said tersely. 'I've told you.'

'When?'

'After Christmas. There's no point in spoiling his Christmas. Not that anyone will be here, except his bloody mother.'

'Does it make any difference,' he asked, 'before Christmas or after?'

For a moment his mother was silent, then abruptly stood and began to tidy around him. She clattered the toys into a box. 'Christmas used to be special, didn't it?' she said. 'I don't see why you can't stay an extra day. You're not going anywhere else.'

'It's our first Christmas as a family,' Ashley said quietly. 'We wanted to spend it together, just the three of us.'

'You have a family here,' said his mother.

Ashley gathered Maggie into his arms. He tilted the bottle and watched as she drank. 'But after Christmas, Mum,' he said finally, 'where will you go? Have you thought about it?'

She snatched the teddy from the pushchair and hurled it into the box, took his cup and her own to the kitchen. 'Well, not to either of my sons!' she shouted. 'I know that much.'

Do you realize (Question Ten) that our home town is now in the geography-curriculum textbooks? It used to be that we only existed on the football-results page of the Sunday People, a passing mention in tiny grey type at the foot of the minor-league round-up. But suddenly there it is, two whole pages in one, half a chapter in another, a dozen additional listings in the indexes, famous for being a company town as well as a new town and subsequently a ghost town. It's a model of its kind, an instructive example of modern industrial decline. It's no surprise people leave it; the greater puzzle is why people stay. But I wonder what in your nature drove you to leave it so completely? Since the holidays began, and I resolved to steer clear of the toolbox, I've been at a loose end (excepting my turns at parenting) with nothing better to do than rummage restlessly about in my mind for the origin of your adventurousness. But there really isn't very much there. Just one thing. It was possibly the only occasion we ever visited the actual countryside. You were still a small boy, and Mum and Dad took us to a faraway field without tables or swings or ice-cream vans, not even a souvenir stall. We didn't know where we were going until we arrived; and then we sat idly in the grass, unsure what to do or how to behave. I wanted to go home, of course, the sun was too hot and there was rustic dust in suspension in the air. But Mum and Dad were determined we should admire the view, and for a minute or so I tried to. And whilst I was trying, making an effort, you disappeared, you got up and wandered away. Mum panicked, Dad shouted, and eventually, resentfully, I found you, chumming up with some sheep in a neighbouring field, for which you were given the inevitable Damn Good Hiding. And that was the end of our first and last rural excursion, Mum said we couldn't be trusted, we were <u>*too irresponsible*</u>*. Which remains to this day a key word in the Brookian lexicon. Irresponsible. Responsible. Respectable. Sensible. Normal. Only I'm not sure any more what these words are supposed to mean. Do you, Douglas (Question Eleven)? Did you ever? And does our mother?*

JANUARY

I MADE A *New Year's resolution, Douglas. I resolved I must try harder at school. After two years of skiving, petty pilfering, corner-cutting and spurious sick-lines, after six months of half-weeks and general half-heartedness, I resolved to find job satisfaction through goals, objectives and lesson plans; through diligence, perseverance and good pupil–teacher rapport. So what do I do when I wake from next-to-no-sleep to a power cut and the world is in darkness and my bus is due in five minutes and I stumble out of the house wearing the wrong coat and there's no bus pass in my pocket and no keys and I don't realize this until I reach the top of the street and have to wake Jay to get back in the house and consequently fall out with Jay and then miss my bus by less than a microsecond and get very wet waiting for the next one because the roads and pavements are damp and grey, the sky is damp and grey, and everything between them is soaking? What do I do when my connection in town is forty minutes late and it's ten past ten before I get to the school and my head of department (or 'line manager', as she's now to be known) is waiting to upbraid me and the headmaster is waiting to interrogate me and, worst of all, my class can't wait to humiliate me? What do I do when I then find one of my best pot-plants upturned and beyond reviving and I suspect a fifth-year with a grudge but can't prove it and so sack my first-year classroom tidy-uppers instead and immediately feel guilty and try to reinstate them, only to be told they don't want their badges anyway, tidy-upping stinks? And when at lunchtime, for no particular reason, the head girl tells me I'm 'sarcastic' and her best friend, my favourite girl in all the school, tells me I'm 'snide', and all the time I thought I was being my most wittily charming? And my second-years are then at their most unruly? And my fish-tank monitors report the aquarium mysteriously short of one ceramic castle and one sunken galleon and tell me, no, they don't want to take another trip to the Fish Franchise, they're not interested any more, they've finally had enough? And they hand in their badges? And when, in the last lesson of the day, my ceiling suddenly collapses under the weight of the rain and the multiblock beneath the tank begins sparking, there's a flash, an explosion, the aerator stops humming and a wet splat of grey rubble lands on my only clean trousers? And when, to cheer myself up, I accept a late request to make up the numbers in the staff five-a-side and promptly fall on my arse, my ankle knackered, and can't stand and feel like a total prick and have to be dropped off at the hospital to get myself x-rayed or put down and spend nearly two hours being pushed around like a pea on a plate and take off my trousers five times and come away with no more than a tubigrip and an aspirin? And finally, what do I do when I get home and realize I've mislaid my evening's marking in the agony of the moment and Jay is in another foul temper because she was supposed to be going out over an hour ago and the Grub is in the kitchen emptying an entire box of washing powder onto her head, which I think is funny and Jay absolutely does not? Douglas, you're a man of the world, what do I do?*

★

The wind blew in gusts across the park, whipping Jay's hair, flapping her skirt round her knees. Maggie paddled her legs in the air and laughed as she swung. Water rippled in the sandpit behind her; the chains of the other swings jingled. On the far side of the enclosure a boy was juggling a football in front of his mother, scuffing his trainers on the grit of the tarmac. The woman sat hunched forwards on the end of a chute, gazing at nothing, and barely moved when the ball struck her shoulder. The boy stopped playing and hugged her; then Maggie's buggy caught the breeze and rattled towards them; paused, and rolled closer. Ashley hesitated, and went to retrieve it. He glanced at the woman. She was crying, quietly weeping. As he limped back to his bench the boy patted her arm and returned to his football, kicking it now at the railings and chasing the rebounds. His mother wiped her eyes and got to her feet. She brushed the seat of her coat and slowly walked off. A few moments later the boy trailed after her.

'Did you see that?' Ashley said.

Jay lifted Maggie from the swing. 'Was she crying?'

'I should've asked if she was all right.'

'She wouldn't have welcomed it, Ashley.'

'No,' he said, and they watched as the woman crossed a zebra in the distance, the boy running to catch her. A man in overalls stopped and looked at them too, then continued sweeping the pavement, pushing the litter to the kerbside. The bin-lorry had called that morning, and the street was blowing with pieces of styrofoam. Ashley adjusted the tubigrip round his ankle. 'Shall we walk now?' he said.

'If you feel up to it.'

'I'll use my Zimmer,' he said, and took the handles of the buggy. They went towards the crossing. Some way after the road-sweeper there came a small van, two spinning brushes in front, a water sprinkler behind. The driver sat smoking in a glass-walled cab and stared at Jay as they passed him. Her skirt was bright red and she was wearing green leggings, a waxed yellow anorak. Ashley raised his voice above the drone of the vacuum, the rotor flap of the brushes. 'I could always get a job on the bins,' he said.

'Underqualified,' Jay told him, and took hold of his arm, squeezing it tightly. 'No muscles.'

'Don't lean on me,' he murmured; then seeing her annoyance, he said, 'Sorry, it was dragging. The weight.' He steered the buggy around a pile of dogshit and they turned down an alley smelling of washing powder. Beyond the ramshackle fences the yards were strung with damp clothes. Looking up to the houses Ashley saw the flexing shadow of a telephone line, smoke tumbling from a chimney. 'What about plumbing?' he asked then. 'Kitchen conversions?'

Jay shook her head. 'Did you realize your pipes were leaking? I had to put a bowl under the sink-trap.'

'The sink-trap?'

'I looked it up in your book.'

'What does it do exactly?'

'It leaks,' she said, and he nodded. At the end of the alley they clambered around a broken wardrobe, a scattering of coat-hangers, and emerged to a street lined on both sides with odd bits of furniture. They passed an armchair and sofa, a white enamel toilet bowl and two plastic cisterns. There was a sink and a cooker, a sodden teddy bear, and dozens of pieces of hardboard. Similar junk would appear every few weeks, standing for days until a Council lorry arrived to collect it. Once, shortly after they had moved to their home, Jay had found a wicker armchair near the top of Telegraph Lane. She had given it to Ashley to carry and a woman had run out of her house to reclaim it. It wasn't theirs to steal, she'd said, and dumped it back on the pavement. Ashley had apologized, but she'd continued to watch them until they reached their front door.

'Your mother would have a field day with this,' he said now.

'They'd lynch her,' Jay said. 'Can you imagine?'

'Wouldn't be such a bad thing,' he smiled.

'Ashley!' She stopped and stared at him; then shook her head and walked on, pushing her hands in her pockets.

'Sorry,' he said, struggling to keep up. 'It's the pain, you know, it makes me cantankerous.'

'Your ankle has nothing to do with it, Ashley.'

'No,' he said. There was a fridge lying face-up on the pavement. The door was dented and cupping water, and Ashley sat down on its edge. He fastened the brake on the buggy and hugged his arms round his chest. 'It's everything else,' he said then. 'My life is arthritic.'

'Don't be pathetic, Ash. Come on, we're getting cold.'

'Just a minute.' He stretched his leg in front of him. 'It really is sore, you know.'

'Shame,' she said, and crouched next to the buggy. She warmed Maggie's hands in her own. The low sun glanced from the windows behind her. 'I don't know what you were thinking of, Ashley. You're such a mug sometimes. When did you last play any football?'

He shrugged. 'I was ingratiating myself, Jay. I was being one of the lads, associating with my fellows.'

'And was it worth it? Are *they* worth it?'

'Not really.' He blew on his fingers and stood up, let Jay take the buggy. 'Where to now?' he said. They'd been out for almost an hour.

'Where do you want to go?'

'I don't know,' he replied, and gazed around at the terraces, the alleys and corners. On his days alone with Maggie he often pushed her out in the afternoons, touring the same few streets, usually ending up at the park. Once, when it was sunny, they had followed the course of the river, out past the sewage works and the derelict factories, as far as the start of the new bypass. They had caught the bus back; there had been nothing to see, just a blank strip of tarmac. He hadn't told Jay. 'The usual,' he'd said. 'Round the block and back again.'

'Ashley?' she said now.

'You choose,' he smiled. 'I'll follow you.' And she took them up a street parallel to their own, empty but for a couple of workmen. One was measuring the dimensions of the pot-holes in the road with a trundle-wheel, the other jotting the numbers on to a clipboard. TOUGH was written on the bonnet and doors of their truck. Ashley pointed and said, 'There's jobs in construction, Jay. Or security. I could get one of those.'

She looked at him sternly. 'Your daughter would never forgive you.'

'You'd like to think so,' he said. 'But look at her now.' Maggie was bouncing backwards and forwards in her seat, jolting the buggy, her cheeks flushed red with the effort. 'She's a speed-freak already,' he said. 'She'll probably do all her school projects on cars just to spite you.'

'*I'll* never forgive you then,' Jay said.

They turned towards the off-licence. The names *Killy*, *Winky* and *Groucho* were freshly painted over the shutters, and the neighbouring shop had a new signboard, sponsored by a cigarette brand and encased behind a wire cage. At the kerbside, the newsagent Ajaz was unloading some boxes from the back of his car. Ashley said, 'Okay, final suggestion – what about community arts? I could be your other half at the project. We could do a mural on those shutters, for instance, do some nice trees and things.'

'You're not a woman,' she told him. 'We wouldn't have you.'

'I could try,' he said.

Jay's hair blew over her face. She ducked her head and flicked it away, glanced at him quickly. 'Anyway, they've already asked me if I'd like to be my own other half.'

'What?' he said. 'When?' Jay crossed the road at the

junction. Her project had never been able to fund both her maternity leave and a temporary replacement; and since she'd returned in September, they'd delayed advertising the other half of her job too. Students had come and gone, volunteers were plentiful, and so the work had continued, no more chaotic than usual. Ashley had thought the arrangement was permanent. At the door to the newsagent's he said, 'Jay, what did you say? What did you tell them?'

'I said I would think about it.' She guided the buggy through the narrow entrance and parked it next to a slot machine. The covers of the magazines curled back in the draught.

'You might've told me,' he said.

'Why?'

'Because it affects all of us,' Ashley whispered. Ajaz came in behind them. He heaved three crates of cans on to a shelf, stripped back the cellophane wrapping and went out again.

'Not yet it doesn't,' Jay said.

An old woman stood before them at the counter, short and very fat, her raincoat stretched taut on her back. She was almost bald. Ashley stared at the flakes of skin on her shoulders. 'A block of cheese,' she shouted. 'And give me six rolls. Make sure they're soft ones.' Maggie began whining in her corner. Frowning, Ashley went to pick her up. He jigged her in his arms and waited beside Jay as she rummaged through a sack of potatoes. They were spongy, sprouting roots. Before he could speak the fat lady pushed by him, sorting her change. She tried to put some money in the slot machine. 'I can't reach,' she complained, and Ashley pulled the buggy out of her way.

'Jay, I'd like you to do it,' he said then.

'I thought you might.' She smiled to Ajaz's wife at the till. 'Have you any fresh spuds?'

'Oven-ready chips,' she replied.

'Just milk then.'

'Two?'

'One, please.'

Ashley followed Jay out of the shop, dragging the buggy behind him. 'So?' he said.

'So I need to think it through, you know?' Her voice was raised in the wind, sounding impatient. Ajaz looked up from the boot of his car, tapped a pen on his notebook. Behind the wheel a small girl sat wearing an oversized pair of driving gloves, her door open to the pavement. Ashley noticed the boy called Groucho strutting towards them. 'I mean,' Jay said then, 'you might like the idea of being a house-husband now, but can you imagine being stuck in that hole five days a week? And doing this every day? Traipsing round these streets every afternoon for a bit of fresh air?'

'It'd be fine,' he said, clipping Maggie into her straps. 'Really.'

'And the money, Ashley . . .' But Groucho suddenly kicked out at the car, slamming the door on the girl. He made a swipe at Ajaz as he passed him, missing by inches and laughing. 'You prick!' Jay yelled after him, and he raised a finger in the air and swivelled it, not looking back. The girl gazed wide-eyed at her father through the window. Ajaz put down his pad and ushered her into the shop, then returned to examine the door. He licked his thumb and rubbed a mark from the metal. A smouldering cigarette landed on the pavement beside him, tossed down from one of the flats. He didn't glance up, and he didn't look at Ashley or Jay.

'Come on,' she said heavily, pushing the buggy. 'We'll talk about it later.'

'No,' he said, hurrying beside her. 'I mean it. There's nothing to talk about. You *want* to work full-time. And I want to jack in work altogether. So that's it. Jay, listen, Daddy's putting his foot down. It's sorted.' And he grabbed her roughly by the shoulders, planted a kiss on her ear. 'Do you hear me?'

'I hear you,' she said. 'But there'll be no more trips to the beer shop, not on my wages.'

'Tea,' he said happily. 'Water. I'll drink boiled water. I'll make some now, to celebrate. Two cups of boiled water.'

'We'll see,' she smiled.

Babycare is an endless worry, Douglas. Our daughter celebrated her own New Year by catching her first-ever real-life lurgy, a genuine hair-raising affliction of every bodily inch and function. She couldn't eat or sleep and wouldn't stop crying, she became feverish, threw up, lost weight, went limp in our arms, rolled her eyes, and suddenly erupted in spots upon spots, from her nose to her toes. It was scary. And because we know about meningitis, because this is the disease we've most read up on, and which we've adopted as our eventual undoing, we naturally assumed she was a goner, our journey into parenthood ended. Two minutes in the doctor's waiting room effected a miracle cure, however, and she promptly recovered with energies redoubled – she no longer crawls exactly, but scurries and scampers, hurtles and beetles, a bug in a perpetual hurry, yelping and burbling, tearing pot-plants and newspapers to pieces, upending ornaments and emptying boxfiles, bumping her head and losing her temper, laying waste to all about her whilst Mummy and Daddy sit in their corners practising what they hope is benign neglect and inevitably accusing each other whenever anything goes too painfully wrong. She has an unerring nose for hazards of every description, mechanical, chemical and electrical, and seeks them out with terrier-like dedication. And no matter what brightly coloured distractions we scatter about the floor of the living room, we no sooner turn our backs than she worms her way into the corner beneath the table where the multi-block is hidden and attempts to suck the plugs from their sockets, or makes another dash to the kitchen for the washing powder. This gets her extremely excited and she sits on her bum in the midst of the mess she has wrought, emitting ear-piercing shrieks in ten-second bursts and flapping her arms like an absolute hen. Very cute. Her few moments of relative repose are no less unrelaxing for her parents as her favourite pastime is to play her Tommy Tippee trumpet, at which she's become quite the virtuoso, though she's yet to produce anything remotely resembling a tune. It's all a blare. Not that she cares. Really she's uncannily cheerful and clearly believes herself to be indestructible. Which is worrying, endlessly.

If only her good humour was contagious. This has been an uncommonly grim winter I feel, and even though Maggie accepted her eviction from our bed to the cot without so much as a bleat, the longer nights have rarely been quite long enough, I hardly ever sleep soundly and I wake all out of kilter, unrested, barely unwound, the accumulated woes of the previous day still unresolved. You might almost say I've been depressed, except that the month for depression is surely not January but February, the grimmest, miserablest month of them all, an absolute Sunday teatime amongst months. Although, as Jay keeps reminding me, this February shall be different, not only the occasion of major readjustments in our living arrangements, of which more later, but the occasion of the Dug's homecoming, whatever home now means to him. We've been thinking you might like to prolong your tour, and thus remain forever in transit, by visiting the People's Free Republic of Hogslea – declared independent under international law on Sunday, 1st January, a free state with over 1,000 passport-holding citizens and thirty-three permanent residents, as notified in writing to the Organization of Non-Aligned States, the European Union, the Guardian newspaper, and to the Foreign Secretary of the belligerent British Government, from whose monarch all allegiance has been formally absolved. The passports were printed by Jay herself in her lunchtimes at work, and in her role as cultural attaché and common-law sister-in-law I'm sure she'd be only too pleased to act as your guide and interpreter. You will, of course, need to be careful to respect local customs, lavish money on the natives, take your litter away, not wander too far into virgin territory, leave your camera at home, accept any work assigned to you,

*purchase any trinket offered to you, refuse to bargain, and tell
no one afterwards. Or tell everyone afterwards. I might even
join you. But then we've heard not a peep from you in nearly
six weeks, no word from Ecuador or anywhere else, and we no
longer quite know where you are. Perhaps you have been
mugged or otherwise waylaid. Perhaps you've decided to linger
longer in Guatemala − or Little Kitchen, as we call it. I hope
the latter. In literal translation, do you realize, Guatemala
means 'land of many trees'. It's a veritable Hogslea amongst far
and distant lands. Did you know that? You can answer in
person. I shall depend upon it.*

Maggie fell silent and Ashley sat very still. Jay lay beneath
him. There was a steady hiss from the heater, scratching
branches outside, the distant wind, Jay's breath and his own.
He could hear his heart pulsing. Rain beat on the window,
and then Maggie sighed, turning on to her side. The cot
creaked and she snored. Ashley leant his weight again into
Jay's shoulders. He gripped the pelt of flesh at her neck and
pulled outwards, squeezed again and pressed in. He squinted
at the clock on the floor. Fifteen minutes had passed and his
ankle was beginning to ache. His thumbs were tiring. He
worked them slowly down the knuckles of her spine, rubbing
in circles, his fingers spread wide, and when his hands
spanned her waist he smoothed them up to her shoulders and
slumped forwards. He grazed his teeth on her neck, tasting
her scent, the warmth from her skin. Jay moaned as if smiling
and he linked his fingers through hers. She raised her buttocks against him. 'Turn over,' she whispered.

Ashley lay on his back. Jay closed her hand round his penis.
As it hardened she stroked the pad of her thumb on its tip,
over the glans, and then he felt the moist ring of her lips
descending, her teeth, and the pouch of her palm around his
balls. Her hair settled on to his belly. He took the weight of a
breast in his hand. But it was all too far away. He gripped her

arm gently and tugged, and she gathered the blankets from the foot of the bed and pulled them over her shoulders. She sat across him and smiled and lowered her mouth on to his, closing her eyes. He sought out his own taste on her tongue, and held to the width of her hips. She rubbed herself on his cock and he scratched his nails down her thighs, tucked his arms under hers and hugged her tightly against him. She bit into his neck. He said, 'Ow,' and she did it again.

When she sat up the bedclothes fell in a heap to his legs and the quilt slid to the floor. The heater sputtered. Jay glanced to the cot and they waited; and then she slipped him quickly inside her. She arched her back and Ashley looked up to the swell of her breasts, their slow sway as she rocked. He cupped his hands over her nipples, and she felt for his fingers with hers. He watched her face, her flickering smile, the wisps of hair on her cheeks. She bit her lip, and came forwards, kissing his chin, his lips, his eyelids, the bridge of his nose. She raised herself on her forearms and Ashley lifted his head, taking the dark spread of her nipple into his mouth. Her milk pooled under his tongue, sweet and warm, and as he sucked she pressed slowly back, and around, his cock flexing inside her. He heard her breath quicken, and began thrusting to meet her, dropping his head to the pillows. Her breasts softly lapped on his chest. He held her head, his fingers mussing her hair, and looked into her eyes. She framed his face with her hands, and as she came and he came their eyes were wide open, a few inches apart and fixed on each other.

Afterwards she said, 'So will you come?'

'I just have.'

'To the camp.'

'Maybe.'

She smiled. 'It's very healing, you know.'

'Healing,' he said. 'Fuck's sake, Jay.'

'What?'

'Healing.' He kissed her cheek. 'Fuck's sake.'

FEBRUARY

SALUDOS DE GUATEMALA! said his brother's letter. *From Guatemala, greetings!*

Ashley stood alone on the edge of the camp. The smaller benders were almost invisible now. Dense hummocks in the darkness, they might have been bushes or earth-mounds. A few stalks of lamplight pierced the door-flaps. The smoke from the flues thinned out through the trees. Bulked up with woollens, he felt the chill air on his face and his fingers. It crept around his neck and he shivered. A smell of leafmould rose from the ground as he pissed and he looked across to the clearing, to where the remnants of a bonfire still smouldered, kicked over with dirt an hour before. A shopping trolley lay on its side nearby, spilling a tumble of logs. The metal showed faintly luminous in the dark, like the white-painted stones which marked out the pathways, and the cream-coloured tarps of the kitchen tent. A long vertical banner, three feet wide and pegged to the ground, rose steeply into the trees. There were shelters up there too, tightropes and hand-holds, a whole copse wired together.

He warmed his hands on his breath and cupped them over his nose. He tried to stamp the numbness from his feet. Earlier in the evening there'd been dancing out here, potatoes roasting in the fire. He had sat and looked on with Maggie tucked into his lap. He had clapped her hands for her. It was as much as he could do to join in, and both Hazel and Jay had smiled at him. But later, when they'd hopped up and down with the others, flapping their arms and laughing, Ashley had stared fixedly into the fire, and his own embarrassment had annoyed him. Finally he'd stood, jigging the baby and swaying, but by then it was all over. Now Maggie and Jay were sleeping, and Hazel was drinking tea in the kitchen, from where there came a steady murmur of voices, the tired beat of a drum. The noise drifted into the surrounding stillness and quiet, and everything appeared as if waiting, the tents and the trees, the darkness. Some day soon the camp would be cleared for the diggers. A sheriff's officer had called three mornings before with a notice. Flanked by policemen, he'd declined the offer of breakfast, then read the notice aloud and pinned it to one of the trees. It was an order of eviction. The area was called *the parcel of land described in the Originating Summons as Plot 53A*, and this evening the notice had been used to kindle the bonfire.

Something moved in the woods. Hunching his shoulders, Ashley trod carefully towards it. He paused and widened his eyes at the dark. The forms of the bushes and trees slowly assembled around him, but straight ahead there was blackness. He raised an arm to shield his face and pressed forwards, gingerly testing the ground. Several paces on he came to a clearing and stopped. He listened, and at first there was nothing, then a few faint scufflings and birdcalls, the shushing of the breeze. He didn't know what he'd expected. An owl hooted from the canopy and he started to smile. It was the first time he had heard one. Peering upwards, he saw the night sky, bright stars poking through the web of the branches. He inhaled deeply. There was a smell of moss and earth and fungus, and the cold was beginning to wake him. He decided to walk further and pushed on through the undergrowth, less cautiously now, and stumbling a little. The ground dipped and climbed suddenly. He couldn't see his own feet and he blundered into obstacles, felt the tug of straggling branches, twigs bristling his hair. Then from the distance there came the low hum of a generator and he used this to guide him. Soon a mist of light spread out through the trees. The hum rose to a clatter, and the woods ended abruptly. Ducking his head, he crept forwards, and crouched in the shelter of a tangle of briars.

A long straight passage had been cut into the coppice, fifty or sixty yards wide and enclosed by tall fencing. Gaudy arclights illuminated the site. A speckle of frost lay over the ground, and a couple of guards stood talking by a portakabin. Ashley watched them through the branches. The taller of the two, even viewed from behind, appeared restless, uncomfortable, and not much older than a school leaver. He leant a shoulder into the cabin, but immediately straightened and folded his arms, then looked down at his feet, and nodded, and slouched again on the wall. The other man gestured casually with a cigarette. Ashley strained to hear what he was saying, but his voice was lost to the noise of the generator. Burly in his uniform, he had the squat, rigid stance of a soldier. He wore a heavy moustache, dark stubble, and his trousers were tucked into the top of his boots. Finally he chucked his cigarette aside and flexed his arms, then patted the younger man on the chest and began walking across to the fence. The boy turned lazily to follow and Ashley recognized him at once as one of his sixth-formers.

Euan Eliott had been the first to sign out at the start of the school year. Ashley had met him in a corridor, waving the green form that released him. 'I'm jacking it in, Mr B.,' he'd announced. 'I'm fucking sick of this place.' He hadn't said what he was going to do, and Ashley hadn't bothered to ask, but now he recalled a conversation in the previous term, Euan slyly grinning, talking about the hippies on the Common. Jay had been on television the previous night. 'They're drug addicts, Mr Brook,' Euan had said. 'They're filthy and disgusting and they never take baths. They should all be slammed up.' Smiling, Ashley had suggested he join the police force, but Euan claimed he'd already been promised a job as a guard; he knew someone who worked on the site. The pay was £3 an hour. 'That's rubbish,' Ashley had told him. 'Nah, Mr B.,' Euan replied. 'Loads of overtime, night shifts. You should apply for it too.'

Looking on now, Ashley felt his pulse quicken. They were making a slow tour of the perimeter. The older man tugged at the fence and toe-poked one of the stanchions. The wires shimmered noisily and he did it again, pulling harder this time. Euan fiddled with the zip of his jacket. He kicked at a stone, and for a moment seemed to stare directly at Ashley, then he blinked his eyes and gave a long yawn. As they began walking towards him, Ashley hunched lower and breathed into his hands. He remembered playing hide-and-seek with Douglas in the shrubberies of Ravensby, and accusing his brother of cheating; it had always been too easy, Douglas had always found him too quickly. The guards would surely see him now. His ankle was beginning to ache, and he felt foolish. He ought to stand up. Euan had been one of his pupils. Ashley had been a schoolteacher. There were no tools in his pockets and he wasn't trespassing; an hour earlier he had been helping his daughter into her sleepsuit.

The ache began to spread up his leg. He tried to shift his weight, but they were almost upon him. The ground crunched under their boots, and he tensed, closing his eyes.

They paused a few feet from his bush. The fence rattled again, and the noise made him start. He waited, hardly breathing, and as the shake in the wires subsided he realized they were walking away. They hadn't seen him. He heard a cough several yards on, and finally he moved, easing upwards. Something cracked under his heel. He raised his head. The older guard was looking straight at him. Euan began laughing, and then Ashley backed out, already starting to run. 'It's Mr Brook!' Euan shouted. 'Come back, Mr B.! Don't be frightened. Come and have a cup of tea with the lads!'

I'm sitting on the doorstep of a lean-to shack surrounded by flowering shrubs. There's a hummingbird throbbing away and there's a dead eagle stretched out on the wall. It's a big bird with a four-foot wingspan. It's been gutted and it's been spread out on the wall. I'm not sure what to make of it but there it is. This is not a country for sensitive vegetarian types, Ashley. On the bus journey up there was a sheep riding on the roof with all the cabbages and pottery bowls. The bus lurched round a hairpin and the sheep came hurtling over the side – it was jerked to a halt by the noose round its neck and it dangled just outside my window. Its hooves were scrabbling on the glass. Eek, I thought. Naturally its owner wanted the bus stopped, and 'luckily' we'd run into an army checkpoint so the driver had no choice. The checkpoint was manned by the usual group of bored youths in sunglasses, sub-machineguns casually draped over their shoulders, etc. Everyone got off the bus and one of the youths got on and poked through our baggage, then the men from the bus all stood in a line to have their IDs checked and get patted up for concealed Ray-Bans. Everyone seemed to take this pretty much in their stride, joking and laughing like you do – I suppose because it's part of everyday life out here. There didn't seem to be any tension about it anyway, except that the soldiers wouldn't let the sheep's owner rescue his sheep, not until he'd been thoroughly body-searched. They searched him twice. He made a sheepish sort of fuss about this, as much as you can with your hands on your head and a gun prodding your belly, but then one of the soldiers offered to cut the animal down for him. 'Si, si,' he said. So the soldier hacked its head off. It's a sheep's life.

I described all this later to the people I'm staying with and they just shrugged their shoulders. They told me a story about a cousin of theirs in a neighbouring village who used to run the local bar but refused to pay protection money to the soldiers or give them free drinks. It seems there was a lot of guerrilla activity in this area a few years back – the government had built a big garrison nearby and a lot of people were suddenly 'disappearing'. The cousin was writing letters to an American human rights group, and so one night the soldiers turned up to sort him out, things got a little out of hand, and they chopped his head off too. Apparently the villagers thought they'd got off pretty lightly because the usual reprisal at that time was to massacre whole Indigena families. Which puts things a bit more in perspective, I suppose. A shame about the eagle, though. And the sheep. Otherwise this is still a very beautiful country – 'muy tranquillo,' as they say.

The kettle was dented and encrusted with carbon. An old man called Dave picked it up from the stove and refilled the teapot. The sleeves of his jumper were pulled over his hands, and there were twigs stuck to the wool of his hat, flakes of sawdust in his beard. His expression was serious, deep frown lines creased his forehead and they sometimes called him Ernie for earnest, which made him laugh; Jay said he was never serious about anything. He sat cross-legged on a dhurrie and opened a pouch of tobacco. 'You should've given yourself up, Ashley,' he said. 'They're okay really, they're like train-spotters, you know? They collect us. They would've taken you in and shown you their albums. They've got pictures of everyone in there – names, phone numbers, distinguishing features, favourite colours . . .' The gaps in his teeth showed when he smiled. He licked the gum on his roll-up. 'I saw a nice one of Jay and the kiddie anyway. Very sweet. They'd pinned that up on the wall.'

'But did you see the poster?' Hazel said. She was sitting against a hay-bale with another girl. A tie-dyed sheet covered the lattice of poles behind her. 'There's this massive big tree in the rainforest. And these two muscly great guys with chainsaws. Then underneath it says, *We came, we sawed, we conquered.* I should've ripped it down.'

A young woman sat plumply on the bench beside Ashley, her arm and thigh pressing warmly against him. 'They've got a sense of humour then,' she said. 'That's nice.' She was holding a slab of bread and cheese. There were swirls of henna on the back of her hands, and a jewelled ring through her nose. She was called Ocean and she was training to be a teacher. 'You're still cold,' she said, and shuffled closer, bumping her hip into his.

'You're not.' He smiled.

She gave him a chunk of her bread and said, 'Eat,' then a young man with dreadlocks placed a mug of tea at his feet.

'It's just as well you ran, Ashley,' he said, lifting the locks away from his face. 'They would've taken your photo, but they would've given you a fucking good kicking afterwards. They're evil bastards, especially that one, if that's the same guy. He's the one who did me. *I was in the paras, mate.* Thump. *I know how to kill, mate.* Thump. He was really up for it, yeah? He'd completely lost it, he was out of control. He got me here by the collar and he started swinging me round, going crazy. I was choking, and he was trying to kick my balls in. I blacked out in the end.' He touched his throat. 'I thought I was going to die for a minute, end of story.'

Ashley sipped at his tea, and Ocean nudged him. 'One of them felt me up,' she said. 'Then later he comes over, all apologetic, and asks if he can have my phone number because he really fancies me!' She laughed. 'Can you believe that?'

'I can believe that,' said Dave.

'It wasn't funny, though,' she said. 'I reported him for sexual assault – to a *woman*, mind you, a policewoman. I told her to dust me for fingerprints, his grubby paws were all over me.'

'And?' said Ashley.

'She told me to piss off.'

'They were wild that day,' a bearded man nodded. 'Mental,' he added.

But they had heard all the stories before. In the silence the stove crackled, and Ocean yawned loudly. Dave switched on a cassette player and started another roll-up. A woman passed him some dope and he drew out a couple more papers. Ashley gazed around at the bender. A dim lantern hung down on a chain. Between the tarps and the weave of the beams there were sheets of hessian insulation; rugs and shawls decorated the walls and the duckboards. There were bits of crudely made shelving, water-butts and calor-gas bottles, enamel bowls and a sink, an array of pots and pans and boxes of vegetables. The tables and chairs might have come from the streets around Telegraph Lane. It was like sitting in an upturned basket, he thought, everything tipped on to the floor. Someone began talking about football, the game they were missing on television, and then Ashley heard Hazel's friend mention India. Yawning, he closed his eyes and leaned forward to listen. The warmth of the stove was making him listless.

'I've really got to do it alone,' the girl was saying. 'No way can I go with that guy, Hazel. I want to come back totally different, yeah? Totally sorted. It's like, I need to clear my headspace but I can't do that with him around because he's just ego, you know? He dumps on me. So that's it. Byeski. I'm out of here.'

'Where will you go?' Hazel said.

'Delhi, Goa – everywhere, you know? I'm really up for it. I

just know I'm going to see so much I haven't seen before. Temples, poverty, religion. And real sunshine, yeah?'

'Ashley's brother did India,' Hazel said. 'He sends these letters, he's been all over. Ashley, wake up.' She knelt forward and tugged at his ankle. 'Ashley, where did your brother go in India? Tell Gill.'

He shrugged. 'Delhi, Goa and everywhere,' he said. 'The usual stuff, you know. But I don't think he's got his head-space sorted yet. Not totally and utterly anyway.' Hazel stared at him. She was almost smiling. Her friend drew self-consciously on a cigarette. Ashley patted his knees and stood up. 'Sorry,' he said, 'getting sarcastic again – must be my bedtime.' He raised a hand to the others. 'Night everyone,' he said; then grinning to Hazel and Gill, 'Byeski.'

'Ashley,' Hazel said.

'What?'

'Don't get beaten up, will you?'

'Not tonight,' he said.

But dreams, I know you're interested in these things, Ashley. There's one I wrote down for you. It was a summer's evening and I came to visit you three in the garden of an old country house. The house wasn't yours, and the garden was huge – very neat and manicured, every border sharp as a razor's edge. Ashley, you were wearing a big green rib-knit cardigan with knotty brown leather buttons and you were crouched in a flowerbed with Maggie and Jay. You'd made a little nest in there, and you didn't know who the fuck I was. Like I was too ridiculous to exist. 'But I've got ID,' I kept saying. 'I've got ID.' And I showed you all the letters you'd sent me – they were in my rucksack, nothing but letters and photos of Maggie. 'See,' I said, 'see, Ashley, look at this one, she's very pretty in this one.' 'Yeah, yeah,' you said, 'but Britain's a shit-pit, Douglas. Here, look.' Then you showed me a full-colour blow-up of a steaming dog-turd. It was crawling with little insects and the insects kept flying off the photo and trying to bite me, so I decided to leave, but then you shouted, 'Fuck's sake, Douglas, you're here now so you might as well stay.' Only I couldn't make up my mind – the insects were making so much noise I couldn't think straight. And then I woke up. I really had been bitten. Guatemala is a very beautiful country but they have a definite problem with 'pulgas' – bedbugs to you and me. Or I have a definite problem with pulgas, which is puzzling – it's almost as puzzling as that eagle – because there's really so little left on me worth biting. South America just about finished me off.

Mad to sum up an entire continent from so few countries, but South America really is a mad continent – there seemed nothing holding the place together, it was like you couldn't rely on logic or reason and everything was straining apart, especially me. Sometimes there was a real buzz. The people live their lives so much in the open – you'd go out and there'd be white people, mestizos, tall black people, hawkers of torches and chickens, money-changers, shoe-shiners, biscuit-sellers, girls in tight skirts and flouncy blouses, men in slacks scratching their balls . . . and there's no reserve about it, they don't behave as if their bodies aren't there. But somehow I always seemed to take a wrong turning. I kept getting lost down the winding backstreets. There was no problem finding people to ask for directions because they were all standing around watching me, and some were even following me, but as soon as I opened my mouth I was completely ignored – like I really was too ridiculous to exist. Paranoia descended and I felt like I was riding my luck until something really bad happened, which eventually it did. I was staying in another of these cheap hotels where I couldn't work out who owned it, who worked there, who was a guest and who was just lounging about. There seemed to be a party happening in every room but mine. I was sick anyway and spent the entire night in a fever, getting up every half hour to shit water. By ten the next morning I'd completely lost my place, then one of the parties spilled into the corridor and I went storming out ready to hit someone. Big mistake. I piled

*into some hairy gangster types snorting coke right outside my
door and they beat the last remaining watery shit out of me.
Someone also stole a bag containing my Walkman, camera and
toilet bag – as if the bruises weren't bad enough, they left me
with furry teeth and smurfy hair.*

*By then my personal compass really should've been pointing
to home, but suddenly it was flickering all over the place. I was
neither here nor there, and your letters just seemed to confirm
that, Ashley. They were very unsettling. You wrote that you'd
got used to this version of me, always somewhere you're not, but
I felt I was nowhere at all. It seemed I'd put all this distance
between me and everything I was used to – work, home, possessions, family, friends – and in the end I'd totally lost myself. I
didn't recognize my own reflection in mirrors and everything
about me was suffering fatigue. Obviously I needed to get fat-
tened up, and I needed to find a nice hammock somewhere. But
most of all I needed to make a decision about what to do next.
But I just couldn't do it, because without all that stuff – work,
home, family, etc. – every day becomes a series of really petty
decisions about nothing in particular, the simplest thing takes
an age to decide, and when you're actually faced with a really
big decision you're totally fucked, paralysed. The only good
thing was that my ticket back to Guatemala was about to
expire. I felt I had no choice in the matter, so I dragged myself
onto the next plane, and when I got off the plane I got on to
that bus – simply because it was there, and it was going somewhere I'd already been, and so I didn't think I'd have to cope
with anything new, I could stop 'haring about'. It was a good
move as it turned out, but it's a million miles from where I
began in Nepal. Then I thought I was on the verge of some
blinding insight into the true nature of human existence. Now
I'm just happy if I can remember my own name.*

Hazel's bender resembled a tortoise shell. Even bent double,
Ashley's back would have touched the arch of the poles. He

crawled in on his knees and clambered over Jay's legs. She was sharing a sleeping bag with Maggie, a couple of duvets heaped over them. He padded around in the dark for his own bag and found it tucked into a corner, a pair of Jay's tights bundled inside it. Shivering in the cold, he tugged off his boots, his trousers, and pulled on the tights. He removed a couple of jumpers and hurriedly zipped himself into the bag, then he wriggled under the covers, snuggling into Jay's warmth. The duvets smelled dankly of mould. For the past three years they'd been knotted into bin-liners in their spare bedroom. Ashley hadn't wanted to bring them; and he'd complained again to Jay about her clutter and rubbish, her useless belongings. If ever they managed to move, he'd said, they weren't taking them with them. And she hadn't bothered to argue. He could start sorting them now, she'd said, and discard as much as he wanted. She would be working full-time from next week. Their house was up for sale, and they were already looking for places to rent in other areas.

Maggie snuffled. He released his arms from the bag and felt for her face. He touched Jay's hair and smiled, and rolled on to his back, cupping his hands under his head. He gazed up at the darkness until he saw the faint ribs of the shell. It made noises, seemed to rise and contract like something breathing. He remembered Maggie's first night in their home, lying all three in their bed, her soft wheeze as she slept. In the hospital her first breaths had come in effortful gasps, her chest seeming too small to contain them. He remembered the midwives arriving to wash Jay and ushering him out of the room. He had gone downstairs to the observation ward, to where Maggie lay in a glass crib, perfectly pink on a sheet of pale green. 'Hello,' he had said. 'Hello, Maggie.' Her legs were like wishbones. His finger in her hand was enormous. He had gazed at her feet, the pudgy swell of her cheeks, the pewter-coloured blur of her eyes, and then he'd run back upstairs to tell Jay. But she hadn't been able to listen. He remembered her wincing pain as she climbed from her bed to a wheelchair, and the cold of the corridors, the crash of the lift doors, the shabby sprawl of the maternity ward. The baby had followed in the arms of a nurse, and she'd wailed when he'd kissed her goodbye. He hadn't minded. Walking alone to the bus station, dazed and hungry, he had smiled at strangers and dithered at kerbsides, not trusting himself to the traffic, and then on the top deck of the bus home he had started to sob, picturing Jay as she lay sleeping that morning, the tubes and wires and machines, the vacuum extractor, spotlights and sluices and noise. Douglas was in Singapore by then. A few days later Ashley had woken one morning at dawn, thinking Maggie had stopped breathing. In the gauzy light of their bedroom he had laid his hand on her chest and lowered his ear to her nose. Her heart had fluttered under his palm. Her breath had smelled of ice-cream, white chocolate. Too happy to sleep, he'd slipped out of the bed and carried his typewriter downstairs to the kitchen. He was still writing to Douglas when Maggie began bawling for her breakfast. He remembered making a pot of tea for Jay, and taking it upstairs on a tray with a single flower in a vase and two tubes of bottom cream, one for her haemorrhoids and one for her stitches. It was a Saturday, and they hadn't left their house for the rest of the weekend.

Actually I've enrolled for a few weeks in a Spanish language school. I spent my first few days in a guest house, feet up, mind a blank, but now I'm lodging with an Indigena family who are also trying to teach me the local dialect, which is called Mam. It sounds a bit like dishwater draining out of a blocked sink, so you'd probably understand it quite well, Ashley. Their house is one big room in which they all sleep, a kitchen, and then my room tacked on at the end. The toilet is a hut in the garden with a hole in the floor and a hosepipe to flush it. The family is Domingo and Juliana and four children – Maria, Cesar, René and Sylvia.

René has the most spontaneously good-natured smile of any child I've ever seen. There are also puppies who wriggle and wag their tails whenever anyone goes near them and get kicked if they stray too close. The pattern of the days is pretty regular. After break-fast tortillas I sit on a hill above the village doing my homework. Or if it's raining, I sit on the muddy porch watching Juliana and Maria do their weaving. Or if either of these is too taxing, I go back to bed. Lunch is tortillas. Then the other children come home from their school and I go off to mine to conjugate some more useless verbs. I come back up the hill in the rain for my supper (tortillas) and then sit around in the kitchen until it's time to retire – usually about half eight. By Guatemalan standards the family aren't poor but life is pretty basic. Apart from the radio they have no entertainments, just a home, clothes, and enough food (tortillas) to live on. No cruddy ornaments. But this is, as I may have mentioned already, a very beautiful place – a steep wooded valley surrounded by narrow mountain ridges and topped by fluffy white clouds. I feel pretty much at home here actually. I feel pretty much a part of the family. In fact, you can tell that to Mum and Dad – Douglas has finally settled down with a nice family. I hope yours is safe and well in that flowerbed anyway. I think about you three more than you might imagine, Ashley – if I think of 'home', my real home, that's what I think of – and we'll be four in the spring, I hope. Unless you make another baby in the mean-time. In fact, why don't you make another baby? Isn't that where we came in? Your sperms, my aeroplanes? Might be just the thing . . . There's probably a lot more I could say but the pen is moving very s-l-o-w-l-y over the paper now. So take care, big bro, and keep sending the letters. There's room in my rucksack for a few more of them yet, I've ditched everything else.

A bird was scratching around on the roof of the bender. Its call was shrill and persistent and Ashley opened his eyes. The light beneath the tarps was murky, brown-tinted, and he guessed it must still be early. He hadn't brought his watch or alarm clock. He hadn't used either since he stopped working and he was beginning to miss them, as he missed his own bed, the promise of mail in the morning. A muffled snore came from the other side of the tent, where Hazel was sleeping. He turned his head towards her, and found Jay watching him, smiling. Her gaze flitted over his face in the gloom. 'Hello,' she whispered. Ashley rolled on to his side and looked under the bedding. Maggie was feeding, her hand softly plucking Jay's breast. As he lowered the covers Jay said, 'Nice sleep?'

He swallowed. 'Uncomfortable. I dreamt we were burgled.' He touched her nose with his knuckle. 'You're freezing,' he said.

'Not under here,' she said.

'I've got to visit the shit-pit,' he sighed. 'Too many beans.' His legs itched in Jay's tights and every part of him ached, but he lay a while longer, still heavy with sleep, the warmth of his bag. He began to drowse, but there was a lurch in his gut, a sudden loosening, and he quickly dragged himself upright. He pulled on some clothes. 'I may be gone for some time,' he said, and left with his bootlaces trailing.

The bird took fright as he came out, dipping over the clearing and into some bushes. Frost spangled the ground and streaked the bare trees. A thin, pale light filtered down through the branches. He tucked a toilet roll under his arm and bunched his hands in his pockets, then set off through the woods, in the opposite direction to the previous evening. Planks and boards had been laid over the brooks and the water was frozen, gleaming dully like metal. He scuffed through drifts of brittle leaves, and took the inclines warily. Birds warbled and chirped all around him. There were buds on the twigs, icy blades poking up through the soil. It was peaceful, but perhaps today he would take Maggie back to the house. He hadn't intended to stay more than a couple of days, and was surprised to have lingered so long, but someone ought to be home in case the estate agent called, in case they were burgled.

The latrine was enclosed on three sides by striped windbreaks. There were two plastic seats nailed to a crossbench, a bucket of ash standing between them. Ashley sat with the hem of his jumper stretched over his knees and looked out to a fringe of silvery saplings, a spreading grove of black-and-white birch trees. Frail branches trembled in the cold. A rabbit hopped and crouched still. Yesterday he had walked through the birches with Maggie and Jay until finally they'd emerged to a place which they recognized, a fallen bough in a clearing, a corridor of dark twisted trees. The previous New Year there had been snow on the ground. Ashley had stood with his arms around Jay, his hands on her belly. A plane had ripped through the silence above them, and then he'd felt the baby rippling inside her. It was the first time, and they hadn't known where they were.

A small plane was approaching him now. Looking up, he saw a few wisps of high cloud, birds kiting on a breeze. The noise became louder but nothing appeared, and he realized it was a helicopter, circling somewhere over the camp. He tore a strip from his toilet roll. There was a shout in the distance. He wiped his backside, and tipped some ash in the pit, then heard someone screaming, whistles and yells, the urgent rip of a chainsaw. He started to run, but his feet were slack in his boots, his trousers undone. He slipped in a ditch. Yellow jackets flashed through the trees. With shaking hands he knotted his laces, zipped his fly, and when he stood he saw Ocean, loping into the woods. She was too slow for the men who chased after her, and fell before she was tackled. People were scattering in every direction. He dodged the arm of a bailiff and ran past Hazel's friend Gill. She was sitting alone in the mud with her back to a tree, half-dressed and sobbing.

Ashley had to push to get into the camp. There were too many people. He touched a policeman on the shoulder and said, 'Excuse me.' He noticed leather armguards, straps and buckles, truncheons, handcuffs and visors. A bare-chested man was hauled past him, panting for breath. He heard a girl screeching, '*Leave me alone!*' and saw a knee land on an arm, a face streaked with blood. There was a knot of women yelling for an ambulance. Trees were crashing near the work-site, the bulldozers approaching. He ducked a missile thrown from above, and then he glimpsed Jay holding Maggie, one arm clutching Hazel. He shouted but they couldn't hear him. Bodies pressed against him. He forced a workman aside, and tripped over a leg. An elbow hit his face. He stumbled forwards, landing heavily, and as he got to his feet a young man fell sprawling, charged down by a policeman. Three and four others appeared. 'Stretch out your arms!' one shouted, 'Spread your legs!' Ashley smelled their uniforms. He heard the blows, the young man screaming, and his own voice shouting, 'That's enough! That's too much!' He tried to stop them, he grabbed one by the shoulders, and then there was Hazel, her thin grip on his arm. She yanked him away and pulled him towards Jay. He saw Maggie's toys on the ground, a boot treading into her sleepsuit. The bailiffs were wrenching their bender apart, stamping it flat, and Jay was crying, 'That's our home! They're trashing our fucking home!' Ashley opened his arms. He clasped her tightly against him, he held her head to his cheek. She was cold and trembling, and Maggie was wailing. 'It's finished now, Jay,' he said. 'It's over. We've got to go now.' He eased Maggie from her arms and hitched her on to his shoulder. He looked round for Hazel. She was clutching their coats, waiting beside him. Jay stared at the ground. Ashley said her name. He took her hand, he linked his fingers through hers, and then they were running, out through the debris and noise, the last of the camp, and into the trees.